Incarnate

Book 1 of The Outcasts Series

A.K.Hinchey

DEDICATION

This first novel is dedicated to all the people that have believed in me and spurred me on: my parents Lynne and Michael, my sisters Jennifer and Elizabeth, my awe inspiring nanny Mary, my awesome aunt Helen, my best friend Cheryl, my soulmate Duane and so many more.

Thank you!

CONTENTS

ACKNOWLEDGMENTS

I'd first like to thank my husband Duane for the support he has given me over the last few years, from distracting the kids to listening as I bounced ideas off of him, I could not do it without you love. Next, I would like to thank my mother Lynne who has given me creative guidance, and my father Michael for the unwavering support he has given me over the years. I would like to thank my sisters Jennifer and Elizabeth who have given me support, inspiration and the confidence to follow my dream of releasing my first novel. I'd like to thank my nanny Mary who has always been a loving source of comfort and support. One of my favourite memories is going to your house every weekend. Thank you for always believing in me. To my best friend Cheryl, thank you for the endless support you have given me. I hope our costa dates carry on far into the future.

To my beta readers, my mother Lynne and Jacob Flowers (Alvenecus), thank you for guiding me in the endless ins and outs of storytelling and grammar – grammar not my favourite thing – and thank you for reading my work.

Thank you to Eddy at Branding Acura for designing my epic book cover. You were kind enough to listen to my input as well as exhibiting your creative genius. You conducted yourself in a very professional manner and I could not recommend you more.

Thank you to Amazon and their kindle direct publishing for allowing me a platform to publish my work. I appreciate it more than you could know.

Thank you to the Sunday schooling my sisters and I had at nanny Mary's for the inspiration. I hope I show my appreciation for the learning to a respectful end.

And lastly, thank you for taking time to read my work. I appreciate each and every one of you. Thank you.

"And there was war in heaven: Michael and his angels fought against the dragon; and the dragon fought and his angels, and prevailed not; neither was their place found any more in Heaven. And the great dragon was cast out, that old serpent, called the Devil, and Satan, which deceiveth the whole world: he was cast out into the earth, and his angels were cast out with him"

Revelation 12:7-9

1

Darkness surrounded me. Cold slivers of wintry hot fire were caressing along my back, making me gasp. Lovingly aggressive hands held me in place, only holding my arms, but I felt shackled by a million chains in a million places. I heard a laugh, close to my ear, from miles away.

I struggled fruitlessly against my invisible chains, wishing I knew where I was, or even why I was being held. It made no sense to me and my panic only grew. I couldn't breathe; I was suffocating. I could feel a hand at my throat, both aggressive and tender. It began to tighten its grip, making my breath come short and sharp.

Eventually, through the swirling eddies of sheer blackness, a soft blood red light began. It grew and brightened until I was nearly dazzled by it. I closed my eyes, hoping the assault would be over soon, but the curious, shining light remained bright, relentless and unending. When I dared open my eyes once more, amid the swirling blood red chaos stood, well, a beautiful man. His body was evidently well muscled even under the shining bronze armour which adorned him. His blond hair was slicked back to reveal a masculine beauty that should have made my knees go weak with lust, but all I could do was recoil with fear.

I watched helplessly as he advanced on me, a knowing smile beginning on his soft lips, revealing perfect white teeth.

The wicked gleam in his sharp hazel eyes became brighter the closer he got; I could almost sense his triumph as he moved to engulf me. It seemed not to matter that he had sparkling golden wings, I could see the demon in him raging for release. I could feel my fear mounting and mounting until...

... I sat up in bed, pouring sweat and desperate for air in my struggling lungs. I sighed and rubbed my hand across my forehead willing the effects of the nightmare to disappear. These dreams were becoming more and more frequent and I wish I knew what they meant. Always I dreamed of the blonde stranger and the terror he invoked but never could I seem to place why these dreams were happening.

I glanced at the clock and could see it was two in the morning... again... and Rowan had to be up for work at six. Carefully I got out of bed. I didn't want to wake Rowan, he had a big presentation to do later in the morning and I didn't want to disturb him. He had been acting strangely enough as it was, always checking to see if I was okay and reminding me that he loved me. I didn't know if I should be worried about it or not. If he knew I was up again after another nightmare he would double his efforts to watch me.

Silently I padded into the bathroom. I could feel the terror of the nightmare still choking me. Standing at the mirror, I silently cried, feeling my tears drop onto my clenched hands. I couldn't figure out why a nightmare, granted, a recurring one, would affect me this way. The sobs continued to rack my body and I had to sit on the side of the tub. My knees felt too weak to hold my weight and I knew if I wasn't careful, I would end up a weeping mess on the floor.

Eventually my tears and my terror subsided, and sanity took control once more. Taking a deep, soothing breath I continued to sit, willing myself to take control of my mind. Okay, so the nightmares were becoming more intense, I could now see the stranger in detail and the things he did were not even worth thinking of, but it was no reason to allow myself such erratic emotions. I washed my face and moved to go back to bed. I longed for Rowan's soothing presence. He always had that effect on me; he could calm me in my worst terrors and bathe me in his unending love. I couldn't help miss him when he wasn't there.

I snuck back to bed, willing my body weight not to affect him too greatly. I wasn't a fat woman, but neither was I a skinny supermodel; I was curvy and often revelled in my hourglass figure. It could cause problems, however. Thankfully not today though and Rowan remained blissfully unaware, so I snuggled up to his wonderfully warm form.

At times like this I would ring one of my two best friends Vale and Lyria. They were social outcasts like me, raised in the foster system not knowing who they were, orphans that automatically found solace in each other's friendship. But Vale was covering my shift at Pandemonium and Lyria never answered at night, who knows why. So, I took comfort in

Rowan, his silent strength and slowly drifted back to sleep.

***

I looked up at the large grey building, resplendent in its very dullness, and sighed. It felt like I spent half my life here which was probably right. It hadn't taken long for my enthusiasm for my work to die out. Being a barmaid at the ripe old age of twenty-six was nothing to brag about.

Approaching the darkened doorway, I knocked three times. The clichéd slot in the door slid back and a pair of lizard eyes stared at me.

"What'ssssss the passsssssword?" hissed a deep voice.

"Open the damn door before I cut your tiny little lizard bits off?" I smiled sweetly and waited. The slot slammed shut and the door creaked open (something to delight the customers) allowing my entrance. I pushed through the invisible barrier, magic set up by a shaman to allow only the supernatural in, and stepped into a world far different from the outside. The walls were painted a deep velvet black and burgundy silk drapes hung from the ceiling. The booths around the vast dance floor were flanked in burgundy velvet seats and dark wooden tables. The dance floor was always packed when I got here but I knew it was black marble. If I didn't already know this bar was owned by one of the higher ups I'd swear it was a vampire that owned it.

"You're too cruel to me Anahliaaaaaaa, you know I'm a

mighty python..." he stepped closer to me and I could feel his forked tongue flick out and taste the air around me.

As quick as I could manage, I spun and caught his disgusting tongue before he drew it back.

"I told you Terry, no tasting my aura, you know I'm too rich for you." I lifted my left foot, decked out in slim black stilettos with cheeky red toenails peeking out, and kicked out with all my might. Terry flew backwards and into the crowd of sweaty bodies. Damn snake shifters, they creeped me out enough.

Shaking off the bad vibes, I walked over to the bar, looking to check the two bar seats I always did. I was never disappointed. Sat there were my two lifelines Vale and Lyria. They were closer than family. I waved at them and moved to the back of the bar to remove my black leather jacket. Decked out in tight black jeans and a backless black top, I was properly attired for what I knew would happen tonight. Finally ready I ignored the few customers nursing our drinks and went straight to my friends.

"Yo bitch," Vale greeted, "I see Terry still has a thing for you."

"Yeah well he can take his thing and shove it... he creeps me out." I shuddered.

"Please, you know you would if you could, it's said he's endowed like a python..." Vale started to twiddle her eyebrows. I could feel the bile rise in the back of my throat.

"Leave her alone Val," Lyria butted in. "She's got a tough enough night coming up." I looked at our quietest friend.

Vale and I had pretty much adopted Lyria when they were young as she had been so quiet, so delicate, with her pale skin and white hair. Only later would we discover what that meant.

"Thanks, Lyr," I said as I moved to serve the insistent satre, all but flogging himself to get my attention. I could handle better, though they oozed perverted slime all over the place... literally. Yeah, the mythology books never mentioned that, did they?

I didn't get back to my friends for a couple of hours it turned out. A stag-do full of wolf shifters came in demanding my attention and I had to concentrate to avoid unruly paws. Then I had the 'pleasure' of serving the banshee envoy to some such or other dignitary. I lost appreciation for the conversation sometime after he winked at me. Yes, banshee's can be male too. Shocking.

Stifling a yawn and lamenting the fact it wasn't even late damn it, I trudged back to my friends. I was about to ask how they were when I was intercepted by Lucian, the higher up's demon lap dog.

"Boss wants you to show off again."

"Seriously?" I knew I was whining but did these arseholes not realise how uncomfortable it was for me to 'show off?'

"Seriously. I mean why keep asking me. You're the only winged angelic being not tainted by," he shuddered, "light ... or blissful darkness. At least Boss said you'd get a bonus this time." Lucian sauntered off like he was one of the deities.

"Bastard demon," I muttered and sighed. I knew I'd do

what the boss wanted. I really needed the money. I slapped my head on the counter as soon as I reached my friends.

"Told ya," Lyria chimed as I sipped my cocktail.

"Aw he wants you to flash the feathers huh?"

"Uh huh." Okay, the bar muffled my groan well.

"Well get to it hot stuff Rowan will be here soon, sucks to be you." Did Vale actually just swat my butt? I lifted my head and flung my long ebony spiral curls over my shoulder. I signalled the DJ and the opening piano chords of an alternative rock song began. It was a beautiful song, totally apt for what I was about to do.

I glided to the pole in the middle of the dance floor and thrust myself up the metal. Clasping my legs in an iron grip, I let go and hung upside down giving the drinkers a nice shot of my cleavage. Using just a touch of my magic I began to float, unclasping my legs as I went. I moved so my head faced the roof, beginning to pirouette in place, faster and faster until I was a blur in the air. Just as there was a crescendo in the song and the beautiful female voice sang of being alone though he's still there, I stilled and unfurled my great ebony wings. They kept me afloat as my magic waned. I heard a chorus of 'aaahhhs' as I landed, bored of the whole affair already. I'd landed on one knee with my right hand on the floor and head bowed, aware that the superhero landing pose was first class cheese, but I was paid more for it. I gradually stood and stretched to my entire twelve-foot wingspan, looking at each drinker with the hatred I felt. Okay I didn't know what I was and refused to believe the rumours, but it didn't mean I had to be paraded like that.

My vision continued around the room as it did every time, only this time it faltered when I met the gaze of some piercing golden eyes. A lone figure watched me with great interest. He had delicate male features with a longer viking face and short soft blonde hair. He should have been gorgeous, but a shot of fear streaked up my spine. He watched me too intently, too smugly and much too determined. He also looked scarily like my nightmare. I shivered and settled my wings on my back so I could go back to serving.

My friends must have realised something was up. They actually came over to me.

"Are you alright?" Vale asked, shockingly sounding concerned for once.

"Yeah," I sighed. "Yeah I am. I just saw someone that freaked me out slightly."

"The golden hottie that only had eyes for you?"

"Yeah." My wings twitched in annoyance.

"Why did he freak you out?"

"He just seemed too determined, too intent on me, and something told me to be scared." My friends knew very little about my night terrors. "You should be," Lyria said quietly. I did that a lot, said something cryptic. Often it came to nothing, but I knew this time I should pay attention.

"I'm going to find Lucian." I moved off to the dance floor intent on the slimy bastard when the golden stranger stood from his table and moved. I ignored him and moved quicker. Where was the damn demon? I needed to get out of here like yesterday.

The golden stranger kept pace with me, eyes intent and purpose determined. I'd just reached Lucian as he turned around when a deep voice rang out,

"My father has missed you Lady; he is eager to see you again." There was a small collision in the centre of my chest. Glancing down I saw a ruby firmly planted, coated in sparkling golden light.

"Uh shit," I muttered, turning wide eyes on Lucian. He seemed stunned and was yelling, but I didn't hear him. As the golden light built, I turned to see my friends. Suddenly a bright silver light seemed to almost battle with the gold and I heard Vale shout "An..." in a muffled scream before the world went sparkling black.

***

I didn't know where I was. I seemed to be surrounded in clouds and piercing azure sky. It seemed almost serene in its natural state. Wasn't I just in the bar? I struggled to remember what sent me here. In any case I needed to set off back.

Suddenly the ground I stood on shook. A bright golden light shone from the heavens and a sound as if a loud bell rang, echoed. Pain shot through my heart as I spun in place to see a figure fall from a great height. It was blurred though seemingly the embodiment of darkness.

It gathered speed, hurtling ever downwards, feathers coming from its ... wings? and seemed in danger from impact. It drew level with me, I hadn't realised I didn't stand on ground, and time seemed to freeze. A set of startling silver eyes, the mirror image of mine, looked deep into my soul and an unseen mouth uttered,

"Wake... up... "

****

I shot upright from the grim, sticky floor. A crowd had gathered to stare at the freakish bartender who passed out. Lucian stood glaring at me while Vale was gearing up for a fight. A soothing warmth filled my veins and I looked down to see Lyria clasping my hand. Rowan was knelt beside me looking worried. He must have arrived while I was out. Luckily my wings had retreated while I was unconscious. He knew I was supernatural but not quite sure what. I hadn't wanted to freak him out and soon it was too late to tell the truth. He however was a pyromancer, a very rare fire mage, and had the body heat to go with it. Even in my befuddled state I was happy to see Terry singed.

"What happened?" I managed to ask. Rowan helped me to stand unsteadily, keeping hold of my shoulders. I wasn't surprised when Vale answered.

"The golden hottie threw something at you, light flared, and you collapsed. I was gonna whoop me some hottie ass but Lyr made me wait. The hottie disappeared, Rowan turned up, Terry tried to cop a feel and we almost had Rowan-fried python." That was a lot to take in. I glared at Terry as Lucian spoke up.

"Ravencroft, go home. The bar's closing, I need to consult the higher ups. Be back tomorrow an hour early." With that he turned and headed up the dark oaken stairs. I was still so confused but let Rowan lead me from the bar. Everyone else had already started to head out with Vale and Lyria promising to ring me tomorrow. I could only smile weakly.

I walked down the street arm in arm with Rowan. They had agreed to take it slowly given I still felt uneven. It was such a beautiful night sadly tainted by what had happened. The stars shone in the sky and the moon was a perfect silver crescent smiling at them. I was so incredibly exhausted I just wanted to get home, have a stiff drink and go to sleep. That sounded like heaven right now.

I glanced at my left hand resting gently on his right forearm, my alabaster skin a stark contrast to his beautiful tan. I often wondered how I had managed to attract his attention. I had been such a loner as a child, an orphan due to an absentee father and a mother that died in childbirth. I had lost all hope until that fateful day Vale had rescued me from a bully. She said she saw something familiar in me and felt the need to stick up for me. I wasn't one to argue with that.

Gradually Lyria turned up, a beautiful pale midget new to our home. She was so small, delicate and afraid of everything I could do nothing but adopt her. She was a ray of warm golden sunshine. Which again brought my thoughts back to Rowan. He exuded an aura I couldn't put my finger on. It was warm, familiar and soothing.

I glanced up at him. He was a few inches taller than me and I liked how safe and protected those few inches made me feel. He was a beautiful man on the outside as well as in. He had short dark hair, stunning chocolate eyes, strong nose, soft lips and glasses. The glasses didn't make him look nerdy or bookish. They merely enhanced his masculine beauty and ruggedness. I would probably just look at him forever if I could.

The walk seemed to be taking a while with my unsteady gait. They didn't talk much as he was still fuming over Terry, which I thought was the reason for him acting strangely. Rowan stopped as if he could hear something. I glanced around. I didn't hear or see anything. I was about to say something when Rowan placed a finger to his lips. He turned tentatively towards the alley we had just passed and stared, concentrating, as if he were trying to see something. Suddenly I could hear a discreet whistling and Rowan pushed me out of the way just as what seemed like a spear of pure golden light came flying towards him. I screamed. Rowan was quick however and seemingly produced a spear of pure blistering flame to deflect the incoming missile. As he swung it around to hold it with his right hand the golden spear clattered to the floor and disappeared as if it never was. Several other spears followed, and Rowan easily deflected each with his own spear and the help of what seemed to be a shield. With his left hand he managed to pull me through the air to be engulfed by his flaming light. I so wanted to help him. I was untrained, but I had power the likes of which most had never seen but I was afraid. I had kept a secret and didn't know how he'd react.

Once Rowan seemed happy that I was in the protection of this shield of his he once again turned to the alley, readied his spear and waited. Eventually a figure moved forward out of the dark mist. I was intrigued despite myself. It turned out to be the golden hottie from the bar. He seemed even more reminiscent of my nightmare horror in this light, but something was a little off, I couldn't place what.

"I see you have not lost your edge," the blonde man said, obviously directing his speech at Rowan. I was confused but remained quiet; I didn't dare break the tension.

"I am surprised you expected me to," Rowan replied in the same archaic tone. "What do you want devil spawn? I am shocked to find you here in the Mortal Realm, most Nephilim abhor those they consider beneath them." The tension was still there but the conversation seemed almost civil.

"I do feel..." the stranger seemed to be struggling with a word. "... tainted by being here but I have my orders and *I* am a loyal subject." There seemed to be hidden meaning within those words. That's when Rowan's patience seemed to run out.

"Get to the point demon, I have no patience for these games of yours."

"I'm here for the girl," he said simply. I heard Rowan sigh.

"How did you even know she is here? Not even He knows she is here."

"Our oracles detected a lost magic in a place where it no longer existed, and we were ordered to investigate," the demon said. He held a hand up to his nose and grimaced. "Honestly Michael, how do you stand it here? This place reeks of mortality."

Rowan chuckled "Your stinted view of the worlds will ultimately be your downfall, spawn." His only response was to smirk at Rowan while he seemed to say to the darkness behind him:

"We have our orders; we must take the lady alive. Discard the warrior, his celestial stench is offensive to our very existence." Aly felt Rowan tense at that. Someone had threatened me and that was one thing he didn't stand for... ever. My erratic mind would try and make sense of the rest later.

"You know that is not going to happen spawn," Rowan said with deadly intent in his voice. He grasped the pendant around his neck, the pendant he always wore, and I was shocked to see the gem grow and burn with a deadly flaming light. He heard the hottie gasp.

"Quick, he is still wearing his amulet. Take it from him!" Suddenly, they were surrounded by golden warriors from the unending darkness around them. They were all evidently battle hardened and I almost gave up hope. All carried golden broadswords strapped to their backs and what seemed like some sort of gun at their waists. Their armour was a mix of seemingly ancient Roman clothes with a more archaic golden plate armour. I thought they almost sparkled in the darkness.

I could feel the rage starting to emanate from Rowan as if it were tangible. I began to back away from him but a hand on my arm stopped me. I could hear him muttering something; he threw up his hands and shining fire spread forth in waves. It served to distance the warriors from them before retreating and forming a circle of fire around them. I wanted to scream but didn't dare. Rowan had suddenly taken on a sinister quality, exuding more power than a pyromancer had ever possessed. He glanced at me and I almost screamed; his eyes were glowing with an intense flame that he had never possessed before.

In response the hottie merely smirked and motioned for his warriors to continue. The men all drew intricate symbols in the air in front of them. Golden fire followed their fingers, and a light pattern was left floating in front of them. All moved their hands to either side of them and with blood curdling yells, they punched through the symbols.

Golden fire flew towards Rowan and mein spirals and arcs. It was then that I screamed, mostly in frustration. Rowan pivoted and, muttering again, he held his hand out and turned in a circle. A dome of flame light covered us, and the fire bounced off, as if it never was created to begin with. While we had been distracted by the other warriors I was shocked to see that the hottie had drawn several symbols in the air and was about to punch through them.

"You will be coming with us my lady." With a blood curdling cry of his own, the hottie punched through the symbols and a torrent of golden fire screamed towards us. I cried out and stepped in front of Rowan. I really didn't want to reveal my secret this way, but I knew I had to protect him in any way I could; it was only what he did for me; and I watched in grim determination as the fire shattered Rowan's shield.

I held out my arms in front of my face, crossed at the forearm, and waited for the torrent to hit me. It wasn't an unpleasant feeling. The golden light burned away my doubt while the fire burnt a way into my soul. I waited for it to stop and when it did, I was shocked by what I saw.

Clasped in my hand was a large silver scythe. Untarnished, it glowed with an ethereal light. My clothes had become a sparkling silver breast plate with a black leather strip-skirt, black leather knee high boots and silver gauntlets. Wind caressed my back and I realised it was bare. Well, it was bare apart from my two large ebony wings protruding from it.

I knew I should be worrying about my transformation and Rowans reaction but a feeling I had been trying to suppress all night took over and a warm sense of joyful familiarity filled me. Strangely I felt whole, complete somehow, or at least more so. I looked at Rowan to see his reaction and saw that he was fighting the golden fire from his body. How dare they attack us like this? We had just been trying to walk home and now Rowan was suffering. I felt the beginnings of anger and knew where to direct it. Silver light surrounded my hands and shone from my eyes. I looked at the hottie again and he visibly paled. I laughed, and it was a throaty laugh of pure menace. Lifting the scythe, I pointed the bottom at the hottie.

He made the mistake of laughing.

"Much like a female to be unable to defend herself when it was needed."

I merely grinned. Somehow, I instinctively knew what to do and with a mere thought, a loud explosion sounded, and a bullet of pure silver fire shot towards him and shattered his knee cap. He fell with a bellow of pain and fear. I bent toward him. "I am complete, I will remember, and I will have my vengeance." That was my voice but not my words.

His friends rushed towards him, avoiding me, and they grabbed him and ran off, without a backwards glance to anyone.

I laughed, and then my world went black.

2

The darkness surrounded me once more. I was dressed once again in the shining silver armour, my large ebony wings resplendent in the darkness. I turned and turned but couldn't see where to go. I was lost, and I would never be found.

Suddenly, the ground I had been standing on gave way. I was falling, and I was falling fast. I looked up and could see the purest white light emanating from a spot in the darkness. I longed to get to that light but was falling too far away from it.

Ebony feathers flew past my vision as I fell. I could feel myself becoming more incensed. How could I fall and not be rescued? Gradually the ebony softness of my feathers became silver, and then became silver light. Why was I falling when I was only doing what came naturally to me? I was only as I had been created.

The silver light grew warmer and more intense at my back. I thought this fall would never end, until a pair of strong arms eventually caught me. I was glad to have been saved, until I looked up into a hauntingly familiar face, beautiful and terrifying. It was him, the man from my nightmares.

I opened my mouth to scream...

***

...and woke up cold, scared and unable to breathe. Where was I? The last thing I remembered was the gang in the alley. I refused to think of any of the other occurrences; they could wait. After some hyperventilation I took a deep breath and tried to centre my mind. First, I had to figure out my surroundings. Cold water splashed onto my head which drew my gaze upward. I appeared to be in a cave of sorts, it was large, but rock surrounded me at every angle; damp, dark and foreboding. In the middle of the 'floor' was a crystal blue lake with a rock in the middle. I moved closer and I could see a man; a large, well-toned, naked man; chained to the middle of the rock. I knew I should look away but the stranger was somehow mesmerising even in his prone state, his golden skin calling to the very centre of my being.

A deep, extremely masculine voice rang out. "Greetings Lady Death," he turned to look at me and I was struck with a pair of pure blue eyes. "To what do I owe this pleasure?" my voice caught in my throat. What was I to say to a being such as this? I didn't know who he was, or even who would leave him in such a state.

"I..."

"Ahh, so the rumours were true, I see it now." My mind couldn't quite fathom where this conversation was going but I had to ask.

"Who are you? What rumours?" The same headache I had in the alley returned full force and I had to grab a rock face to ensure I didn't fall. A wing brushed the cold dampness of the rock and I gasped. I now really noticed that I was still in the armour; weaponry, wings and all. Why? What had this to do with me?

"You may call me Azazel fair one, and as to the rumours, you will find out soon enough, it is as unavoidable as fate and twice as cruel. But for now, come closer to me and let my warmth chase away your fears."

I found myself moving towards the centre of the lake when the headache once again forced its way into my mind. Strength filled me, anger overcame me, and a cold, hard certainty caressed my soul.

"You will not have this one demon, I come to you only for advice," I found myself saying. I wanted to hear more, wanted to know why I was saying such odd things almost against my will, but I found myself fading and my world again went sparkling black.

***

I gradually stirred from the deep and unending darkness. I expected to find myself still in the damp cave but instead found myself laid on the bed I shared with Rowan. I was thankful that the darkness this time had not heralded another dream, but I was still extremely confused. How had I gotten here? The last thing I remembered was the darkness of the cave, the strangely attractive man and the dizzying confusion of my own mind.

"Oh good, you're awake." Rowan's relieved voice came from the corner of the bedroom. I kept my eyes fixed on him as he moved towards the bed. "I was worried for you. You've been out for a while." Rowan took hold of my hand as he sat on the bed. "How are you feeling?"

I chanced looking down at my body. I remembered all too well the armour, not to mention the scythe. I prayed it was too much wine, or some crazy dream that had taken me. I was Analilia Ravencroft, a twenty-six-year-old para reject living in the city with my boyfriend. I decided that would be my mantra to repeat to regain my sanity. I would look down my body and see my black work clothes and sexy heels.

Sanity had not returned. The shining silver armour still sparkled up at me. I still wore the black boots and silver gauntlets. I looked to the corner of the room and there was the scythe, taunting me with its shine. *It was taller than me for crying out loud.* I remembered the innate knowledge of how to use it back in the alley, though I had never seen it in my life. I shuddered.

I looked behind me and withdrew my wings, something I could do since birth apparently. Satisfied I looked like any other mortal I turned back to Rowan. Eventually I found my voice and it was rusty and raw.

"H... how did I get here?"

"About an hour ago you stumbled through the front door. The wings and weaponry were still with you. You just flew off from the alley and scared me to death. Do you not remember?" I remembered the cave all too well and the shame I felt about being attracted to someone, or *something*, else but I had thought it was a dream. I looked at Rowan imploringly.

"I don't know what's going on with you," he paused. . *My he is a handsome one*, a voice whispered in my mind, *I have only been accustomed to golden men that love themselves too much. No, I believe I prefer a dark beauty.* What the hell was that? Since when do I talk to myself? *No, you are not crazy, but you are not yet ready to understand. Listen to the boy and know more of the worlds you inhabit.* "Especially since you never told me you had wings," Rowan gave me a pointed look.

"Really? My magic's going awry, and I keep losing control, but you're focusing on my lack of telling you my feathered secret Mr I-know-the-psychotic-golden-hottie-in-the-alley?" I saw Ronan flinch.

"That's a fair point. Want to share?" he asked. I nodded slowly, not sure where to begin. Thankfully for me Rowan decided to take the lead.

"Okay, the guy in the alley is called Kane. He's a half fallen/half demon hybrid bent on causing trouble. I've been going up against him for years. My... guild specialises in battle with such beings. He has been more bothersome than most however."

"Why did he call you Michael?"

"I can't say. Maybe the years of battle and dark magic have twisted his mind. I wish I knew," I got the distinct impression Rowan was hiding something, but he continued. "Now, your turn." I exhaled.

"I'm an orphan. I never knew my parents, my mum died in childbirth. I was found as a new-born alone in a dirty apartment with the body of my mum," that familiar pain struck my heart. "I was taken to an orphanage but around my third birthday I started to sprout my wings. I was transferred to a place that was known for 'special' children like me. It's where I met Vale and Lyria. We were the outsiders in a home that turned out to be for paranormal like us; outsiders in a home for outsiders, how ironic. We stuck together being the odd ones out. My wings grew as I did, keeping their shining ebony colour. I developed a strange kind of power. It thrived on the decay produced by human life. I could use 'waste' as Vale calls it to do pretty much anything. The carbon dioxide we breathe out into the air? It's dead air, a decayed molecule no use to anyone. I can use it to keep me afloat in the air should my wings get tired..." I drifted off thinking back to my feathered performance. I could've used the carbon dioxide in the air to kill everyone there but that wasn't me, which is why the scythe freaked me out.

"So, what are Vale and Lyria?" obviously Rowan thought talking about my best friends would be easier... it wasn't.

"I can't say. Just as they don't tell my own fucked up secret, I won't tell theirs." Rowan seemed displeased with the answer but continued,

"So, you're a fallen?" he asked in a tone that suggested he already knew.

"No. Fallen are as they were when they fell. They've never been babies, toddlers or children. I have."

"Well what about the armour?"

"I've never seen it before. It appeared almost as if to protect me from that magical fire. It felt good... comfortable and familiar... but strange, as if it were angry with me..." Rowan drew into himself, seeming to get angrier the more he thought. I wanted to interrupt him but knew I probably shouldn't, so I waited him out, studying the armour still on me. The breastplate was a gorgeous silver that seemed to emanate a beautiful glow. The scythe was the same. Both sparkled with an energy deeper than life, that had a cruel certainty in nature.

Eventually Rowan sighed and rubbed his forehead.

"We need help!" No shit Sherlock. "I may know someone who could help, but I haven't seen them in a while and they may be angry with that," he sighed.

"What does that mean?"

"Fun," he sighed, which he was getting good at. "I... need us to go back to my old guild. It's been a long time since I've been there but surely, they would help us. The head oracle is ... temperamental at best."

"Right." temperamental... great. I could feel the stress from earlier only intensifying.

"Shall we go now? Best to get a head start on these things." Rowan seemed all too chipper now, perhaps it was the mention of his old home.

"Sure, why not. I can't see me going to work tomorrow anyway," I stood from the bed. "How do we get there?"

"I think I remember the spell," he blushed. Aw he blushed, how sweet. "To be honest I'm a little rusty." I couldn't help but smile, Rowan always seemed so sure of himself.

"Do I need to do anything?"

"No... no... I just," he sighed. "I'm just sorry for what we'll find there." Without saying more, he turned to the nearest wall and began chanting in an unfamiliar tongue. No doubt some secret language so that others would not find his guild. Eyes closed, he pointed at the wall and a line of pure flaming orange light shot to the bottom of the wall. It continued until it had formed the shape of a doorway. He then placed his palm, flat in line with the wall, mere centimetres over the glowing outline and a strange mist shot forth to flesh out the drawn doorway.

Once finished, he turned back to me, a slightly grey tinge to his beautiful skin. "Shall we?" he held out a golden hand. I ignored it and walked towards the wall, transfixed by the beauty of what he had done. The wall still seemed solid below the gold tinged mist, but I held out a tentative hand out regardless. I was amazed to see the wall ripple.

"Will we be okay?" I asked, the nerves getting the better of me.

"Of course," was the reply as his solid hand took hold of mine. However, just as they were about to take our first step the room, and the whole building, began to shake. The intensity grew as they were knocked from our feet. An invisible force thrust them apart and I slammed against a wall.

As stars danced in my eyes, a golden light formed rapidly in the middle of the room. I was almost blinded by it when a figure appeared as if he'd always been there. I was struck by his almost feminine beauty. He had long ebony hair pressed as straight as could be. He had a classically handsome face that was currently shooting evils in my direction. His flaming purple wings ruffled in annoyance while his crackling lightning sword danced in its sheath. What now?

I struggled up the wall to stand and just as I reached my peak, I had to grasp my head as intense pain blinded me…

… "Alethea, think on what you do. He has been cast out for a reason. Do not lose your hallowed place due to ridiculous false feelings."

"How do you know Barachiel? I love him, I will go." Alethea marched towards the end of the balcony, my ebony wings ruffled and my ebony curls flying with the rage I found myself in. I turned my silver almond eyes back on the seraphim prince, indignation present in every syllable I uttered. "I am Death, I have been since the beginning of time, I will remain so until the end." I turned back… and leapt.

Free falling as I was, I missed the look of pure hatred emanating from the prince of lightning's eyes…

… I gasped as the vision faded, the pain receding to the back of my mind so I could focus.

"Barachiel," the stranger nodded, slowly drawing his lightning forged sword.

"I didn't see it then, but you hated me… her…" *Us mortal, us.* My head ached from trying to figure it out.

"Correct. I could not fathom how one could leave such a position for such a paltry emotion as love. I should have been chosen instead," as he raised his sword, I could see a tinge of green light shining from his purple eyes. *Jealousy, I know that emotion well*, my inner crazy was getting louder.

I looked on in shock. My wings were gone, and my scythe was by the gateway. The sword seemed to descend almost in slow motion, and I despaired as I could do nothing. Yes, I had power, but it was unknown and highly untested.

Incredibly, a longsword of pure molten flame stopped

Barachiel mid thrust. Rowan strained against the pure force of the seraphim prince. He moved in front of me all the while waiting for a weak point in Barachiel's strength, allowing me to dive for the scythe. Conscious thought left me as I lifted the bottom of the scythe. A bullet of pure silver light shot towards the angel who was now locked in battle with my soulmate. Bright orange flame grappled with sizzling purple lightening as my bullet hit Barachiel's wing, causing pain laced silver tinged blood to explode behind him.

Rowan took the opportunity to run for me. Grabbing my hand, he ran for the portal while the angel howled in pain. I knew I should be worried about running at a flaming wall, but I knew staying would mean death for us both. Taking a deep breath, I borrowed from Rowan's courage and leapt, mentally screaming at the thought of burning alive.

I had the unpleasant feeling of flying through the air with very little grace before crashing into a brick wall; Rowan tried to cushion the impact and received the bruises for the effort. Passing through the gateway had felt like a lover's caress reminiscent of my Rowan. It was a soothing feeling after the initial terror.

I landed with a resounding thud on top of an already prone Rowan. The green tinged sky spun as I struggled to get my bearings. A pained groan sounded from beneath my and only the ringing in my ears prevented me from realising it came from Rowan for so long.

Scrabbling to get off him, fearing I was doing more harm than good, I bent to help him up.

"Damn, are you okay?" I asked as I brushed some stone dust from his arm. As it turned out, they made a bigger impact site in the wall then they had meant to.

"Yes… yes I'm fine. More to the point, are you?"

"Well, the fear that I crushed you aside, I'm okay I guess." I finally took a moment to view our surroundings. They stood in what appeared to be an alleyway, if somewhat dated. I could see old fashioned market stalls straight out of one of Vale's fantasy games. They sold cloth of all colours, jewelry sparkling in the sun, exotic food stuffs and the like. Every person seemed decked in such wonderous finery, no one seemed wealthier than the other. I wondered if they had gone back in time, the buildings had a dignified and old-world feel, perfect for the clothing. The only thing that felt out of place, aside from me of course, was the guards. Oh, they had armour and weapons much as I did, yet theirs was glaring golden finish. No, what felt out of place on them was the guns.

"Where are we?" while I had been amazed by the beauty of the place, Rowan had been to grab me a cloak. Apparently silver armour wasn't the norm here. I smiled; his thoughtfulness was what attracted me to him in the first place.

"We are exactly two and a half dimensions over. This

realm favours death magic more than any other."

"Why are we here?... wait... two and a half dimensions? How do you get half a dimension??"

"Sweetheart, we don't have the time for me to explain that. We're here because my guild is here." I took in the new information with some trepidation. Rowan was from this dimension? He kept something from me. What else wasn't he telling me? I could feel anxiety trying to claw its way in, my inner crazy staying surprisingly quiet. Rowan moved closer to soothe me, but I moved further, hysteria winning out in the end.

"Oh, your guild is here? So... you're from here? What else aren't you telling me? Hit me now. I'm blacking out, being attacked by blondes, being attacked by seraphim princes and sucked through flaming portals. What's a little more??" I sat on a nearby bench and my head fell into my hands. I missed the absolute stillness that stole over Rowan.

"How did you know he was a seraphim prince?" The suspicion in his voice was both determined and apt. I spoke through my hands.

"I get glimpses... visions... whatever. Someone who could be my mirror image was arguing with that... Barachiel." Go muffled hands voice.

"Then come, we definitely need something confirming." In a show of surprising assertiveness from Rowan, he grabbed my hand and got them moving. We moved through the marketplace so fast all the exciting things they sold blurred into one.

Eventually they came to a quaint shop front, grey and unassuming. Rowan lead us inside, and I was confronted by a balding, middle aged man who was eyeing me with an air of superiority. He gradually turned eyes to Rowan and his face, almost comedically, changed. A familiar look entered his bloodshot eyes; I had seen a similar expression at the bar whenever someone would look at my friends. This man, this weak mage, adored my Rowan. I could feel my rage boiling up from a dark place in my soul. I couldn't blame him, Rowan was magnificent after all, but it didn't stop me wanting to hate him. Jealousy was a harsh mistress.

"Ah master Rowan," he slithered round the counter on his slime ridden fawning. "I did not see you. How do you fare this morn? Indeed, it has been a good ten years since last I saw you." Were we trapped in a freaking classical novel and no one had told me?

"I am well Ronald," Seriously? Ronald? It sounded neither mage-like nor epic. What great mage was named Ronald? "I am retiring to my chambers. Send Illaria to me."

The funny little man glanced at our clasped hands. "Illaria, milord?"

"Yes. Do you have a problem with my direct order?" I didn't know where this sudden aggression had come from, but I was liking it.

"She is still indignant that you left her."

"Nonsense, that happened fifty years ago, she understood my heart belonged not to her. If she denies me, she is welcome to leave my guild and my protection."

I had to admit, I flashed a pretty smug smile at Ronald as Rowan led me through the small door at the back of the shop. I was not prepared for what I found when I went through. A wide hallway of polished white marble was lined with portraits of various people. As Rowan led me further, I asked,

"Um… explain?" he squeezed my hand,

"What do you mean?"

"Oh, I don't know *Master* Rowan…" Oh yes, the sarcasm was rampant today. "The guild, the leadership, the ardent adoration and worship from balding men, your ex… to name a few." He led me through a great oaken door, the aged wood embraced by twisted pure silver. Inside I found a large sitting area with pure purple scatter cushions everywhere, marring the beauty of the pure white marble. There was some dust, I guessed the maid had quit in Rowan's absence, but the place was pretty well kept. Through one of the other arch ways I could see the sleeping area with a large oaken four poster bed. Exhaustion hit me better than a speeding car ever could. I hoped I could rest soon. So much had happened, so much had changed, and I'd not had much chance to dwell on it. I really needed a pamper day with my girls soon.

I had just sat on a beautifully soft throw cushion when a knock sounded on the door. Rowan sat next to me and motioned with his hand. Golden sparks flew from his beautifully long fingers and the door gently opened. Stood ready to enter was a beautiful woman clad only in lace and what seemed to be pure silver fish scales covering very little of her breasts. I hated her already; my lifetime subscription to the local dieting club came back to haunt me. Damn the woman.

"Master Rowan, what a…" the sultry look on my face disappeared as she spotted our clasped hands. "… pleasant surprise, your highness." Wait, what? She sauntered into the room, confident in her looks. And perched on a cushion far too close for my liking.

"How can I help you, *my* lord?" Her hand reached out to stroke his ankle. I took a deep and calming breath. This woman needed to live for the next thirty minutes to tell us what was happening, then I would end her.

"Seer, we need you to confirm something."

"Oh, so formal. Why don't we dismiss the chit and I can show you what I've learnt while you were away?" I saw Rowan wince, and with good reason too. The rage, the darkness that had been bubbling under the surface of my skin, burst forth in a torrent of my silver power. *Ooo goody, I love this bit.* My ebony wings burst forth from my back as the whore flew towards the wall and crashed into it with a satisfying smack. I called my scythe to me - hey I may as well embrace it - and pointed the bladed end at the seer.

"You do not go anywhere near him. Do you understand me?" I could feel my silver power pour from my eyes. "He is mine, now and beyond eternity."

"Oh baby, I love your possessive side," Rowan said from behind me. He stood to one side.

"Can you see why I have returned now seer?" I watched incredulously as the seer, Illaria was it? Fell to her knees in front of me.

"Um, what are you doing?"

"Forgive me, my Lady," she quickly uttered. "I had not realised you had claimed him as your own. Why do you return to us now?"

I was now utterly confused. Obviously, this seer thought I was someone else. I settled my wings into a comfortable position on my back and looked at Rowan. He seemed resolute, almost determined. What was he thinking in his beautiful brain?

"Why are you kneeling Illaria? Who do you think Ana is?"

"Master, have you completely missed the statues of Alethea strewn throughout the city? The armour, the wings, the weaponry... This... this is Alethea returned to us."

Oh Him, I completely forgot that these people see me as some sort of saviour. They seem to have forgotten that they tapped into my magic without permission. Something didn't sound right about that.

"I knew it," Rowan stated with complete conviction.

"Then we are in agreement. Do you remember the story of Alethea and how she fell?"

"Of course, I remember it."

"I've never heard it so could someone enlighten me before I go officially insane," I asked. I could feel an anxiety attack battering down the doors of the mental shield I had put all anxiety in.

"Take a seat my Lady. I may despise you, but I bow to your etherealness. I shall begin the tale at once."

The seer rose from her kneeling position and moved to take position. In the middle of the room Illaria motioned towards the fire pit and beautiful flames that burned black in the darkness sprang to life. I went over to the fire and started to swirl my hands in the smoke.

"Long ago, before we ever existed, there were the First Children; those that God created to be perfect, to be children worthy of his love and affection..."

Ha, perfect. Let her see Lucifer and think he is perfect.

I somehow doubted Lucifer could be classed as perfect too. As I watched, a picture began to form in the smoke, of clouds and golden light, and Illaria began to glow with a faint black aura.

"...He created the choirs of Angels; the Archangels; warriors of Heaven; Guardian Angels... all were created with his love and affection. There were also the Angels that embodied different aspects of the Universe; Vengeance, Justice... but the two most powerful created were the polar opposites- Miltiades, the Angel of Life and Alethea, the Angel of Death. These two would always oppose one another on all aspects of the Hallowed Grounds but it was as it should be."

"At a similar time, the Lord had decided to create the Earth and all the creatures to live upon it. Work was going well, all joyous in the thought of what they would create. A special choir of Angels was chosen to put all our effort into creating something special for one species upon the Earth; Human emotion. They were fascinated by what they created."

"However, one day one of the hallowed Archangels stole into the halls where emotion was being created. He could not understand how Humans were worthy of such an invention and Angels were not. He studied them closely and decided himself that this should be for the Angels. First, he took Pride, and began to wonder why Angels followed the Lord and not him. He was obviously a great being himself. He then found greed and began to decide that he wanted to rule the Hallowed Places. And lastly he found Desire, and began to dream of overthrowing the Lord and those Angels unwilling to follow him."

"This Archangel's betrayal was never found out; he was crafty enough, after being infected with the emotions, to take some and create more. So he watched and waited, trying to see the opportune moment to take the Hallowed Land from our Lord. He was patient enough to wait a while."

"Now one day, Alethea had returned from retrieving the souls of the dead when she and Miltiades had another dispute. He thought it was wrong that she take so many souls and I merely stated, as was right to do so, that 'I was neither good nor evil, I merely was.' The Archangel was transfixed by Alethea's beauty and confidence. He decided that I should be the one to help him overthrow the Lord; he wanted her, and he needed her."

"The Archangel managed to infect her with all the emotions he had stolen, and other Angels eventually joined our cause, and the great battle took place much as stated in the Bible. However, Alethea with her newfound emotion, felt guilt at what she was doing..."

I never realised that at that moment, tears of shame were streaming down my cheeks.

"...and she could not continue. She accepted The Fall willingly, knowing she had taken part in the upheaval and knowing she deserved it. She was cast out with all the angels, including the original Archangel, who was known as Lucifer

Morningstar. The Fall was long, and some of the Angels did not survive it, but Alethea and Lucifer did. Lucifer had been given a special punishment. Now he had to rule a place so vile that only the evillest of souls would reside there. It was called Hell."

"Alethea was lost. She was not an evil soul, but she did not know what else to do, so she stayed with Lucifer and his obsession with her grew."

"Eventually she escaped him, to which Lucifer had the most vengeful action planned. He cursed our Lady, using the most powerful Hellfire magic he could summon, to experience the pain of birth, mortal life and death until she was once again reincarnated into her rightful body."

"Now, while this does not sound like such a terrible thing, Alethea was the embodiment of Death and fated to bring Death to all those she cared for in her multiple mortal lives. She would be alone, unknowing of her power until she was awoken for the Second Coming."

The smoke that had pictured all of this dissipated and Illaria fell to her knees exhausted.

"How do you know all of this?" I asked through trembling lips.

"Illaria is our most prominent seer second only to me in power. She knows things of the past, the present and the future. We can trust what she says as the truth," Rowan answered for me.

It is... unnerving to have a mortal understand so much of what transgressed between Lucifer and I. She missed out some painful, painful detail but what she said is the truth. I rebelled and I will be eternally ashamed for the rest of my never-ending life.

I stood to take a short walk back and forth, looking as if I was trying to wear a hole in the floor. This deluded woman with far too much history with Rowan believed that I was the reincarnation of the angel of death. *You are.* Yes, the woman in the vision was my carbon copy, yes, they shared the ebony wings, but she couldn't be serious, could she?

Of course I am the Angel of Death. Well, technically WE are the Angel of Death. You have control of the body, I for once get to sit back and make the sarcastic comments. Every reincarnation I went through created a soul for the body while I slept in the mind. Now however it seems that Lucifer's nefarious plans are coming to fruition and I have awoken. I do not know what this means for you Child but know I will help you as much as I can.

I stopped as Rowan rose from the floor and began,

"I have finally found…"

A loud explosion sounded, almost like a large bell being hit with them inside, and all three were cast back to the walls. They seemed held there as if strong wind held them. A pure white light started right in the centre, as small as a firefly, getting bigger and bigger with each blink of an eye. Eventually the light grew two people, two people whom I needed now more than ever.

"Vale... Lyria..." I shouted in both excitement and to draw the fact that they were still pinned to their location.

"Lyr, turn it off," Vale shouted over the tornado volume. Lyria shut her eyes again and a faint white light appeared to hover over her forehead. I muttered some words, as if to myself, and the wind died as if it never was. Once released, all fell to the ground extremely ungracefully. Vale looked at me with an I'm-pissed-off-I-had-to-find-you look.

"Stand up so I can knock you on your ass again."

"What did I do?" I shouted back, mildly offended.

"Lyria couldn't sense you anymore. I thought you were dead, WE thought you were dead. I... gahhhhhhhhhh." It was as if Vale couldn't express her rage and grief. I jumped up to hold her, letting Vale vent her rage on me. The three of them had been together forever, her rage was understandable, plus Vale didn't do tears... ever.

"Feel better now?" I asked, fearing yet another beating.

"Some... You'll still pay for this later you know."

"I know," Vale lifted her head from my shoulder and finally took a look around the place. Her eyes landed on Illaria.

"Who's the skank in the fish scales?"

"That's Illaria; this realm's most prominent seer and Rowan's ex." I knew that would get a reaction.

"Well, she can keep her hands to herself where he's concerned, or I'll wake the beast." A growl could be heard echoing around the room and Illaria crawled backward away from Vale in fear. I knew Vale had managed a partial shift of her face and knew what lie within. Vale was so protective.

We watched slightly bemused as Illaria stood as gracefully as she could, straightened her ridiculous robes and left with a humph. I turned to my best friends in relief and love.

"How did you find me?"

"Lyr thought to check in other realms for your life essence. I never knew other realms existed."

"Me either. Did you know we're two and a half realms over? I mean how do you even…?"

"Ladies," Rowan almost shouted to get our attention. "Now we've quite happily pissed my head seer off, shall I show you your rooms?"

"What do you mean?" I asked with rampant confusion. "Aren't we going home?"

"With celestials attacking you. I don't think so. You'll all stay here where we have the strongest person in the realm protecting you."

"Mmm I don't know love, Vale and Lyria need their rest and I'm pretty sure Illaria would rather hand me over than protect me." Gosh I loved baiting him.

"Erm my love? You just wait until our friends are in their rooms." He had a naughty twinkle in his eye, the type I loved to evoke in him. It was going to be a good night.

_3_

I stood in the archway of the overtly extravagant Roman home. I was from Gaul and never quite cared for the luxuries these Romans indulged in, however, it made my enforced Roman husband happy; and when he was happy, I was not beaten.

He was inside, ordering the slaves to prepare the hall for our newest celebration. He had just returned from war under the hated Julius Caesar and he had been victorious... again. He had brought brand new slaves from Gaul and he could not understand why it made me feel uncomfortable. If not for my beauty, large bosom, and small waist, I too would have been a slave. Instead I was now his wife, forced to take the hated Roman name Lucretia by my dictator husband.

He came forward when he saw me, pride in himself evident in every step,

"You must dress well tonight my love," he said as he caressed my cheek. "Caesar honours us with his presence in light of my victory. He will be here tonight, and the banquet must be perfect. Wear the silks I bought from the conquest in Egypt, they will enhance your beauty and promote to Caesar more of my worth." His hand continued downward, caressing over my breasts and down my thigh.

"My love," I began hesitantly, blatantly lying in the process. "There is something of import I must speak to you about."

"Do not vex me about the slaves again Lucretia. Feel lucky you are not one of them."

"It is not the slaves which haunt me this night. I..." I hoped I was not crazy admitting this to him. "I am plagued with doubt about how we live. Some of your men hail you as immortal. Your conquests have spanned decades and yet you do not age. I myself have lost track as to what age I am. How... how do we live so long?"

My husband, Maximus, gave me a long and calculating look. "You are wiser than I allow myself to believe. Come with me," he took my hand delicately, as if he were afraid I would break.

He led me gently towards the back of the great hall and took a torch from the wall. He then lightly pressed one of the stones in the middle and the wall moved. Lucretia was scared. I had not known there was a secret room here. It was of carved granite and marble, much as the rest of our home was, but in the furthest wall was an entrance to a cave. This shocked me. Maximus had said he had built the home with the cliff face to the rear as he could more adequately protect it should he be attacked, but he never mentioned a cave being here.

He propelled them forward, into the mouth of the cave, and squeezed my hand gently as it led downward. They seemed to travel forever, always going lower and lower, until they came to a boulder in our path. Surely Maximus could not move that, I knew he was strong, but even that was beyond his limits.

He did move it however, and he took my hand once more to lead me into the main room of the never-ending cave.

"This is how we stay young my love." There were torches by the doorway, so Maximus threw the one he had carried toward the far wall and what was there was lit up. Lucretia gasped. Stood there was the most beautiful woman Lucretia had ever seen. She had cascades of ebony curls and soft ivory skin. Her lips were soft and pink as a rose. Around her neck and wrists burned manacles that were more than what they seemed. She wore a gown of pure silver silk, though from her captivity it was torn and bloodied. The thing that really shocked her however was from the creature's back there were two large ebony wings, sparkling with a rare silver feather. The grief and anger from the creature poured over me in waves, though I knew it was not directed at me but Maximus.

"This is Alethea, the Angel of Death..."

***

I gasped and sat up in bed, struggling to breathe. It had been me chained in that cavern, my exact mirror image. I knew it was just a dream but seeing myself had both shocked and scared me.

It was a dream and it was not, the-voice-that-shall-not-be-named said. *Now that I am awake, it seems that my memories are leaking into your subconscious mind. I had almost forgotten Lucifer had done that to me. I am sorry.*

I looked at Rowan, huddled against me for warmth and protection, and wondered if I should tell him. He hadn't slept since all this began and I worried for him. I needed to let him rest.

Settling back into the excessive black bedding I tried to think what the dream meant. If these visions were true then I was indeed somehow linked to the angel of death. If this was one of my memories, why was I seeing it from someone else's perspective?

I am Death, she answered simply. *The memories of the souls I touch tend to linger and become my own; and I like your modern mind. I am learning so much, how do you think I picked up modern English so easily? Keep your modern views; they may prove a shield when most you need it.*

I sighed as the disturbing darkness consumed my mind once again.

***

... "Maximus, what... what have you done?" I demanded. I did not know what the creature was that was chained to the wall, but I could see it was in pain and suffering; and my husband was willingly doing it. This creature was beautiful and deserved to be set free.

"I have made a deal with a powerful being known as Lucifer. In return for keeping this creature chained and bound, he would teach me the magic to give us eternal life. Observe..." Maximus closed his eyes and began to chant. A blood red aura began to surround his hands and he pointed towards the woman. She gasped in pain and waved her hand; silver fire followed her movements and instantly I felt better, I felt younger and more alive. By Jupiter, what had my husband done?

"Come. We have a banquet to prepare for," Maximus led me from the cave as he had led me into it and for once I made a decision about my own life. I did not know what might happen to me or the secret I carried but I determined that I would free the woman and hope that Pluto would take mercy on my soul.

***

That night, while my husband was away with a concubine, I seduced a young gladiator into following me. I took him through the secret wall and down into the cave. I promised him many wonderful delights should he move the boulder for me. This he did, and I gave him the ultimate freedom; I thrust a dagger into his heart. I felt sorrow for the task but death with a kiss from a woman would be preferable to death ripped apart by lions.

I walked carefully into the cave and my eyes rested once again on the woman.

"Have you come to stare at me mortal?" She asked in a velvet voice. "Have you come to demand more life? Be gone, soon I will be free, and my vengeance will be terrible to behold."

"I am here to demand nothing. I have come to help you," I replied. "We must make haste; my husband will soon realise I am gone. How do I free you?"

"In the simplest manner," she replied, "The key there on the outcropping; Lucifer made these manacles of Hellfire magic; I cannot break them. Nor can I use my power, he has warded against it. So, they merely need to be unlocked, yet the key is out of my reach." I hurried to the key and picked it up. It tingled in my hands, but I ignored it. I knew Maximus must be getting closer now and I feared his wrath.

I looked at Alethea, who had fallen to her knees in pain, and asked,

"Do they hurt?"

"More than you could know," was the reply. "Be wary mortal. The manacles will burn you." I was not afraid; one of Maximus' greatest delights was burning me when he had no other amusement.

Hurriedly I worked, gritting my teeth through the pain and hoping I was not causing the woman more. I had just come to the final ankle manacle when a loud voice roared from the doorway,

"Lucretia, how could you?" I turned to find Maximus with a torch and a look of pure rage. Hurriedly I undid the last manacle and smiled in triumph as it fell to the floor. The woman stretched to her full height, a little taller than I, and stretched her wings as if sore, as if she had not done so in a very long time.

Maximus missed all of this and he lunged straight for me, a look of pure hatred marring his handsome face. I closed my eyes and waited for the attack, but it never came. Instead I found that the woman had caught Maximus by the throat and was holding him aloft, as if he weighed nothing at all.

"Cease your hatred mortal and listen to me," I said. "You enjoy soliciting Lucifer's company so much? Then I will send you to him now. I take back all that was stolen from me. Give Lucifer my regards and tell him I will speak to him soonest." I watched in horror as Maximus crumpled in on himself. He seemed to age rapidly and then disintegrate to nothing.

I flinched when the woman turned to me.

"Be not afraid gentle Lucretia. I cannot stop you reverting to your natural age, but I can slow it. Your baby will be born naturally. After that, you will have rewards befitting someone of your kind nature." Lucretia watched in awe as the woman disappeared, consumed in silver flame. Already I was feeling tired and knew I would have to lie down...

***

… Unconsciously I moved closer to Rowan, seeking comfort in my sleep. My magic worked to soothe my mind as much as it could but alas, I knew these dreams would keep coming; perhaps it would make things easier. In the meantime, I had chance to study the nightmare's held within my own mind...

***

... Some months later, I was lying on my couch surrounded by my handmaidens. I now resembled an old woman rather than the young woman they knew me to be. My baby, my son, had just been born. Lucian would grow up in the care of my most trusted friend, not knowing the depravity his parents had cavorted in for so long.

I felt myself grow weaker and a silver shine caught my eye. Invisible to all but myself stood the lady from the cave so long ago now. I knew she would come back. I waved to where she was stood in the corner of the hall, and then... I died.

I found it an odd experience being stood looking down at my own dead body. I looked at what I was now and was surprised to see I was that same young woman again, though rather translucent. Alethea walked up to me.

"I am returned Lucretia," she said. "I swore you would receive rewards for such a kind act as freeing me. It was a kindness I had not thought mortals were capable of." She began to trace silver symbols in the air in front of me, "I am saving you from the never-ending cycle of life and death and you will have a place in His hallowed halls." Soft white wings began to appear from my back, "you will be a guardian Angel, an honoured position. Perfect for someone with your caring nature. Perform your duties well and you will always have His love."

"Wait," I cried. "Do not you come as well?"

"I... cannot. I am no longer welcome in His presence."

"May I ask a service of you then?"

"You may, my friend."

"Look after my son, my family. I am gone and he has no one left."

"I will look after your family for as long as I am able." Alethea watched as I began to rise into the Heavens.

"Be well, my friend" …

***

I woke up in bed yet again, this time with less shock. Rowan was asleep next to me, but I could tell it wasn't late morning, it being barely light outside. I lay there for a while thinking about the dream. What did it mean? Does it have significance for what may come? Why was it all in English? Weren't they ancient Romans?

Ah Child, you clearly think too much, came Alethea's tart reply. *It was in English because I understood and could speak Latin but here in your mind, we use English. It would not have made any sense to leave the memory in Latin. As to its significance, that I do not know. I swore to Lucretia that I would protect her family and the guilt consumes me that I have not been there to do so recently. She was a wonderful woman, one that opened my eyes to the greatness which mortals could achieve.*

This was pushing on the last remnants of my sanity. Maybe Rowan could shed some light on it, though I wondered if he'd find me crazy. I should be used to strange things happening. I'm the only one of my kind that I know of so far. The question is what happened to me to become me if I was the angel of Death before?

I looked around marvelling at the pure marble of the walls. This World seemed so different from ours and yet, somehow vaguely familiar to me. I laughed when a dishevelled purple head and a confused bright white head looked in through the archway and moved one of my wings to cover the still naked form of my love. Hey, they've seen me naked before but is it totally okay to be possessive? Rowan is mine!

"What do you two hobo's want?" I laughed, throwing cushions at them. They looked put out that I had a great aim.

"Bitch I am warning you, I have not had my morning coffee," Vale said, grumpily picking the cushions up. "Is there even coffee here?" It was a good question; one I'd ask Rowan just as soon as he finished quickly dressing behind my wing. Did we even have a plan anymore?

"Fear not fair maidens," Rowan said with intense dramatic effect as he stepped from behind me. "I shall get you coffee," and with a bow and a flourish he was gone through the archway. Dammit, I meant to ask him about the whole your highness thing.

"Ugh, put the lovesick eyes away and get some clothes on. No one wants to see that," Vale's grumpiness was really starting to get on my nerves. I sighed and stood to perform one of the few spells I knew that required none of my own darker power. Muttering to myself, I drew the hand the length of me and was gratified to see clothes form over my, I'll admit, rather comfy nakedness. However, just as my luck had been since that fateful shift, this didn't turn out either. I had aimed for jeans, instead I got the armour. I sighed while the other two gasped.

"Explain woman!!" Vale was worried, you could tell; she was being loud.

"She means why do you have armour?" came Lyria's much softer voice.

"It's complicated," I breathed through a grimace. Where would I even begin in explaining?

"TRY AGAIN," Vale was shouting now, and I had to take deep breaths to calm my swiftly rising anger. We are very much alike as we are both very fiery; Lyria is like coolness on a hot summer's day. She was powerful, she could stop us with just one word.

"Please…" Aw she did the eyes too, dammit. I lost first.

"That night I got attacked in the bar by Vale's hottie; we were walking home when the same guy attacked us in an alleyway. We defeated them but I blacked out. Rowan brought me here to find some answers."

"And… the armour?" I swear Lyria's voice jingles like a bell.

"The armour is harder to explain," I said, wishing I knew a spell to make them know instantly. "I… I think I might be the reincarnation of the angel of death." *Finally, she listens.*

There was silence; it was thick with confusion and stray thoughts.

"Piss off," Vale said and laughed like the maniac I'm pretty sure she is. "If you don't want to tell us it's fine. Just keep the armour on alright. Something's wrong with the world and it has my fur bristling." *I like this one, very admirable companions to have.*

I have to admit I was pretty annoyed she didn't believe me, but I didn't have time to dwell as Rowan picked this time to return. He had take-out cups of coffee.

"You've popped back home," I accused. My heart leapt into my throat as I pictured him being ambushed just to sate our need for caffeine.

"I masked my presence love, and made sure to open a portal near the coffee shop."

I didn't hear him. I pictured his lifeless body on the floor and felt an overwhelming flood of anxiety hit; a shockingly familiar old friend I hadn't felt since before they had met Lyria.

I pictured him; his shining chestnut hair limp and matted with flowing blood, endless cuts to his bronzed skin and precious ruby liquid flowing from his life stream, his stunning chocolate eyes staring into mine begging for my help. I placed my head between my knees and breathed heavily, willing the panic to go away.

I felt light pressure on my head and the inside of my eyelids shone with a pure, translucent white light. My Lyria, the purest person I know. She had helped with the anxiety ever since we met. No one took a paranormal being with a mental health disorder seriously. No antianxiety drugs seemed to work on me, the effects burnt off within a matter of minutes. That's why I found Lyria to be the priceless gem she is.

"Better?"

"Yes, much better, thank you."

"What just happened?" asked Rowan, the only confused one in the room. It was sort of adorable when I thought about it.

"What just happened?" It was only right he demanded to know I guess, he was just a little snappy. I sighed, and realised I sighed a lot.

"It was when I was younger. I think maybe two or three. I had already started to experience strange visions, dark emotions surrounded by fire and death. The carers at the orphanage had labelled me as crazy already, a child barely able to talk, and would shut me in darkened closets a lot. They thought it would build character. I played outside a lot, away from others. Back then only 'normal' paranormals were accepted in the para homes so I was alone a lot before I met Vale. It turns out there had been a spate of kidnappings in the area, no one cared as it was para kids, and no one ever found those kids again. I was just the latest to be snatched. It becomes vague after that, but I remember being buried alive. Apparently, it was hate crime related, I don't know. Anyway, to cut a long story short I developed claustrophobia and anxiety. It's been difficult, no one takes a paranormal with a mental health problem seriously. We didn't meet Lyria until our teenage years and it was completely by accident that we learnt she could sooth my attacks. Her light is indispensable to me and I will always protect her." I stopped to silence. I guess it had gotten heavy quickly but in my defence he did ask.

"Wow." Rowan sat down still holding the coffees we'd managed to not completely devour on site. He seemed to be thinking hard about something. Given the amount of information he had just received it really didn't surprise me. Thankfully before he could ask any probing questions Lyria piped up.

"So what do we do now?" She took one of the cups.

"Honestly, I have no idea," I answered, my mind still ablaze with anxiety and light. Rowan sat next to me and took my hand. "But Rowan I need to ask, why did Illaria call you your highness?"

"And the surprises keep happening," replied a snappy Vale.

"Well… erm… you see…" he hedged. Really Rowan? "Ana I love you, you know I do, but I haven't been wholly honest about my past. I haven't exactly lied to you, but I haven't really told you about it either. To be honest I never want to return to this life, but it seems Fate would have it a different way. Do you know the section in Revelations, about the war in Heaven?" I nodded my head. "Well, we call it the Great Unbalance. Chaos reigned as the fallen angels descended to the earth. The barriers between their dimension and ours

58

weakened and Humans were able to tap into the magical energy that emanated from these beings. This changed the DNA of those Humans, and new species appeared within Human society."

He is not lying to you, despite what your logical side is trying to tell you. He has some details wrong; the mortals were changed by my impact when I fell and my power spilled out of me, I knew she was wrong before, *but essentially, he is right. Listen closer.*

"From Miltiades, the Angel of Life, developed the Nephilim, those that could affect Life magic and the essence of all that life touched. They're a pompous lot that believed they were far superior to all, and called themselves such; Illuminati, Druids... they liked to promote their own self-worth."

Well, anything even remotely linked to that braggart Miltiades is going to be a pompous ass. You will soon discover my horrendous taste in men.

"Now, another species developed alongside this one; the Necromancers. They had tapped into the far superior magical energy of the Angel of Death, Alethea. They were brilliant scholars, accomplished sorcerers... They took on aspects such as the ancient Aztecs, Egyptian priests... Always honouring their patron Alethea."

Oh. Now he is talking with his own sense of inflated pride. Why it is that it is always the men that must brag about how wonderful they are?

"This is where I come from. Legally, in the city, I am Rowan Belmont, technical designer of a large company and your boyfriend. I was born..." he stopped, as if it were difficult to continue. My head was reeling so far, why stop now?

"I was born Prince Mikhail el Rayan. I am, or was, the crown Prince of the Court of Madness, centre of power for those dedicated to Death magic. I should have been next in line to rule, but I did not agree with my father's ways, and so I ran and I have been running ever since. I never expected to return here to be honest. My father is stark raving mad, known as the mad king, but I am positive we are shielded well, at least for now." That was a lot of information to take in. My Rowan was a prince of this death riddled half dimension? I was so confused. Lyria was the sensible one, repeating,

"What do we do now?"

"Well… if we work on the theory that Ana used to be the angel of death I see that we have two options. First, we could go and talk to that simpering fop Miltiades. He's the angel of life and he gets on my nerves…" Rowan trailed off.

"And second?" I asked, not liking the look in his eye.

"Second we could slum it and go and talk to Lucifer. I really rather we not do that though. His obsession with Alethea may mask the fact that you aren't her." Wow, so we're screwed either way. I couldn't go and see Lucifer. *No, we could not!* That could trigger who knows what, not forgetting he is still an evil bastard. Yet, the thought of going to see the other one made my blood boil for some reason. I wish I knew why. *You'll find out.*

"I don't know." Honesty, the best policy my ass. Everyone's face dropped, not to mention Rowan dropped my hand.

"I had best consult Illaria then." He got up to leave and that lingering anxiety had me panicking that I had let him down somehow, though whoever said I should have all the answers needed shooting. I moved to say something, anything, that would promote myself in his favour once again but as always Vale beat me to it.

"Tell her to behave or I WILL eat her." There was no levity in her voice as it was a grave threat. If I had not known Vale forever, it would have scared me.

After he left, we sat huddled together, drinking the much needed caffeine and talking about not much at all. It was nice. It was almost like before the World turned upside down. We did however talk about my sex life. Like a lot. My best friends are nosy you see. I was telling them to mind their own businesses fuck you very much when Rowan returned. He was sighing repeatedly and tiredly rubbing his head. Oh great, the seer was up to something.

"Well?" I asked, already dreading the answer.

"She's gone," he sighed.

"So?"

"Well seers tend to stick to the guild they are assigned to when going through the trials, their magic is closely tied to the guild. Her being gone would indicate a higher power gave her enough strength to leave."

"What does this mean for us?" Vale asked, seeming to grow in size as her anger grew.

"There was no sign of a struggle, so we have to assume she ran to said higher power with news of Ana," he looked at me with such sorrow in his eyes. The ache in my heart made me move to hug him. It was all I could do right now.

"Why would news of me send her to go against everything she's believed in?" Why do I keep asking these questions when I really don't want to know the answer?

"Because if I'm right and you were Alethea, it means Lucifer will start the second coming, which will bring literal Hell for us all..." he let his voice drift off, allowing what he said to truly sink in. What if he was right? Did it all hinge on me? I felt the power within me surge at the prospect. This scared me, it had always laid dormant allowing me to take from it what I needed. If it was reacting now, Rowan was right after all.

***

... They had failed. Somehow, he knew they would. He still did not know why he had decided to use his hapless offspring. He was of a worthless partner and allowed himself to succumb to his emotions far too often. Perhaps time in the seventh ring would calm his temperament. His feathers ruffled. He supposed Alethea was too much for a Nephilim, even in this form.

Damn them, it was a simple matter of obtaining her thanks to the resurrection spell he had cursed her with. How had they failed so miserably? The blonde man took hold of the nearest rock and threw it at the wall, watching in satisfaction as the rock burst into green tinged sand. Were the descendants of his loins that incompetent?

He did not like to admit it, but he had been foolish. Eager in his need to get her back he had summoned the one being he could easily manipulate to him. He hated him as he radiated life and revelled in all that was connected to life; that is why the damnable fool would stroll around completely naked. The blonde man grimaced as he remembered how their meeting had transpired. A ball of golden light had appeared before him and he felt sickened just at the sight of it. His usual response was to attack but he had had to hold himself back this time. He needed something and he was determined he would get it. Eventually the form of a man appeared in the light and he found himself looking into his own mirror image; well, his own mirror image if he were stupidly naked with unkempt hair.

"You!!!!" shouted his twin, Miltiades. "How dare you summon me?" Out of nowhere he produced a large golden sword alight with golden flame. How had he produced that? He was naked for His sake. There was a clash of swords as the blonde man went to defend himself. He needed something but it was not a sword in his side.

"Calm yourself Life Lord," he began. "I have not brought you here to have to defend myself. I have brought you here to discuss something we both need."

The Life Lord faltered at that and lowered his sword somewhat, unsure at what the blonde man could offer him. Was he trying to deceive him or was he being honest? You could never tell with him; his insidious spirit always blurred his meanings.

"What..." the Life Lord stuttered. "What could you have that would hold any meaning to me?" The blonde man smirked,

"What is it that you crave? What do you need more than anything in the worlds?" At this the Life Lord dropped his sword and stalked away,

"Do not mention *her* to me," he bellowed once more. "Due to you and her I am doomed to this never-ending life of bitter cravings. I have gone mad, slept and then gone mad once more. I cannot begin to describe the sheer Hell of what I have gone through. It has eased since she has been gone... Do not... *Do not* tell me she has returned."

The blonde man lowered his sword. "I have not had

anything to do with your suffering brother. It was all her and believe me when I say she had done it on purpose. she had not a care for what you went through and thought to use you as a shield against me." The blonde man walked the few steps to the Life Lord and said, "Does it not make you angry? Does not your blood boil at the mere thought of her? Do you not want to make her suffer as you have suffered? She has not returned yet..." and the blonde man circled the Life Lord to whisper in his ear, "...but she soon will."

They had spoken, for want of a better word, for only a few minutes longer, each accusing the other of unspeakable acts. The blonde man smiled; at least on his part they were mostly true. He had not survived in such a hostile place as his domain without forgoing his moral conscience long ago. None of his celestial brethren understood this. The heated back and forth finally finished and Miltiades grudgingly agreed to help before disappearing in a flurry of intensely hot golden flame; he must have been angry.

He had to smile. It had been so easy to acquire the Life Lord's help. He had to admit he was not sure if Miltiades would follow their plan, but he would make him pay if he did not. He was to bring her to the blonde man, and he would see to ridding the Life Lord of his 'Demons'. In truth he could not, he suffered with the same urges the Life Lord did, but he would let him believe that if it meant getting her back. His hands began to itch at the thought of holding her once more; he needed to see her.

He walked into the hallway avoiding all beings as he went. He had no desire to interact with another right now and all knew to stay away from him. He walked straight to the first statue he had made of her and touched one marble leg with grief and longing. How much longer would he have to endure his loneliness and suffering? How long before he could set his plans in motion?

With one last caress he turned to go back. If the Life Lord failed him, he would make him suffer. He also had to talk to that fool Barachiel who spurred the mortal to lose control but for now he had to concentrate on his next step. Thankfully, he had added a wild card into the mix...

4

I managed to escape outside of the guild to get some fresh air. The notion that I was at the centre of this really affected my psyche. The magic shop temple had started to feel claustrophobic after Rowan's announcement. I wandered down the golden pavement, passing people and ignoring their looks, adrift in the sea of my own mind. I didn't even realise my wings were still out but really, who cares?

Why was I so important? I really was no one to anyone except for my friends. I was a freak of nature alone in both my powers and my mind, though I guess that didn't count now thanks to my crazy voice, lucky enough to be adopted by two fellow freaks. Oh, don't get me wrong, I wasn't doing the self-pitying thing. I loved my power. It revelled in decay but could produce such beauty. I once used a decaying cloud to produce a stunning rainbow for a child going through chemotherapy. He promised not to tell. I smiled. I once removed the necrotising bite from a woman's leg leaving it healthy and whole. I could do wonderful things with power so deadly, but was that enough to place me smack dab in the middle of some sort of… I don't know… prophecy? I questioned whether I was strong enough to protect my loved ones from what was to come.

I followed the golden path south, past quaint looking shops and beautiful cottages. I stopped at what appeared to be a bakery and looked in. Wow, those cakes looked amazing. Glancing at the baker my heart stopped. There was a flash of wing and I swore it was Azazel stood there. What could he want? I hadn't seen him since that time I blacked out. Was he here to cause trouble or was he here to help? I blinked again and the baker was just an ordinary man staring at me like I had grown another head. Ooops, maybe I was just seeing things. I was very tired. I moved on with a sigh, noticing more as I went. Were the guards carrying guns? It looked funny compared with the breastplates and the swords. I made a mental note to ask Rowan about it later.

I continued to follow the cobbles as they gave way to little walked tracks. The beautiful emerald forest had appeared as if from nowhere, glittering with remnants of a beautiful golden power. I fingered the dew off a nearby mint coloured leaf and levitated it into the air. This power was startingly familiar to me but it was not mine; if anything it was my polar opposite. This was life, pure creativity and vivacity. I let the dew drop gradually fall like a tear streaking down the cheek of the sky. I was partially jealous; I loved my power, but I couldn't create anything as grand as this. I walked on considering my vast and terrible power.

The gorgeous nature soon fell away to a battle-scarred clearing. Was this level of destruction done by someone's magic? The ground was far more blackened than luscious green. Craters held blackened lumps I did not want to pay too much attention to. The silver ruins spoke of a grandiose culture ruined by death and decay. Sadness emanated in this vast area. Call me a coward but I wanted to turn away from here. My power felt at home here but my conscience told me to go, much grief was experienced here.

I crouched to the floor and scooped up some blackened earth. I was not prepared for the vision that followed…

***

The murky grey sky was a turbulent abyss tonight. I had best make a move and hurry to the temple. The guild master had called an emergency meeting and as the scribe I was needed there to record it all. He was to address us all finally, he had been away for so long on his search. Instructions and guidance were greatly needed tonight.

Suddenly, a golden light pierced the angry darkness, as sharp as any dagger. Two figures emerged mid battle, each sporting blistering wounds and flaming weapons. One had a large flaming broadsword and nothing on, the other had a flaming pitchfork and whip. One flung shining golden magic while the other deflected with green tinged fire.

The blatantly naked one shouted,

"What have you done with her?" He had a terrifyingly desperate gleam in his eye.

"I know not life lord," shouted the other who would have been the first's twin if not for the dulled armour he wore.

Both seemed to have shining golden wings.

"Milah quickly," the guild master shouted from the archway of the temple, beckoning me inside. However, it was too late for me, I could not draw my eyes away from the scene.

"If you will not talk Hell lord then you will die," screamed the naked one and he launched a large pure golden fireball at his twin.

This was deflected by a tinged green sword with a loud crash of metal and alas, as the guild master screamed my name I was engulfed in flame and pain and darkness.

***

… I fell backward out of the vision, gasping for air through the residual pain. I dropped the dirt as I fell. What was that? Somehow, I had a vision that was not mine or Alethea's. Yes, I'd dreamed of Lucretia but that was a dream, not while I was awake.

"Let me guess, you saw Milah," came Rowan's deep voice from behind me. He must have come upon me in the vision and waited until it had subsided. At least I knew I was safe. My vastly inappropriate mind noticed how sexy Rowan looked right now. The best thing was he was naturally sexy, he didn't need to try.

"How did you know?" I asked, trying to rise from my sprawl on the ground with as much grace as I could muster. I obtained the level of demented chicken.

"I was the guildmaster who shouted her name," he said walking towards the ruins. He stopped in the archway, "I stood right here just shouting. Why didn't I protect her?" He came near the mound on the ground, his head bowed. "I was desperate to save her, but the damn celestials power was too much, too fast," his voice cracked. "She was only eighteen, a child when compared to our longevity, she deserved better. She was due to be wed to her childhood sweetheart. He died trying to protect her too…" he pointed to a blackened mound nearby. "This pushed me over the edge and created my deep-seated hatred of many celestials… but not you, never you…" A crystalline tear fell from his beautiful eyes and I could feel his grief from where I stood: I could tell he felt deeply about this. "Some of the more superstitious of our guild called it the war of the ancients…" Oh come on, this was not a time for me to laugh yet I could feel the tremors starting in the pit of my belly.

I can feel the laughter coming from the core of your being, came the tart reply. Evidently my uninvited guest didn't like that I was finding this all a little hard to believe. *Uninvited guest? This body is mine Child and you would do well to remember it.* I couldn't help it; the tremors grew stronger. I really had to get a hold of myself.

I threw my arms around him, finally sharing his grief while fighting and yielding to the strong emotions within the vision. I now knew the reason for the destruction of the temple, but it all remained so… so pointless. I prayed the rest of the blackened lumps weren't once human. *Pray all you like Child,* came the reply. *He will not answer.*

"Come on, lets go back and plan our next move before Vale gets angry and comes to find us." I tugged on his hand and he gradually moved, still staring at the blackened mound on the ground. I have to admit, I had to shake the vision clear. One of us needed to be focused to get back and I knew Rowan still swam in grief. As Rowan moved I swear I saw an echo of golden wings. What the Hell was that? Was it his power manifesting in some strange new ways? Did he have wings and didn't tell me? Perhaps these questions were just my imagination going wild. Though as we passed the ruins of the former guild a small sliver of silver mist appeared. This quickly morphed into a rapidly gesturing figure. It was the girl from the vision, Milah. I stopped but I couldn't hear her speak. Getting closer I heard only one word… Michael…

We went back to the shop temple laden with cakes from the bakery. The baker had not turned into Azazel again which did make me question my sanity, but the biggest chocolate cake served to distract me. I was looking forward to the cake when we were greeted by a very angry Vale holding a very red Ronald up by the throat. In the darkened corner was a flustered Lyria shining with white light trying to calm Vale down.

"Where are they?" Vale roared, vibrating with feral power. She was close to revealing her secret if she wasn't careful. Her freak of nature essence was more out there than my own.

"Chill bitch," I yelled, trying to insert some of our usual banter back into our situation. I needed not to panic; this was a good way to try. "Put the mage down." I added a sliver of my magic into the command, revelling in the deadly edge. Vale's head snapped around and she snarled at me as she lowered the mage to the ground. Shit I hadn't realised she was that close to changing. Banter was not the right way to go. I called on my own power to protect me. Vale was deadly when she wanted to be. I felt it pool in my hands changing to form a light silver force field around me and Rowan. I felt my swords at my waist and the reassuring weight of my scythe on my back. Wait, when did it become MY scythe??

This situation didn't scare me, our hostility was a tale as old as time. We are too similar you see. Our main difference was the nature of our gifts. My gift was deadly, routed in the certainty that death follows all life. Her gift was more animalistic, routed in her dual nature and nature as a whole. It was certain that our gifts didn't mesh well. Vale had taken a few half-hearted swipes at me while I was getting my shield in place. Now we were about to go at it again when Lyria stood between us. She released a wave of pure white light that sent both of us flying to opposite ends of the room. We lay there stunned, trying to calm ourselves down. Luckily Lyria always knew how to start it off.

I was about to stand and smile, all hostile thought vanished, when I saw Rowan move to attack Lyria, needing to defend her at any cost. The look of pure rage on his face scared even me. Once again, I saw the faintest echo of golden wings, then I was moving without thought. I would never let harm come to Lyria. She had to be the purest source of goodness in this and any other world. But how could I stop the man who owned my soul? It doesn't come naturally in any case.

I thrust the blade of my scythe in front of Lyria and watched as his golden flame bounced off. I was relieved that it worked but feared how Rowan would react.

He turned his manic eyes on me and moved to attack before realising who I was. I saw in his clearing eyes the smallest bit of his soul chip off at the perceived attack. I knew I would brush it off, he knew I would brush it off, but that little bit of damage had been done. I wish I knew what it meant.

"Oh...oh no..." Rowan gasped. "Oh no, I'm so sorry." He dropped his golden blade and it clattered to the ground, extinguishing from existence.

"Love it's okay," I tried to comfort him, but I could see that my words were having no effect. He would be depressed for a while; each time hurt my heart just that bit more. Instead I decided to concentrate my efforts on the other wounded party.

"Sorry Vale, I know better than to issue you an order,

especially snaking some of my power through it." Another sigh echoed, my own.

"I'm sorry too. I shouldn't have shaken the little man. You just have a nasty habit of disappearing woman." She sat and rubbed her forehead, stress and a little anxiety leaving her.

"I love you too." A hug only worked sometimes with Vale, damn she must be tired. I sat and enveloped her, trying to convey in the one action how sorry I was and how much I loved her. She rested her head on my shoulder, much as she does when in animal form. That conveyed without words that she forgave me. We eventually parted and I was gladdened to see Rowan had recovered by then.

"So, again... what's out next strep?"

"We need to stock up on weapons and supplies. If Ana is herself reincarnated it's possible that the second coming is... well...coming." Rowan mimicked Vale's head rub so well.

"How do you know?" asked Lyria, the ever calm, pragmatic one.

"It was written in the spell Lucifer cursed Alethea the first angel of death to pseudo-reincarnation with. Though part of me thinks he thought she would just come again, whole and complete. That could work to our advantage. He made the spell public knowledge. Perhaps he was unafraid, so certain in his power. Who knows." He went silent for a moment and his head dropped.

"Carascu, Carascu, comde danu oui, dalum mala lau."

"Erm, English?"

"Well there's no direct translation from Demish but in essence it's 'go, go, Hell will come when she returns.' That is me simplifying it a heck of a lot."

We sat in silence a moment, never questioning the source of Rowan's knowledge. Perhaps we should have. Had we questioned more… well anyway…

"So," he carried on. "We need to go to the market today and stock up as much as we can. Food, blankets, reagents, weapons… whatever we'll need for pretty much any scenario. I'm unsure whether Lucifer will come for Ana or not but I'll be damned if I make this easy on him…"

The market turned out to be one of those open aired ones. Think quaint RPG fantasy market and you weren't far off. The stalls were bundled together neatly, and I was awash with colourful marquees, beautiful fare and fantastical characters. I smiled as Rowan talked Lyria and Vale through the different weapons that were on display. He needn't have bothered. He spent ages trying to figure out Lyria's light and Vale's animalistic tendencies, but he was really no closer to figuring out what they were, they didn't need weapons. To appease his overprotectiveness, they each bought daggers made of sparkling silver and stashed them in their boots.

My own scythe never left me though I found a handy dandy way of storing it. The solid silver shaft that shoots bullets (I know, right?) at a mere thought softens, making my scythe a bladed whip. It was amazing! It currently hung at my waist receiving lustful glances off the merchant. He can right royally do one if he thinks he's getting his grubby little hands on it. The greedy vendor was our last stop. We had everything we needed plus ingredients to make something called a poultice. Please don't ask! According to Rowan it would heal us of anything. I guess he himself said I was death. Didn't that mean I was impervious? Who knew. He worried for me in any case. It was sweet.

Now we were to head back to the temple shop and rest before moving on tomorrow. Rowan didn't want to stay in one place too long in case we attracted Lucifer's attention.

It struck me that my life as it was seemed like a distant dream. We now inhabited a realm of subterfuge and danger. I sort of missed my bar job.

I wasn't worried about it though per se. Surely we as the proverbial 'good guys' would prevail right… right?

5

...I stood with my eyes closed, trying to regain some of the calm I had lost. The cold wind gently caressed my skin, making my hair flow in the breeze. Today my armour was quite heavy, signifying the danger I was in and the weight on my heart.

I lifted my hand, the sword comforting, and began turning it in a figure of eight around me. I expected an attack any second, knowing the anger I had caused so many beings in so short a time. Sensing danger, I thrust my hand to the right, in time to stop an attack from a demon, silver sword hitting corrupted Hellfire metal. I opened my eyes to see my attacker and was shocked to see it was one of the Angels that fell at the same time as me. His wings were covered in filth now, horns adorning what was once vibrant golden hair, and his heavenly aura had vanished.

"Rest well, my brother," I said as I brought up my other hand. Clasped in it was my scythe. Taking advantage of the demon's prone state, I thrust the blade of my scythe into what had been his heart. I watched the recognition of what I had done register on the demon's face, and with cold passivity I watched as he crumbled to the floor.

I was stood in the ruins of a city once populated with millions of people. All around me the buildings had fallen, the ground was scorched, and the dead were strewn across the ground as far as the eye could see. Tortured silver souls reached out to me to give them the peace they so readily deserved. They formed a sea of silver in my vision and I longed to help them. I could not however, I had to ensure that life, all life, continued for mortals everywhere. Lucifer could not succeed in his plans.

Again, I began to twirl my sword in a figure of eight, guarding against any unknown attacks that may come. My scythe I kept ready knowing the secrets it held would prove useful in the battle. I turned to block the attack of another demon, my sword stopping his blade while the blade of my scythe buried into his chest; I used the bottom of my scythe to blow a hole in another attacking demon, loving the effect the magic bullets had on my enemy.

The battle continued like this, the green tinged magic of Lucifer's demons clashing with the heavenly gold. Interspersed were the odd flashes of silver when I myself had to intervene. All seemed evenly matched; sometimes Angels won, sometimes the Demons. All who stood against me fell. I was bathed in their black blood with a circle of their bodies around me. Yet still I fought.

Eventually Lucifer appeared in the fray, casually side stepping all who attacked and any battle he came too close to. He had one goal in mind and that was me. The old sense of terror which had always plagued me resurfaced and I found myself frozen. He smiled his most seductive smile and I found my attention drawn to his lips. He may have been the most obsessive, evil former lover but he had managed to retain his soft mouth.

A demon took this distraction as a distinct advantage and plunged his Hellfire sword straight into my heart. I could feel the maliciousness of the metal as it tore through flesh and bone and found my heart live and beating. I coughed, blood dripping down my chin to the scorched ground below. I heard Lucifer's snicker, his admission of his victory over me. I fell to my knees, the blade still buried deeply within my chest.

In my rapidly blurring vision, I could see Lucifer come to his knees beside me. He caressed my cheek softly, running his hands down my ivory skin, seeming to revel in its softness. He lowered his mouth to mine and gave me the briefest kiss, while his hand reached to the back of him. He grinned at me, the grin he was famous for, and pulled out... Rowan's dripping severed head... my heart, though already pierced, shattered...

***

... and I sat up on the sleeping pad, gasping. What the hell was that? Absently I pawed at my chest above my heart, probably trying to get the dream blade out. Tears streamed down my cheeks, not from the phantom pain in my heart, but from the horror of seeing Rowan dead. Was it some sort of vision of the future or was it something that could be avoided? I needed to make sure that never happened.

It could be the future Child, Alethea replied. *I have the gift of Sight; this is how these seers could tell the future so well. It is possible that is what may happen if we side with Him in the second coming. Trust me when I say you do not want to pick sides in this. I have been lost for so long but even I can see the value of mortal life and its necessity to keep going. If we side with one or the other, all life will stop. This I guarantee.* That was some relief.

Afraid that my crying would wake Rowan I moved off the pad, donning my armour as I went. Oh, I'm sure I could find something less metallic around here, but the dream scared me. I feel I should be ready for anything. Armour, check. I wish I had remembered my weapons.

Glancing to make sure Rowan still slept gloriously naked and yet wanting to re-join him, I left to get some fresh air and calm myself down. The sheer terror of the dream would not leave me.

I moved to the doorway and donned my black leather boots that had been carelessly left behind in lustful passion. Finally ready I moved out into the World, taking a deep relaxing breath. After the dream the inside of the temple had made me feel somewhat claustrophobic and panic had begun to set in. Being outside now calmed me somewhat and allowed me to think, thus successfully avoiding the anxiety attack.

They were still within this city Rowan had brought us to, but my gaze was drawn to the seemingly out of place forest behind the shop. I moved towards it as if in a daze and I found a small path to follow. To my eye it was a quaint dirt path surrounded by beautiful flowers; I missed the translucent, green tinged cobbles that appeared beneath my feet. I passed under a leaf covered archway twenty feet in the air. Only then did I realise it was one tree that had collapsed onto another. I smiled; they were intertwined, much like a lover's embrace, much like myself and Rowan had been earlier. It touched my heart and I knew I could grow to love these woods eventually, if Rowan wanted to stay here that is.

I paused as I realised everything had a magical underlying of silver. I don't think it was my vision. Why would there be silver? *Of course there is silver energy underneath everything*, came the dry reply to my thought. I sighed. *I created this realm after I Fell. I needed a respite from Lucifer's constant attentions. This World shimmers silver as it is created with my power, the power of Death. I vaguely remember these mortals being brought here... it was I and Miltiades... Why Miltiades?... they had to be brought here because when I fell my magic cascaded over your World and irrevocably changed the DNA of certain mortals. They could wield my power to a very lesser degree and so could not be left in your World... I'm sorry child, my memory has not yet fully returned to me. Perhaps it will in time.* I hoped so, perhaps it would help.

Shaking my head, I continued down the path, noting some beautiful red and white flowers that were growing out of a tree stump. At the bottom of the stump there was a silver plaque, I leant over and read the words on it:

"*Though you may be gone, your heart will forever remain,*

I'll love you through all time, and take comfort from all the pain..."

I breathed an almost romantic, whimsical sound. I could see the spirit of a woman looking down at the flowers and smiling, her silver shine almost blinding. It was disconcerting for me as I could almost feel the love coming from the shade; this dedication must have been set by the shades love, a painful yet loving and eternal thing to do. I actually had to wipe a tear from my cheek. I gingerly moved on, unwilling to interrupt the ghost's moment.

I continued down the path, almost compelled to do so. I was too busy looking at all the vibrant colours around me, or I would have noticed the hoof prints beneath my feet which were rapidly disappearing, much like the cobbles. Moving forward, the trees eventually gave way to reveal a large field. I wandered into it almost gingerly, stooping to pluck a blade from the tussock grass around me. The cobblestones urged me onward. I marveled at the sheer yellow of the petals on the gorse bush; I didn't think that I would find such beauty in such a place as this, so built up and industrialised. I sat on one small hill ready to relax and take in the peace around me.

In the distance I could see an ancient burial mound. It glowed silver in my rapidly altering vision. Somehow, I just knew the silver sheen was souls rising out of it. Was this what happened when the angel of death was absent? Was this my duty now? I could see the souls so surely that meant I had to do something.

This is what happens when I am gone for so long, Alethea stated. *I have a duty to these people, they were changed because of me, and yet I was not here to see that these souls were properly taken care of. They long for the freedom of the otherlife, or long for the cycle to continue, but without being released they are stagnant there, stuck in their mound until we release them. Can we?*

I knew I shouldn't do anything which might endanger myself or my friends, but I was moved by the plight of the trapped souls. I stood and took a step forward, reminding myself to ask Rowan why I saw souls all the time, when there was a piercing shriek on the morning air. To my astonishment I knew the souls seemed to be warning me of something, but I didn't know what.

They sense danger to us Child, Alethea added. *They know not from where but they want us to be cautious, we are their only salvation, and you can see souls because we ARE Death.*

Perhaps they warned me of danger to myself and wanted me to be cautious. They drifted without focus, suggesting they didn't know where the danger came from. They seemed to be worried as they saw me as their only salvation. *I just said that!*

I shuddered at that last thought and found clasped in my hands my scythe. I knew I must have summoned it somehow and was glad for the unconscious input. I held it aloft in front of me, willing all danger to be gone. The sliver of silver souls began to drift to the right, almost like smoke coming from the ground. I followed their movement and found, on the horizon, a dark clad rider. I was transfixed by him. He sat atop a horse made of pure red flame, the heat neither burning nor seeming to bother him in the slightest.

He merely sat there observing me, watching as I was caught by his spell. I could feel a desire begin in me; not the deep desire I shared with Rowan but a lust I had never felt, and one that didn't sit well with me. I found myself stepping toward him as his horse began to canter directly towards me. I knew I should flee but I felt overpowered with the desire to be near him. His horse broke into a trot then a gallop, and all the while I moved closer to him.

As the horse became faster the riders hood fell back to reveal a classically handsome man with a strong nose, soft lips and a close-cropped goatee. A part of me panicked.

It's War, the voice, whom I was rapidly thinking of as Alethea, screamed but I didn't pay attention to her, caught in his thrall like I was.

As the warning finally sunk in, I realised it was too late. The horse had reached me, and as the Horseman grabbed my arm, the World went shining black.

***

Alethea

Something was wrong. I span in a circle. When had I gained control of our body? The last thing I remembered was War galloping toward us. No, she must still be in the dark corner of Anahlia's mind, slowly gaining strength for the confrontation with Lucifer I knew must come.

Something was wrong because I had never had a physical presence when I was not in control. What could happen to cause this? Was Anahlia's soul waning so much? I stood in the centre of the dark clearing while silver mist floated around me. *What was happening?* I cast my power out from me in a bright silver wave and could feel Anahlia was merely unconscious and definitely still present. I could also feel that something was now encroaching on this dark place that I assumed must indeed be a dream. I wanted to scream and shout; it appeared I could not even seek peace in this dark and secluded place.

I never noticed the blood red spark that started just behind me, nor watched as it grew into an elaborate arch. A long-dreaded figure appeared within the light and started to stalk his intended goal but what he found was not what he expected.

"Alethea?" I span around at that all too familiar voice.

"Lucifer! So that is it, I have taken the place of the mortal in this twisted nightmare." I watched as the wicked grin he often subjected me to emerged on his sultry face.

"I will admit I have been tormenting the mortal. A broken soul is far easier to tame. Were you to regain consciousness and she were weak; I could more easily take you both." I grimaced and looked straight into his eyes.

"Do not mistake me Lucifer, you will never have her," only then did I realise that the terror from the curse was not present within me, more it surrounded me in the atmosphere, as if it were affecting Anahlia instead. I smiled and drew her scythe.

"You will not corrupt her as you did me..." Lucifer only smiled.

"Ah Lady Death, how much you have forgotten..." he walked slowly towards me and without me realising, placed a hand upon my brow...

***

I grimaced once again. How many times was Miltiades going to argue with me about my calling? Throughout my existence I had been told that the other Angels were far more superior, their masculinity made them honourable and even that they could not be as easily corrupted as I. Were I one to speculate I would think that the emotions created for man had leaked into our hallowed ranks. However, this was not for me to determine, I had my tasks to perform and would not deviate.

"I merely think that you take too many souls at once Alethea," Miltiades stated once again.

"I care not what you think," I stated simply and walked off. I could not understand Miltiades' obsession with my personal tasks. I sheathed my great flaming scythe and sat at one of the golden tables. I would eat as I always did, deposit the souls in their allotted places and then rest. I blatantly ignored Miltiades as he stormed off. I quite enjoyed that he became perturbed at my willingness to avoid him. I knew I was probably the only one happy to do so.

"May I join you?" asked a deep voice. It was vaguely familiar to me but I tended to stay away from other Angels as they liked to remind me that I was His cruel joke.

"Do as you wish," I replied. Part of me wanted to deny him, I had a disturbing feeling about this meeting, but I ignored it. Perhaps I was just tired.

"Thank you," the voice replied as a shadow crossed my vision. I refused to grant him my sight, what was the point in it?

"My name is Samael," the Angel continued. "I am an Archangel in the service of Him and Michael. I saw your argument with the Life Angel."

"Pay it no mind," I replied as I began to eat the food that had appeared.

"I think he is jealous of your position." Despite myself, I found that I was intrigued by this notion. Miltiades jealous? Is not that one of the emotions that were being created for man? Even so I could not imagine him being jealous of anyone. He was always telling everyone how exceptional he was.

"What makes you think so?" I found myself asking. The Angel... Samael was it?... only smirked in reply. I sighed, I had no time for these games, and stood to carry on with my duties.

I soon forgot about those cryptic words and the Angel that seemed all too familiar. I had spent a long time in purgatory explaining to the souls why they could not return to their loved ones. It was a part of the calling that I hated. These souls were very primitive and lacked the understanding I longed for in a soul. Why He considered them a superior race was beyond me.

I had just stepped through the portal to Heaven when I heard two of Miltiades' attendants approaching. I knew they were his as there was a soft chime sound as they walked. I could not imagine a more ridiculous display of power than that. Turning around only confirmed my knowledge as they were walking around completely naked. I frowned and cloaked myself in my power, disappearing from sight. I could not understand why Miltiades insisted on nudity. What if Heaven were attacked? The only thing he would be good for is getting a sword in the side.

I listened intently as they whispered together.

"Is it true? Is there a meeting of the greater powers?"

"Indeed. It is believed they will proclaim Lord Miltiades as the supreme power."

"Well was there any comparison? Lady Death is nothing compared to him." The attendants laughed together.

"You are right, as if a mere woman..." the voices trailed off as they walked past and away from me. A strange feeling began deep in my heart. It was true I and Miltiades were polar opposites but neither had dominion over the other. He was the life to my death.

Could... could it be that they had no faith in me? Were they going to replace me? I felt faint from the shock. What would I do? What could I do? Samael's words came rushing back to me. Did Miltiades bring it on through his jealousy? If only I were more powerful. Maybe... maybe Samael would know, he seemed to see things no others did...

***

… I snuck into the golden Hall of the Orders. What was I doing? My logical side screamed at me. Wait, I was always governed by logic. Why now did I suddenly seem to have an emotional side. I shook my head to clear them of my erratic thoughts. Samael had had no helpful ideas so I had left him in disgust.

This is why I found myself in the great Hall. Perhaps the emotions they created would be enough to tip my power above that of Miltiades. I did not want all of them, there were too many to count, but I just needed the one to boost my already considerable power. I checked them all. Finally, I came to a raging silver emotion contained within its holding sphere. There was a plaque in front stating it was Desire, that it made one more assertive in our lives, needs and beliefs.

I had to smile; this was perfect for me; this would make me greater. I took only a handful and looking to make sure I was still alone I placed it over my heart. With great slowness it started to sink inwards. What was I doing? Once done I rushed back to Samael. What would he think of this?…

***

… I gasped and pulled myself back from Lucifer's palm. He looked at me with a wicked grin. He had to be mistaken. I could not have been the one to steal the emotions, it just was not in my nature. I felt tears falling down my cheeks.

"It... it cannot be..." I muttered, almost to myself. I had brought about their downfall and Lucifer had suffered for it??? I cursed my memories being so hazy. Being trapped in a mortal's mind had not helped my recover any either. What would I do?

I heard Lucifer chuckle to himself and turn to leave.

"Well, I have an unconscious mortal to torment... it is a good thing that she has your body..." and with that he disappeared in a flash of blood red magic. I gasped. I had best give Anahlia a memory I did have, no one need suffer the horrors that Lucifer can inflict...

6

Rowan

Sunlight filtered slowly into my subconscious. I stretched, a slow languorous movement which came only after a night of lovemaking with someone you were so closely tied to. Yawning quite ungracefully, I opened my eyes and rolled to find ... nothing. The space where Ana was supposed to be was cold, meaning she had been gone quite a while. She was probably with her friends, those three were as thick as thieves.

I stood from the sleeping plinth and conjured clothes for myself as the sheet fell; a simple trick I learned from the fae. They were a clever lot and I made a mental note to see them when we moved on today. The clothing spell was easy enough, though I gave it my own spin conjuring lace up black leather pants and a black silk shirt to go with my pendant, but I had a feeling the war spells would be a lot harder. It was worth it though, I will protect us all.

Pausing at the archway to the room, I looked back at the bed. My love for Ana welled up at impossible rates; not the death toting, flying avenging angel but the pizza loving perfectly figured barmaid from the city. I had the undeniable truth of knowing how lucky I was and no one would take that away from me.

I don't think I will ever be able to scour my eyeballs enough to get rid of the sight that greeted me when I reached the archway of Vale's room. Clearly naked under the silken sheet, she lay asleep next to an equally naked Ronald. Bile rose in the back of my throat and I turned to view the wall. Ana saw Vale and Lyria as sisters which made them my sisters. I put on my angry guild master voice.

"Ronald you sniveling weasel. Disengage yourself from my family and clothe yourself before I 'port your shriveled man thing to the dark side of the second moon…" pause for dramatic effect "…NOW!!!" I gave them five seconds before turning, and sure enough I turned to find a sweaty but thankfully clothed Ronald wheezing by the bedside. I also found a naked Vale… don't worry I only ever feel anything with Ana… brimming with angry shifter energy. Well that answered one of my questions, Vale was a shifter but why wouldn't Ana just tell me?

I jumped out of the way to avoid a snarl and elongated claws. I couldn't use my shield, Ana would kill me, so I shouted,

"Wait, wait, wait."

"Do NOT think to tell me what to do Rowan high and mighty pyro mage," she took another swing "…you best get Ana to me before I rip you to shreds," another attempted swipe.

"Wait… she's not here?" I asked, a niggling sense of dread starting in my gut.

"No, as you pervert peeked, I had different company last night. She's not with you?"

"No... she'll be with Lyria obviously... I... I'll leave you two to it."

I'm not ashamed to admit that I ran, a roar of rage and a crash of ceramic echoing down the hall behind me. Damn shifters!

I was more cautious when approaching Lyria's room. She was so small and delicate, I didn't really want to see what pot bellied member of my guild took advantage of her light.

Thankfully all I found was Lyria meditating; her floating in the middle of the room alight in golden flame. It was serene and I found myself calming just watching her.

"She's not here," Lyria said without cracking an eye open. My calm mind couldn't figure out who she meant.

"I mean Ana, you know, my surrogate sister, your soulmate."

Soulmate?

"Yes!! Oh gees I forgot." Her light was abruptly switched off, almost as if it actually had a switch. She sank to the floor, stood and righted her clothes. My mind came back to me with an almighty slap.

"Ana!!"

"I told you, she's not with me."

"Damn, she's not here then," I surmised, all but panicking now. I felt along the line of magic that connected us tightly, only to find it severed.

"The binding spell I placed on us is broken, I can't feel her." My heart stuttered. One reason was death but it couldn't be that… surely…

Let me try," Lyria said, sitting cross-legged on the floor once more. There was not hovering this time but the golden flame engulfed her again. After a few moments she came back to herself.

"I can't feel her either. What do we do?"

Panic!!

Does this mean I would have to reveal my true self? I wasn't sure Ana could die, even if she wasn't the reincarnation of the angel of death. Her power seemed rooted in the decay of life. Then of course there were her wings and the weapons…

I had placed a binding spell on us the moment I realised she was the one, she was mine and any who stood in my way of her would be ended swiftly. With it now broken it screamed of Ana's death but I refused to believe it. If anything, Lucifer had grabbed her… damn…

"We have a problem and if I'm honest I don't know how best to approach it."

"What now fireling?" Vale had joined us by then, her anger beginning to amp up once again. Obviously she had an inkling about the shit storm we now found ourselves in.

"I think Lucifer has taken Ana."

"What makes you think that?" I had to admit, Lyria was a beacon of calm in the storm.

"I'm not entirely sure Ana can die, so our binding spell being broken worries me. If she is incarnate as well, then Lucifer will want to control her once again."

"So I ask again, what now Firelord?" Vale was angrier now, her fingers transformed by massive claws. It really was sweet. Her love and worry for Ana shone through.

"We go and get her back."

"Just the three of us?"

"We will be enough…" I knew that I smiled a sadistic smile, for Lucifer knew not what he had gotten himself into.

I approached the interdimensional focal point to Pandemonium, the city of the dead, creeping in the dead of night, praying (ironically) that we weren't seen. I was flanked by Vale and Lyria. Him, I hoped I wasn't leading them to their deaths.

What would await us as I tried to enact the

transportation spell? It was in fact the best time to attack me, while I was vulnerable. I shook my head. These paranoid thoughts had no place in my mind right now. It wouldn't surprise me if Kane attacked. Was Cerberus still alive? I couldn't quite remember.

The last person I expected to see was Azazel, basking in the light of the hellish power. Why wasn't he still chained to his rock?

"Oh, I have been released for quite nefarious purposes," he said with a light chuckle. That was always Azazel's way, sewing discontent with a smile and a laugh. I drew my great flaming sword with a growl. If Azazel was intent on keeping me from Ana then he would have a fight on his hands.

"Calm yourself Firelord," Azazel crooned with his hands in the air. "I am merely here with a warning. Turn back," he paused for dramatic effect. "Turn back, this path is nothing but pain for you. I do this out of allegiance to another so know this, Lucifer causes nothing but pain."

"I will not believe you foul demon-spawned get," I shouted, affected by his warning but Ana needed me.

"Suit yourself," he said and grinned, then he was gone in a flash of sour green flame. I turned to my companions to see their reactions but they were frozen, much as usually happened when a celestial appeared. It was how they could affect the course of civilisation so much.

I moved my hand, flat and straight, from right to left with my golden flame following in it's wake. Time resumed. Vale and Lyria kept creeping forward, intent on their goal. Shaking Azazel and his cryptic warning off, I reached my hand forward and snaked it around a single strand of hellish magic. I started chanting the intricate spell, focused inside myself for my flaming strength, when a blast of golden power pushed me back several yards.

I rolled to my feet, unsheathing my great broadsword as I went. I was in time to avoid several more volleys of golden flame attacks. I knew who this was; it figures he would turn up as soon as I tried to enter his father's domain.

"Show yourself demon spawn," I shouted into the darkness. If I didn't stop Kane here, he would slither off and tell his father anyway.

"No need to shout Michael, I am right here." I turned to find him right behind me and my golden flame met his equally golden blade.

"The name's Rowan." As quips went it was mediocre at best. I could see the look of disbelief in his eye.

"Be that as it may, why do you sneak into my father's domain with the halfling and the horse?" Horse? Surely he didn't mean Vale? She was far too angry to turn into such a docile creature.

"Oh you know, I just thought I'd give an old friend a

visit."

"Indeed? How *nice* of you." I could feel him pushing on the blades just as much as I was. "So it has nothing to do with the return of the lady?" Well, he had me figured out pretty quickly, may as well drop the ruse.

"So you know my girlfriend is there. She's mine and I will have her back." I managed to convey deadly intent in such a mundane conversation. Might as well put it out there.

"How quaint. Care to see how well that goes?" Well it did get to violence quickly. I shouldn't be surprised really, he was half Lucifer after all. There wasn't much more to say really. This was just one more fight to finish so that I got to her sooner...

7

Alethea

I sighed a vexed sigh; one that I was almost positive I would repeat over the next few millennia. I possessed very little patience to begin with and now I had to endure not only the presence of a stain on my existence, but he had to blather on too.

Each day I woke hoping it was a dream; each day I was bitterly disappointed. Here I remained and here I would be for all time unless I could think of some form of escape. The smell of Hellfire was positively choking me, and I longed to get away from it and the pain I was chained to.

I sighed again as I listened to him address his minions. He was spewing some filth about them being the ultimate beings in all the realms and their power was undefeatable blah blah blah; frankly I was unimpressed.

"Go forth," Lucifer continued. "Go forth and spread my will across this tainted World. Go and sow the seeds of contempt, of destruction and know you are doing your Lords bidding." To a cry of pure pleasure from his horrendously devoted minions, Lucifer turned back to our shared thrones and took his place on his. He seemed to almost glow with a self-love that turned my stomach. After seeming to mentally congratulate himself on a successful speech he turned to me. It was a strange experience for me to look at him; he was the same handsome Archangel he had ever been but his aura had changed and his hazel eyes now radiated so much gleeful evil I could no longer see how he had once been a celestial being.

"What think you of that, my love?"

"Do not vex me with your inane chatter Lucifer," I replied. "I may be tormented with your presence, but I refuse to have to converse on your twisted dealings in this literal Hell hole." I could see Lucifer sigh. He seemed plagued daily by the emotions he foolishly stole and pride was always the one he happily succumbed to. I had to mentally rebuke myself; sometimes he did not seem so totally evil when I looked at him, he seemed merely like someone who longed for something he could not have.

I shook myself. I had to remember this was the image he wanted to show, that of an innocent being taken down by temptation. He was evil and would always be. I started to shake. Lucifer sighed even louder.

"I am sorrowful in the harried way I retrieved you my love," Lucifer began. "I was angry at Maximus and Lucretia's incompetence at safeguarding you... I would have punished Lucretia also..."

"*Never* mistake me Lucifer," I shouted, interrupting him and conveying my anger, "I am joyful I saved that good woman from your clutches. I have seen what you allow your minions, what you yourself do, to unfortunate souls down here and I would *never* let a good soul like Lucretia's suffer here." I sat back in my throne and turned away from him, brimming with anger. I wanted to scream my frustration at my situation. Lucifer had specially warded the manacles against my power, my weapons and my escape. I was helpless until a situation presented itself that I could use. I could be patient; I was eternal and unending.

I felt so much embarrassment at the way Lucifer had caught me. I had stormed into his dark palace, righteous fury at my heel, and had tried to battle him for my pride and honour at being bound for so long. He had fought me, never using his magic and only his blade, and I had been so forceful in my anger that I had never noticed. He had parried me towards the thrones and I had not noticed, using blade and magic in an attempt to end him. He had moved me closer to the thrones, where he had laid his trap; a manacle of Hellfire magic flew toward me at his bidding and clamped around my wrist. Almost instantly my weapons disappeared and my aura faded. My strength left me and I was dragged down to the throne he had originally created for me. I had let out a scream of anger, but that had been all I had been able to manage. In triumph Lucifer had taken the other end of the manacle and clamped it around his own wrist; he then sat down in his own throne. Now we would be eternally bound.

Lucifer almost huffed his own frustration and went to wipe some dust off of his own shining armour. If I could say anything positive about him it was that he always kept himself very immaculate unlike his minions. His golden hair was still soft and full, his golden wings still intact; his only physical drawback was that his celestial radiance had gone, replaced by a malicious sour green aura that was hidden from all save myself and him. I felt saddened in spite of myself and almost missed the Lucifer from before the Fall, from before his own stupidity; and my own.

My reverie was interrupted by a loud sound, almost resembling the clang of blade against blade. I knew what was to come and watched in trepidation as the emerald green tinged aura emerged. It grew and grew and became a large green tinged light. Echoing around the cavernous throne room was a screech of horse hooves and the neighs of a devilish beast. I sighed; this horseman had picked up Lucifer's misguided flair for the dramatic it would seem. Despite my contempt for the being that was about to appear, I felt the stirrings of a desire I had not felt in a while. I had always assumed that the desire I had been infected with from Lucifer would be for him only and unending; however, it now seemed to have completely disappeared for Lucifer and directed itself towards War. I had to admit, he was a handsome being with a well-muscled body under magnificent armour, soft eyes, strong nose and soft lips surrounded by a goatee. Yes, I could see myself quite happily in his arms, much more so than Lucifer's.

Finally, after much pomp and ceremony, War's blazing horse crashed through the green tinged light and landed at the foot of my and Lucifer's dais. I never understood the colour of War's magic; he had a flaming steed and a flaming broadsword and yet his magic was emerald green. If I ever got away from Lucifer long enough to ask, I would.

War dismounted with his usual confidence and strode towards us I smiled; I could now play my usual game that I liked to, one that would both annoy and anger Lucifer.

"Darling War," I said in my most sultry voice. "What... delights have you brought for me this day?" I used my sly smile, one that I knew had an effect on both Lucifer and War. His piercing almond eyes looked deep into mine and I knew he pictured all the things he wanted to do with me, all the things they wanted to do to one another.

"My lady," he stuttered. "I have brought a soul to our Lord for judgement." I did not like that he had used the word 'our' Lord, as if Lucifer had dominion over me and all things. The amount he curried favour with Lucifer always made my stomach turn a little bit. I sighed, as if disappointed by something,

"Fine dear War, step forth and receive *your* Lord's blessing." I chanced a glance at Lucifer and noted he took in all the details of our exchange with suspicion and the beginnings of anger. I smiled sweetly at him.

"Lucifer?"

He looked closely at me, seemingly unsure whether to

be suspicious of my motives or angry that I dare flirt with another being. He watched closely as War mounted the steps of the dais, threw his cloak from around him and knelt with his head bowed and hands up in offering to Lucifer. Emerald green flames began in the centre of his palm and grew. When they were no bigger than a dagger, they became green light and, in the midst, a small soul appeared. I was tempted to stop paying attention; Lucifer received souls all the time and in my severely weakened state there was not much I could do about it. However, the small confused and scared soul looked somehow familiar to me. I was not entirely certain but the soul resembled Lucretia in so many uncanny ways. What little magic I still had at my disposal screamed at me to save the soul. I was certain now that this soul was somehow related to Lucretia. Was this a descendant? How long had Lucifer kept me down here?

Lucifer finally turned to War.

"What crime has this soul committed?" he asked, almost bored of the task he was set long ago.

"Theft, contempt and adultery my Lord."

"Fine," he sighed. "Eternity in the deepest pit of Hell."

I watched as the small soul screamed quietly and against my better judgement knew I had to do something.

"Lucifer," I began, adopting what I hoped was a seductive pose on my throne. "That seems a little excessive do you not think?" I began massaging my neck slightly, as if tired, and watched how he saw every movement.

"Adultery and theft go against the commandments my love and are things I am well within my rights to punish for. I know this is a necromancer soul, one of yours, but they are subject to my rule also," he replied, not taking his eyes off me. He watched as my hands slowly moved down to my breastplate and caressed the clasps holding it there. I ignored the jibe about the necromancer, necromancers only existed due to my power leaking out last time Lucifer caught me.

"Why not leave the soul for now? Why not place it in purgatory and come give me a massage? Sitting in this throne all day gives me such aches in my wings." I undid the clasps then, watched as my breastplate fell to the ground and stretched, allowing my considerable wingspan to be reached. Lucifer seemed transfixed. Now all I wore were my boots, my gauntlets, my skirt and my small scrap of black silk I wore under my breast plate. I ran my hand over a breast hoping he would take that as a positive, seductive sign. I still had not realised that War followed each move with just as much rapt attention as Lucifer did.

I moaned out loud and moved my hand over my flat stomach. The nausea at the thought of what I was about to do surfaced; could I really do the one thing in all the universes that I dreaded? Sometimes it was unavoidable, he would catch me at one of my weaker moments, usually after an escape attempt, when that small bit of magic I still had access to was all but spent. Then my soul would leave my body and travel to the one place I knew to escape; my realm of Death made for me and by me. It was Death in essence and I felt invincible there, as if Lucifer would never get me again. I knew that I would have to do that again, but only so long as it takes to do the nasty deed, then I would need all my wits about me to proceed with the plan that was rapidly forming in my head.

Lucifer lifted his hand negligently,

"War, do as she says, place the soul in Purgatory." When he received no reply, he looked to see where War had gone. He was not happy to find him staring at me with blatant lust.

"War, do as I bid!" Lucifer put some of his power behind his command and reluctantly War left, his eyes never leaving me, my beauty or obvious appeal. Rather unwillingly, he went through the portal to Purgatory.

Lucifer turned back to me, a look of longing, lust, and excitement in his eye. I almost wanted to laugh in his face; he had such happiness at the thought of my willingly submitting to him that I was almost incredulous. I wondered what he would do now if I took it all back.

I watched as he moved slowly towards me, bile rising in my throat. I tried my hardest to push it away and attempt to look amorous, I could not falter now. His own shining breast plate was removed and discarded on the floor, to reveal a bronze muscled chest. Had I been any other female I would have felt swamped by desire and a need to please him. As he reached me and descended, his chest skewing my vision, all I felt was disgusted to the very core of my soul...

***

...I had to catch myself as I staggered, leaning on one of the rock columns lining the hallway. I had never felt so weak; my spirit felt as if it were slowly leaving me. It never would but the sheer weakness I felt scared me. I had had to go deep both into the magic left to me and my realm. I had exuded so much seduction that I was well aware that Lucifer did unspeakable things to me so I fled further than I ever had into my realm and basked in the Deathly glow. Coming back had required magic I did not have so I tapped into the essence of the realm and hoped that it didn't weaken it forever.

I had returned to my body in time to see Lucifer's smug and satisfied smile as he slept. I had wept silently and gathered my crystal tears in my palm. With these I chanted a spell of hibernation and dripped them into Lucifer's mouth. It was all that was left to me and I prayed it would keep him asleep long enough for what I had to do.

My wing brushed a vaguely humanoid figure and I froze in fear. I had nothing left, no magic to call on, to the extent I couldn't even mask my wings and weapons from sight. I had nothing, and if this were one of the minions, I would be in trouble. Cautiously I glanced to my side and was immediately swamped with relief. It wasn't a minion; it was something far more pompous and bloated with self-worth; a golden statue of Lucifer himself. I smirked in loathing. He never caught on that no one wanted to see him, let alone many golden carvings of him in our lifetimes. If I had my magic at full power, I would have melted it where it stood.

Onward I moved, slowly, as if every step was painful. I was getting closer to the throne room; I could feel the very essence of evil emanating from it. I did not want to go back there, Lucifer was at his most powerful there but I had get to Purgatory. That soul would not suffer if I could help it. How had War come into possession of the soul anyway? Necromancer souls were mine and mine alone thanks to Him.

Onward I staggered, intent on my goal. I became vaguely aware of a soft scratching sound behind me. I glanced behind to find Lucifer's end of the manacle dragging behind me, ash dropping off at regular intervals. I actually shuddered; I was Death itself and yet I still shuddered at what I had done to Lucifer. I had made sure he was asleep, drugged by my enchanted tears, and without regret I had used my longsword with all my might, slashing straight through Lucifer's wrist. In a moment of naiveté, I had half expected ruby red blood to pour forth from the wound, but the hand had merely dropped to the floor turning to ash in its wake.

This hallway was far too long, where was that damnable throne room? Just as I almost gave up, I stumbled across an outcropping and straight through Lucifer's blood red magical barrier. It stung a little as it hit me, but my mind laughed at Lucifer's attempts. What was the point of the barrier? Who in their right mind would break into the throne room of Hell? I realised I myself was breaking into it, but I had good reason; plus, I had never really believed I was in my right mind. I merely blew at the barrier and it dissipated. I had needed a display like that to remind me of my own power. I smiled.

I calmed my mind as I looked around. It was as it would always be, foul and reeking of him. I needed to get this manacle off of me. My power felt suppressed and I felt almost mortal because of it. I couldn't afford such weakness in the presence of Lucifer. Hoping that this manacle was similar to the last I searched for a key. There had to be one somewhere. I spent what seemed like ages searching. Sure enough, I found a small Hellfire key in the secret compartment of Lucifer's throne; I laughed, surely he did not think himself the first ruler to be corrupt enough to hide things.

Quickly I unlocked the manacle and it fell to the floor with a resounding thud. I hoped no one had heard it but I was ecstatic to have my power returning to me. I also smiled at the fact that Maximus had not told Lucifer how I had escaped the last time. Perhaps Fate was finally on my side, at least for this day; I would have to ask him next time I saw him. At that mere thought, I laughed.

Once I had luxuriated enough in my newfound freedom I turned to the thrones; the portal to purgatory stood open next to them, swirling with its rainbow-coloured magic. I had never been to purgatory, I had never thought to go; I had merely sent souls there to await salvation or damnation, whatever may come of it. The thought of going there, where nothing ever changed, made me pause; my life was long enough, did I really want to make it any longer?

I had to be careful when looking into a portal such as this; the ever-changing nature and colour of it could draw someone in, depositing them Him-knew-where. I shook myself, as much to break the spell as to remind me I had very little time and moved towards the portal. I could feel my triumph mounting, bolstered by the imminent freedom I felt. I would do this; I could do this, and it would feel so *good*.

I held out my hand to the swirling eddies of Purgatory and felt my fingers sink into the endless void. It was soft, warm and almost welcoming to a lost soul such as I. I moved to sink into it but could move no further. While I had been staring into the hypnotic portal, two steel bands of corded muscle had surrounded me, holding me to a wall of solid warmth. It was familiar and the part of me wanted nothing more than to sink into that warmth. However I resisted and turned in the tight embrace to see who I already knew held me; War. He held me tightly, almost as if he was afraid to let go, but he was still conscious of my wings. He had always said my wings were a source of great beauty that reflected my moods no matter the occasion. He had said he had always enjoyed to make me angry as my feathers turned silver and caught alight with our curious fire. He should be ecstatic then if I ever tapped into my full power and rage.

War was looking straight into my eyes, he always had the most expressive chocolate eyes I had ever seen, and he was looking at me with the same lust he always did. Now however he had my earlier display centred solely in his mind.

"War…" I breathed. "Let me go. I have to save that soul and I *need* to be free of him. I crave it more than anything." I had no way of knowing if my words sank in. The only response I received was the fire in his eyes growing brighter. It intensified as he slowly, torturously, lowered his mouth to mine.

I had to close my eyes in almost sheer enjoyment. His lips were so soft, perhaps too soft for the average male mouth but nothing about War was average. I could feel him respond to our closeness and to the heat we generated. His breath grew shallow, his kiss hardened, and his body grew tense, almost as if he were waiting to pounce upon me. The hard evidence of his arousal pressed insistently into my stomach. I couldn't afford to let myself be distracted in this fashion but the more he held me the less in danger I felt. I knew I had to break his mesmerising hold but found myself succumbing to his thorough kiss.

"War…" I breathed again and caressed his cheek. The skin beneath his dark goatee was soft and unblemished. It was so easy to forget that he was the harbinger of War, the sole horseman with the most amount of devastation at his command. He would always emanate a soft emerald green aura; I never could figure out what green had to do with War, but then what did silver have to do with Death?

Just as I gave into his embrace once more, there was a resounding blast that echoed through the throne room. War and I were blasted to opposite ends and both were encased in sour green crystallite. I sighed; I had wanted to avoid a confrontation with Lucifer if I could, my power had not yet fully returned to me and I did not know how much I would need if I were to rescue the soul. Expanding my wings, I broke through the crystallite in time to see War do the same with his massive flaming broadsword. The only difference was he immediately bowed to Lucifer.

"My Lord, I caught the Queen escaping." I refused to even acknowledge Lucifer, staring at him defiantly and daring him to say something. I may not have had my magic but at least my weapons were easily accessible, my scythe a reassuring weight on my back.

"Would someone care to explain…?" Lucifer asked in his most contemptuous voice. He stood clothed only in a sheer blood red robe, clasping his left arm. No blood poured forth from the wound I had given to him. And where was his armour? White lines appeared around his eyes and mouth signalling the strain he was under using the magic to quell the pain and to try and control myself and War. I was going to take great enjoyment from this. I stayed silent to see how this would play out; I wanted to see if War would turn into the pitiful minion he always did.

"The Queen was about to abscond into Purgatory my Lord. She was about to steal the soul you placed there for later judgement." War seemed to get lower on his knees, if that was at all possible. He always seemed to fawn over Lucifer, desperate to have some sort of love and praise from him. He would never get it however, even I had never received love from him only lust, and sickening lust at that.

"Is this true my love?" Lucifer asked as he moved between me and the portal. I could see he was trying to place himself in the way hoping that would prevent me from going through. With him in his weakened state and my power gradually returning, I was not going to miss this opportunity.

"I need not answer that Lucifer," I replied, calling once more on the sultry voice from before. "My actions are my own, not to be dictated by the likes of you." I watched as War moved to join his master. They both stood in front of the portal now in their effort to block me from my goal. I could see the swirling colours behind them. I knew if I did not act quickly Lucifer would have that manacle once more around my wrist and I could not, would not be bound by him again.

I took hold of my scythe in my right hand and my longsword in my left. Both sparkled from the pure silver they were made from and looked as if they had never been used for battle. With how angry I was, both blades sparkled with pure silver flame; my magic would come to my aid eventually, I reassured myself. Flipping my scythe, I held it so the blade stuck out from me near my elbow. My longsword I held in the warrior prone position; I knew each blade would convince Lucifer that I had given up. Hopefully, both he and War would relax their guards enough to allow me what I was planning.

I sighed and put all my will and resignation in it. I wanted nothing to alert them to what I planned; this had to go right, and it had to go well. I slowly placed my right foot slightly forward and braced my weight on it. I had to be prepared to start as soon as I said what I needed to, and what my childish side wanted to.

"I will never be bound by you again Lucifer, this I vow to you."

With my last word I threw myself forward. If I had my full power available, I would have merely blown them out of the way, however I didn't and this would have to do. I used my wings to take flight, no mean feat in the seemingly crowded throne room, and with one powerful pump of my wings I gained enough momentum to slice both Lucifer's and War's necks. I was not disillusioned, I knew this would not kill them, but it would slow them down and it would take time for them to heal.

I did not pause to see my handiwork and allowed the momentum to carry me on through the portal. It was a strange sensation, almost like sinking through a thick layer of treacle.

Just as the pressure mounted and I thought my ears might pop, I was through and what met me was not what I expected. For all of my existence I had been told that Purgatory was a grey place; a soulless echo of the World mortals inhabited. I expected mist and I expected a sense of loneliness and longing. I had not expected the pure serenity of it all to overtake me. Purgatory was beautiful. The lush emerald grass beneath my feet surprised me, the sapphire of the sky soothed me and the golden aura of the sun worked to warm my eternally broken soul. I had to rub my eyes twice to ensure that I was not dreaming, not that Angels ever dreamt of course. Purgatory truly was a stunning place to discover after the sheer nightmare that was that throne room.

I took a deep breath and allowed my soul to calm. A place like this would make sense even to someone as damaged as I. There should be no grey mist when someone's soul is in the midst of judgement. It should be peaceful, allowing the soul to be at rest and not fear that it may end up in the claws of Lucifer's minions. I almost wished I could stay here forever, it had been so long since I had felt this degree of absolute peace, but I had something I must do and I would not fail at it.

Purgatory spread for an alarming distance and I could not see the soul readily before me. I spread my wings and took flight knowing I could cover more ground this way and hoping I did not miss the soul. I longed for my full power as I could have called him to me but flying was an agreeable alternative.

Soon I came upon a crystal blue lake shimmering in the

sunlight. I came upon many souls in my flight but not the one I sought. I alighted by the lake and once again allowed the serenity to take me. I knew I would find the soul, I just had to relax and wait for it to come to me. I was Death, souls were drawn to me for absolution. I sat, spreading my wings so I did not accidentally sit on them; I never had but I was a great believer that there was a first time for everything. Picking up a small pebble I threw it across the lake, watching it skip into oblivion.

"E… excuse me?" asked a small, timid voice. I turned to study the speaker. He was a tall, slim man with mousy brown hair and an unassuming nature. He was also the soul I had been looking for.

That did not take long, I thought, and then remembered I had to reply.

"Yes?" I answered.

"Can you tell me where we are please?" he continued. "I'm lost and I need to get back to my family."

"We are in Purgatory mortal. You are dead and awaiting judgement."

"Dead?" he seemed to doubt my word. "How can I be dead?"

"Sometimes Fate can be cruel to us."

"I… I cannot believe it -"

I didn't have time for this. Taking a deep breath, I waved my hand in front of the soul and a wall of silver cloud appeared. Within the cloud an image slowly formed. The soul was running from what appeared to be warriors. The soul had clasped to him some bread and cheese and wore a look of pure terror. He ran from four horsemen- *Four horsemen again? Really? I would have to break mortals of that ridiculous number* – who chased him with weapons unsheathed. They appeared to be the Knights of a local Lord. There was shouting, the leader of the warriors seeming to get angrier and angrier. *"The Lord knows what you have done,"* he bellowed. I doubted he meant Him, somehow.

The soul tripped in a ditch and the bread and cheese spread out before him to a fanfare of gasps. The warriors stopped their mounts and dismounted, brandishing their aggressive weapons in front of them. I could tell the signs of those who tormented the weak for pleasure and these four were no different. They circled him, not even allowing him time to stand up, and all skewered the man where he lay. I held up my hand and the image paused. I had caught a glimpse of something I wanted to see and the soul had gone pale at watching his own demise.

I held up my left hand and motioned in a circle; the vision pivoted, and I could see a hovel of a home where in the doorway were four children crying and screaming at the same time. They must have been the souls' four children, he had been stealing food for them, and their hearts had evidently shattered at seeing his death. I sighed.

"Can you take me back to them?" the soul asked with almost painful hope shining from his eyes.

"You cannot return to them," I stated, perhaps too bluntly. "You are dead, the only thing I can do for you is save you from Lucifer's grasp." The soul visibly shrank at the news and I felt the stirrings of sadness for a being other than myself for the first time. I held my hand to the soul's cheek and allowed him to be bathed in the warm silver light of my power. He smiled and held it to him. I smiled in return and allowed my power to overtake him. An oval of the purest silver power I could muster surrounded him, and I smiled at him while he shrank into a small silver ball of energy. I did not want him to be frightened of what was happening, I wanted him to be reassured that what was happening was good and would inevitably end up well for him.

I placed the small silver ball in the dagger sheath of my boot. It would be safe there in a small space and if attacked no one would think to look for it there. Straightening once more I had to assess the situation. I was now in Purgatory, a place not protected by Lucifer's magics, so I should be able to transport out. I would need to call Metatron to help me once I was out too; I did not know if he would but he was perhaps one of the only Angels left I could trust not to betray me.

I stood quietly, arms and wings down, and closed my eyes. I looked deep within myself to the very source of my power, to the very essence of Death, and brought it forth with as much force as I could. I willed myself to return to the World that mortals inhabited, not my realm of death as Metatron would not dare step one golden sandal there, but to Earth.

A small silver whirl began at my feet. I thought of the mortal World and all the wonders you could actually find; the kindness, laughter and love so many showed. The whirl grew bigger and encompassed my whole body. Soon all I could see was silver light as it rose above my head. I prayed it worked, I had not used a transportation spell in a while and I was, to all intents and purposes, rusty.

I remained bathed in my power for what seemed like hours. Soon my vision cleared, and I found myself on a street. It looked vaguely like the area I saw in the soul's vision though there appeared to be some development for the better. How long exactly had I been bound? And how long ago had the soul actually died? I had not known that Lucifer had placed a stasis spell on his halls. They were both immortal, doomed to live a never-ending existence and yet he felt the need to prolong that? I shook my head in disgust; he would do anything just to prolong my suffering.

I moved into a darkened area between two hovels, aware that Lucifer could track me now that I was out of Purgatory and my power had returned. In fact, he could've tracked me when I had used the transportation spell. Why had he not?

I shook myself and concentrated on the task I had to do. I took the small silver ball from my boot and held it aloft in my palm. I smiled and light poured forth from my eyes, bathing my hand and the soul in warmth. The soul grew bigger and bigger and eventually emerged into the World.

"We are home," he breathed with a look of relief. I almost did not want to do what I had to do next.

"Metatron, Herald of the Lord, He who Guides and protects us. Appear before me!" I commanded, well aware that Metatron would not like the demand in my voice. *Well, that should just make him appear sooner*, I thought and smiled. I liked to goad Metatron; it was almost a sport.

We waited a while, I repeated my command often and with more impatience each time. Okay, I had been banished for several ages now but surely, they had not forgotten who I was? What I represented? *An end to all things.*

I was just about to summon him once more when I noticed time was beginning to slow down, an obvious sign that one of my kind was about to appear. A bird circled overhead, getting slower and slower with each pass. The soul too was slowing down; he may be dead, but he was still a mortal, subject to our laws of time control.

Eventually everything stopped and I waited for Metatron to appear. A golden sparkle began in the corner of my eye and elongated to create a golden light beam. I waited patiently; it was both well-known and well documented that

Metatron loved to appear in the most dramatic way possible - most Angels did - well, the ones who had not Fallen did. Eventually a figure emerged, parting the light as if it were nothing more than window drapery. I was surprised to say the very least. I had expected Metatron to appear with all of his pomp and ceremony but instead Lucretia appeared, donned with the regalia of the Guardian Angels. Gone were her pure silk togas enforced on her by Maximus; now she wore a simple white dress with golden embroidery. It was a nice match to go with her white wings. I noticed that a few golden feathers sparkled amid the white meaning Lucretia had been working hard as an angel to ensure the safety of souls.

"My friend, it is good to see you once more," Lucretia exclaimed while embracing me. I actually had to smile with genuine delight. Lucretia had been the one mortal to open my eyes to the goodness they could accomplish. I embraced her back.

"Lucretia, what brings you here?"

"I received this message on behalf of Metatron," Lucretia stated, pulling back to look me in the eye.

"Does Metatron know this?"

"Ah… no," she replied and quickly hugged me again. I could not be angry, I had so few true friends that I treasured each and every one.

"Pay it no mind," I said, disentangling myself from

Lucretia. "But why do you come here this day?"

"I came to thank you in person for keeping your promise so well."

"How...?"

"This is Nathaniel, a descendant of mine through a necromancer from your realm. I had not realised that my line stemmed from one of those mortals that changed when you Fell. We are more connected than you know." Lucretia turned to Nathaniel and caressed his cheek, much as I had done. She however had taken a motherly glow about her, happy to see one of her line saved. The soul shrunk again, this time into a small ball of golden magic. Lucretia placed it into the locket around her neck. She turned back to me and smiled.

"Thank you once again my friend." Lucretia disappeared back into her beam of light with the soul. The absence of time allowed her to actually move on the beam of light. I could've sent Lucretia back but light beams are always vastly more comfortable then transportation spells.

I glanced at the ground, unsure now of what to do. Now there was only myself to deal with. What *would* I do now? I had been bound to Lucifer for so long I barely knew the World I now stood in. I could stay in my own realm, its aura of Death shielding even my own powerful essence, but Lucifer would find my there eventually too and I had done enough to the inhabitants already. No, I must move and keep moving. If I did not stay in the same place for too long, then he could not hold me to one place.

I started to walk, I dare not fly anymore, and I did not know where I walked. I was in my own little stupor never noticing the beautiful scenery that passed me. Emerald green both in trees and in grass went unnoticed, the sapphire blue of the sky went not looked upon and even the golden radiance of the sun was diminished with my dark thoughts. After a while though I began to notice almost a rhythmic drumming in my ears, my heartbeat moved to match it and my step followed it completely. I thought I could hear chanting but perhaps that was just my imagination. I could not stop thinking of my captivity, how it had happened and why it had happened. How dare Lucifer keep me for so long? I knew I should be concentrating on my freedom, but I had an almost obsessive need to see Lucifer suffer as I had. Call it vengeful, call it what you will, but it was there all the same and I had to follow it.

The rhythm and the chanting became louder and I had to grab my arm as pain flared; it was excruciating and burned me to my very soul. Gingerly moving my hand, expecting my life's blood to flow from some unknown wound, I was surprised and angered to see the mark of infinity burned into my arm in blood red magic. Lucifer was finally making his move. I screamed my frustration to the skies. I still could not hear the chanting clearly, it had to be done by his minions in Hell for me not to hear the words, but I could pick out the old Hebrew word for Reincarnation. Lucifer was condemning me to reincarnation for escaping him again? Could he do that? Was he powerful enough?

I went to conjure a counter spell but was felled to my knees, too weak from the undercurrents of the spell. This was new magic, a mix of Life magic, Death magic and Lucifer's own Hellfire. I did not know how to combat it and so knew I would inevitably succumb to it.

"I… will not be gone forever Lucifer… I… I… will be back to have my vengeance upon you," I managed to mutter as my entire World went shining black…

8

Anahlia

I slowly came to, not really knowing where I was or how I had even come to be there. I vaguely remembered a field and a dark rider on a flaming horse but where I was now was completely different yet also familiar. Thanks to my elongated dream I knew I was in Lucifer's throne room which meant I was in Hell. I was sore and my body ached more then I realised. What had happened to me while I was unconscious?

Do not ask that question Child, Alethea answered. _Suffice it to say I gave you that memory for a reason, it contains a lot of the answers you will need, and it kept you from experiencing Lucifer's sick pleasures._ I cringed at the thought of what may have happened then agreed that ignorance was bliss. _I would also not look to your left but that is your choice Child, not mine._ I had the reaction most people would when told not to look to the left: I looked to the left.

I found myself back in my armour, sat in the throne from my dream and manacled just as Alethea was to Lucifer. He was dressed, much as he had been in my dream, in his shining armour and devilish grin. He looked at me as if he owned me, had always owned me and always would.

I shuddered; no man should look at me like that unless

it was Rowan, and he was not here. Where was he? Had he been injured or worse? I felt the need to get to him take over, a need that was slowly turning into a panic. I focused in front of me, on a slightly green glowing rock, and tried my hardest not to hyperventilate. The appearance of ghosts and Angels made me want to hide, especially now I was in Hell, and seek comfort in Rowan's arms.

I felt the being next to me brush my arm, and the feeling of the soft delicate touch made me look at him again. He was a rugged picture of male beauty; tall, muscled and with golden blond hair to match his golden wings. He had a cocky, almost self-assured grin and an air of hidden power about him. I felt myself succumbing to the power of his male beauty and shuddered again. Despite my celestial memories, I was just human and susceptible to human needs. I focused more on Rowan, thinking of his smile, his eyes, the way he could make me laugh if I were upset with him and the way they always connected. I felt the minor attraction I had started to feel toward my captor fade, and I knew I would be okay.

"Why do you look so down, my love? You are back where you belong, in ultimate power by my side," Lucifer said, talking to me as if I were actually Alethea.

"Leave me out of this Demon," I found myself saying. "It has nothing to do with me and I should not be subjected to your whims."

"Ah Alethea, you are not yet fully awake. You have no

idea how happy that makes me."

"I don't care for your happiness devil. I only care to escape this literal hell." I really must be bolstered by my magic somehow, I've never had this much confidence before.

"What do I care for your mortal tendencies my love? This soul is nothing more than something to be discarded once you regain your rightful body," Lucifer finished coldly, and I gasped. It had never occurred to me to wonder what would happen if and when Lucifer's curse took over. Perhaps his spell was not yet complete, and I would be destined to leave this body, and in doing so leave Rowan. There was no way in hell (pun intended) that I would let that happen. *Fear not Child*, Alethea said to me silently. *I tire of this endless existence. If there is some way for you to keep your mortal body, we will find it and maybe, finally, I can be granted the peace I have so desperately wanted for so long.*

"Alethea speaks to you, does she not?" I wished Alethea would take over. I didn't know how to talk to such a powerful being; especially one that I had believed was nothing but a story until recently.

"That is none of your concern Lucifer," I replied, to which Lucifer just laughed.

"You know the more dreams you have Alethea the more your soul grows while the mortal weakens." Was that part of the curse? Was it true that my mortal soul would die as the dreams accumulated? *I do not know*, Alethea replied regretfully. *It could be a possibility; I know not what Lucifer wove into the spell. Do not worry, I will not take over unless I need to, for now my talking through you should not affect anything, I swear it.*

I just didn't know. Anything was a possibility given I didn't know what Lucifer wove into the spell. I was not less panicked. In a way, what Lucifer said made sense. Alethea was the Angel of Death so as her power grew stronger why wouldn't my soul die? I hoped that somehow I could find a way to save myself; I could not be without Rowan on any plain of existence.

"Lucifer," I began. "You need to release me now. You cannot even begin to imagine the repercussions of your actions." I don't know where this newfound certainty came from but my power was based on the death of all things, as Alethea's was, so surely I could hold my own as well.

"Spare me my love," Lucifer began with disdain. "This is my realm, my laws and my power. No one would dare question me on any of these and no would dare challenge my power to rescue you. Not that you have many willing rescuers in those Halls. You are as spurned as I am." I gasped at the sheer sadness that overwhelmed me at his words. I picked out from the memories of my dreams that Alethea had indeed been spurned by those angels in the hallowed halls and the depression she had felt had been overwhelming. She had rebelled with Lucifer, believing herself thoroughly in love. If she had not been stricken with guilt at what she had done, and accepted The Fall willingly, she too would have been restricted to Hell as Lucifer had been. I wanted to reassure myself, saying that she was only human, but she was not. She was the sole embodiment of Death and the new emotion had consumed her. I wanted to cry at the grief I now felt.

I glanced at my left hand as memory surfaced and I panicked. Thankfully my engagement ring was still there, a beacon of shining hope to me in this dire time. I looked at the two hearts once more and thought of Rowan. I longed to see him again, to know he was safe and to hold him. The two hearts sparkled brighter at me and I was astonished to see the silver sparkle now had flecks of golden fire in it. Was this Rowan trying to protect me? I hugged the ring to my chest.

Lucifer snickered and turned back to his own throne. I had not realised he had left it in his study of me. He had inched closer as I had been lost in Alethea's memories and had even stroked my arm again. I felt physically sick and really wanted to cut my arm off now. I glared at him as he sat down once more, wishing that even a powerful being as him would just up and die.

"Stop glaring mortal. I recognise Alethea's glares, and yours are not a shade on hers. Glaring will not free you." I sighed. I may as well wait until Alethea figures out how to free us which hopefully would be soon; I couldn't take much more of the walking ego sat next to me. I concentrated instead on my situation. I was literally in Hell with the source of all death in my mind. *You are death as much as I mortal.* I didn't know where Rowan was. I seemed to be eternally stuck. My head began to hurt. What person could deal with the events going on around me? I was surprised I had lasted this long.

Shaking myself, I decided to try something I had wanted to back in the field. Surely if I was in control of the body, at least for now, and Alethea's power was contained in my body, shouldn't I be able to control her power as well as mine? I knew that I could control my power without thinking, especially when I was angry, but willing to use hers didn't seem to work before.

That is a novel concept Child, Alethea remarked with a hint of amusement. *Please, try it.* I decided I would, if only to try and prove the all-knowing Angel wrong. I concentrated on my wings, willing them to disappear. I concentrated so hard I grew warm and began to sweat. I knew Lucifer must be wondering what I was up to and what I had planned. I chanced a glance at him and he was immersed in looking at me, to the extent he didn't notice much else.

Did you just think wings? Alethea asked in alarm. *Our wings should be hidden. Even manacled to the fiend as we are I usually had at least enough power to hide them. Be prepared Child. I may have to thrust you to the back of our mind quicker and harsher than I would like.*

Normally I would've argued, it was *my* mind after all, and I will not be told what to do, but the alarm in Alethea's voice and the fact that an angel could get alarmed, worried me so I merely internally nodded. Lucifer thought I was merely trying to call more power to me and began to laugh harder. I was becoming a little chagrined that I was such a point of amusement for him, until I noticed the gathering golden beam. I knew from Alethea's memories that this meant one of the angels was coming to visit.

I didn't know if I should laugh or cry. Both myself and Alethea were in complete agreement that anything would be better than being manacled to Lucifer for the rest of our lives but I didn't know what to expect from one of them, especially with me being in control for now. I prayed that they were here to help.

Lucifer sat there still laughing to himself, bloated with his overextended sense of self pride. He hadn't noticed the golden beam and seemed intent on a small fire of blood red flame in the palm of his hand.

I sighed. The light from the hellfire seemed to brighten in my pessimistic view; and brighten and brighten some more. The intensity coalesced into a definite point. What the hell was happening? The pinpoint lengthened, creating a slim column. This widened and I swear I started to see three specs in the light. Three? It couldn't be. Sure enough, the specs started to grow and I could make out Lyria's light, Vale's nature and Rowan's fire. Him, I hoped with everything I had that this rescue attempt would be successful. However, that hope vanished the moment a second column of golden light appeared. It battled with Rowan's light for dominance and I was left distraught when Rowan's column blasted into the throne room ceiling and disappeared as if it never was. The second column took that opportunity to expand, spanning half of the throne room, at least it seemed to.

Suddenly, a piercing yell came from the golden beam; it wasn't a scream exactly but more like a very loud melody emitted from the throat of a man. *War cry,* Alethea managed to say before bodies poured forth from the beam. There had to be twenty in total, all well-built men with emerald green wings and tarnished bronze breastplates. The leader had more design on his breastplate than most; it depicted a scene of great battle, between what looked like Heaven and Hell, with Heaven seemingly triumphant. The leader's flowing golden hair belied the warrior soul reflected in his eyes. *Gabriel,* came the reply, heavy with a hint of contempt and something I dare not examine too closely. I concluded that my guest was not a big fan of this angel but was willing to see what happened, as long as it led to our freedom. The leader was followed by another archangel; this one was heavily set. He had far too many muscles for an angel but other than that I was shocked to see he had golden wings reminiscent of Lucifer's and a protective air towards the leader. *Raphael,* Alethea managed to say dryly. There was definitely hatred for this being and nothing else in Alethea's voice. I wondered why.

I chanced a glance at Lucifer. He seemed frozen in shock. Obviously he had not expected to be raided in his ++++++1+Hall, with his power and his laws, blah blah blah. I secretly smiled at the turn of events. This may prove interesting and hopefully freeing.

A soft green aura began to emanate just in front of the thrones. It grew until it stretched the length of the throne room and small beings appeared in it. They grew and grew until I could clearly see War, and what she assumed must be Conquest and Famine along with several minions, all ready to meet the threat head on. Lucifer rose.

"Attack them. Remove them from our Halls, our home."

All figures moved forward, intent and almost eager to meet the battle head on. The room echoed with the sound of pure silver hitting Hellfire and shouts and screams, both sides revelling in the slaughter. I wanted to run and hide. This was not my world; I didn't belong here and did not want to be a part of it. I wished for Rowan even harder; I didn't know what he could do in a situation like this but I always felt so safe with him, so secure.

The leader of the angels turned to me with a raised hand.

"To the back of your mind mortal; give me the certainty of Deaths cold embrace..." golden light poured forth, however it wasn't the gentle caress of magic I was expecting but a forceful push. The sensation of flying backwards in my own mind was odd but it was odder still feeling Alethea brush past me as she moved to the front.

Alethea

I stood and stretched in no way hampered by the manacle I still wore. I really enjoyed having control of the body, regardless of the consequences for Anahlia. It felt right and good. I stood there with a smirk as angel fought minion.

"Well, help us Alethea," Gabriel shouted, perturbed that I had not moved to do so yet.

"Gabriel, to begin with I am still laughing at your choice of vocabulary, and secondly," I said with some sarcastic chagrin, "I cannot. Or have you forgotten the damnable manacle attaching me to that -" I pointed at Lucifer "- thing?". I waved the chain at him for emphasis and watched him visibly sigh.

"How do we free you?"

"The key on the outcropping there, but you'll have to get to it before Lucifer does," I could not help but laugh watching the two men scrambling for so small a key. I watched for a minute or two, perhaps longer than I should have, and let both men squirm; I would help Gabriel eventually but I had no great love for him so he had to work for it. I could feel Anahlia laughing at the back of my mind and wondered what she knew that I did not.

When it seemed that both were evenly matched, I wrapped my chain around both hands affording myself a solid grip. I placed one foot forward and braced myself, almost looking forward to what I was about to do. Then I yanked the chain back with as much strength as I could muster and watched as Lucifer flew backward at great speed with a gigantic smile on my face. His head cracked off of one of his precious Hellfire rocks and for now at least he was unconscious. Gabriel grabbed the key and threw it to me.

I watched as the manacle fell to the floor and the full extent of my power began to return to me. I could not help but smile even greater. One day I would defeat Lucifer, I knew it. Remembering where I was, I shook myself out of my reverie and retrieved my scythe and sword. I jumped down and sped towards Gabriel. I could see Raphael trying to fell his demon quickly as he thought I was attacking Gabriel. Did he really think me dense enough to attack the person that for the moment had saved me? I aimed the bottom of my scythe at the minion attacking him and blew him away. I could not help but smile at the look on Gabriel's face, he did not yet know of the influence Anahlia's soul had on both my weaponry and myself. As soon as I reached Gabriel we went back to back, a stance we had opted for in many wars in the past so we could defend each other.

Two minions attacked at the same time, thinking to take us down with combined force and perhaps forgetting who we were. I blocked the attacker's sword with a sweep of my scythe while Gabriel brought his own sword up, deflecting the blade and plunging it into what was the heart of the minion. I span with Gabriel in place, allowing the blade of my sword to sink into the neck of the minion while Gabriel dropped his blade and used it to stab my enemy. We had always worked well that way, working in sync like a well-oiled machine. It felt good to fight that way again, I was loath to admit. The fight had always given me fluidity in life, a way to tap into the very core of myself without losing my personality; after being stuck for so long in the mind of mortals the purity of battle infused me with a flush of pleasure.

The battle continued and miraculously none of the angels were felled. I fought on their side for the simple reason that for now at least they were not trying to imprison me; anyone that was not trying to chain me got my help in some situations at least, and they were trying to free me, though for the life of me I could not figure out why. Surely, they knew that I would not side with them, I was still trapped in the mind of the mortal barely able to access my own power when I wished it. I would not fight for them in any case, I had been banished even though I Fell willingly and not one of them had come to my aid when I experienced the hell of reincarnation over and over again.

We fought on, the melodious sound of pure silver echoing harshly against the wail of the Hellfire blades. I revelled in it and even in the pools of black blood that thickly coated the floor. I had missed the din of battle and the victorious feeling of attaining any sort of victory over Lucifer, and any minion that fell *was* a victory over Lucifer. I did have to admit however that the angels were horrendously outnumbered. Minion after minion piled into the throne room and they were pushed back to the far wall. I could fight them forever if I had full control of my own body but I was well aware of Anahlia in my mind; I was death, I was not evil. I could not condemn the poor soul to nothingness while I revelled in full control of my body once more.

"Fall back," I shouted. I had not really expected them to follow my orders as they did Gabriel's so I was pleasantly surprised when they followed suit, even Raphael. Gabriel broke away from me to battle a minion and I knew I had to get him out safely also. I threw up my hand and silver light raced across the room to where Gabriel now stood, a dripping minion head in his hands. It encompassed him perfectly, almost like a lover's caress, and I raised my hand, raising Gabriel into the air. The golden light beam they had arrived in remained open and I thrust Gabriel through the air towards, and then through it. The rest of the archangels she just looked at and smiled; I did not know if they knew my true identity but would enjoy the process of educating them.

"How..." one of them started, foolishly and with a little pride, much to my shock. "How did you do that woman? No one is stronger than our leader." I heard Raphael sigh at the prideful comment. We may never have gotten on but Raphael was well aware of my wrath.

"Try to leave them in one piece Lady Death," he said as he casually strolled through the golden beam. He had no patience for pride.

I knew I should take mercy on this soul, he was new to the ranks of the archangel, after my time, and did not know who I was; however the entire room, Lucifer and the horsemen included, had frozen in shock. Had not I been through enough? Did I have to eternally endure the censure of others? I sighed and drew my power round me like a cloak; I closed my eyes and concentrated on the angel, head lowered.

Suddenly, I pulled my head up and I was on fire, pure silver fire emanating from my very being and pouring forth from my eyes.

"I am the angel of death youngling, I am neither good nor evil, I merely am. Let my purifying flame cleanse you of the suffocating pride I see." The fire poured from my eyes down my body; it reached the ground and spread, spearing towards the younger angels. A torrent surrounded each being, burning something away though when it finished none were entirely sure what I had actually done.

"What have you done to us?" demanded the same angel.

"I have purified your immortal souls," I replied. "You had the beginnings of pride in you, not noticeable to the average angel unless one had experienced it as I had. No, no," I held up my hand, "no need to thank me. I know I have done you a great service." I watched amused as the angels looked at each other in confusion. Obviously, sarcasm was not rampant in His realm.

"Tell Gabriel what I have done for you..." With a smile, I lightly blew in the direction of the angels and watched with pleasure as a silver gale picked each one up and thrust them through their golden beam. Hurriedly I closed the beam so no minion could follow and turned to face the crowd. Each one looked at me with evident victory in their stares. I however would not be defeated this time. I lightly pirouetted in place, sweeping my scythe and sword behind me. A sea of silver fire sprang forth cutting off my enemies in all directions; I was protected, at least for a time, and now I could perform the transportation spell.

Where was Lucifer? Ah, I could see him now. He had moved directly towards me, trying to fight his way through my silver sea. I smiled and whistled for his attention, and like the good little pet he was he immediately looked into my eyes. I laughed the sultry, throaty laugh that always had an effect on him and I held up my left hand. Slowly, silver flames began to appear, growing in intensity and light the more I laughed at Lucifer.

When I had a ball of pure silver flame in my hand I blew him a kiss, span quickly and hurled the ball at the wall. The flames spread until they had reached 'human' height and merged to become silver light. Looking over my shoulder, I waved at Lucifer and threw myself through the light. I was free and I would make damn sure I stayed that way...

9

Anahlia

I woke up in a prone position surrounded by scented emerald grass. I sighed; lying on my back was something I was becoming accustomed to and I wished fervently that that wouldn't become the case. It starts to damage the psyche if one begins to believe they'll always be on their back, I thought.

I sighed again and sat up. The spell had deposited me back in the field where I had been taken. I could see the silver tinted burial mound and again longed to help but knew I had to find Rowan. He had been in that transportation spell that had been deflected and vanquished, I hope he's okay.

What was the last thing I remembered? I could see Alethea's battle as if a spectator; at one point I even cheered when Alethea got the upper hand over one minion. I actually smiled as I remembered Alethea's joy at being in battle once more; being a natural pacifist I had no desire to fight or hurt anyone but could see it was an essential part of Alethea and that one could not be death without a little violence.

Chuckling to myself, I shook myself from my reverie and stood to find Rowan. I still wore the armour, thankfully, and would be protected if anyone should try to take me again. The scythe and sword were still present, and I hoped I wouldn't need to use them; I was no fighter even if I could access Alethea's knowledge.

I quickly found my way back to the wooded path. I avoided fallen branches and trunks, found the flowers planted in the stump and eventually realised that the path was a lot longer than I thought it had been. Where was the shop temple? Was I lost? Gradually the city began to emerge from the emerald of the forest. Now I was tired and again I was positive I hadn't walked that much previously. The city was a welcome sight. I walked along cobbled street after cobbled street, avoiding the guards just in case. Rowan said he was the prince of this place but he must have left for a reason, I saw no need to agitate that.

Eventually I came upon a familiar house and prayed it was Rowan's temple house. If so, Rowan should be inside and Him only knows I hoped he was safe. I worried since the golden beam disappeared. Was Lyria and Vale inside too? I stood in the doorway and let my eyes adjust to the darkness within. I leant against the wooden doorframe and took off the breastplate that to me was heavy and cumbersome. Honestly, how outdated was Alethea? I felt a mental kick from the lady herself and smiled that I could rile up the power of death so easily. I definitely needed a revamp in the armour department though.

Clad in skirt, boots and what was laughably an 'undershirt', I moved further into the temple. I was eager to see Rowan now; his warmth, his strength, he just comforted me in a way no other could. My soul called to his and it was eager for him now.

Not ten minutes later I was scared and panicking. Rowan was not here, neither was Vale or Lyria. I had searched, but I couldn't see any sign of him. He must have returned here after the spell. Something tweaked and I knew that there was the presence of magic but it was too weak to sense it properly. Where was he? Who had taken him? And who would I willingly fight to get him back? I knew I had to take a deep breath, calm myself and logically decide where I needed to look; however, all I could think was I *had* to find him *now.*

Preparing to fly out of the house in a panic, literally if need be, I caught sight of a silver sparkle in the corner of my vision. I turned and found my gaze driven directly toward the portrait of Rowan's guild. I had no desire to touch it as it was quite domineering, but the bottom left corner of the portrait was shining at me. I moved towards it gingerly and reached out my hand. I expected the silver mist to take over my vision once more but before my fingers made contact with the portrait, they hit an invisible barrier. Almost instinctively I grasped the silver sparkle and peeled it back almost like a layer of invisible fabric. Part of it did indeed snag on something but I eventually succeeded in peeling it away.

To my astonishment it was a letter, cleverly disguised by Rowan.

'Ana,

I woke to find the spell gone wrong, luckily Vale and Lyria were with me. I'm afraid that my father was tipped off by the power of the transport spell and will come looking. I am trying to send Vale and Lyria into hiding but they're having none of it. They're determined to mount another rescue for you. If we don't rescue you and you escape Lucifer, look for us at the mad king's court.

I love you always,

Rowan'

I did begin to panic then. Why had Rowan gone there? Did he think his father that much of a threat? How was I supposed to get there? I had no idea how to get past the waves of guards surrounding the palace and even if I did, I doubted I would be able to find the throne room in the sprawling labyrinth.

Calm down Child, Alethea stated too calmly. *Our way into the Court is about to arrive. Do you have the strength to face one of my brethren on your own? I feel that the penultimate confrontation with Lucifer is approaching and if you are to survive, I must conserve my strength.*

I nodded my agreement even though I was far from sure if I could face down an angel. I didn't like the quiver in Alethea's voice however, and if Death was unsure about something, I knew I should be damn well terrified.

He comes... Alethea's ominous warning was all the notice I had. Suddenly a golden light exploded next to me and I was flung across the living area. I felt my head connect and I crumpled to the floor, translucent silver stars dancing passionately in my vision. Why wasn't I dead? My neck should have snapped from the force of the throw but apart from a mild headache I was fine. *I... believe it may be the essence of my power, my aura taking over Child. I am sorry as much as I fight it appears that that at least will take over no matter what. We cannot die, we* are *death.*

I gasped as I felt a hand take my arm and lift me to my feet. I hoped it was Rowan, I prayed it was him, but something felt wrong. The hand was too rough, too uncaring and I hoped I wasn't going insane when I felt a wing brush my back.

"Forgive me mortal I had not intended to appear so close to you, I can no more sense Alethea's power now than I used to be able to."

I turned around slowly, recognising the voice from our time in Hell and wishing I was wrong. I wasn't, however, and there stood the archangel Gabriel and what seemed to be his permanent shadow Raphael. Gabriel's emerald green wings moved almost of their own accord, shifting slightly then moving once more, settling into a comfortable position. His armour was almost the same as Alethea's, but his breastplate was tarnished bronze. I had a brief glimpse of a memory in my mind; Alethea and Gabriel were back to back once more. Alethea had already Fallen and was not happy that Gabriel was there to goad her. I knew they were somewhere in Hell, but I wasn't sure where; both times I'd seen it I had only seen Lucifer's throne room. Alethea, in a tactic to make him falter, taunted him at discarding his pure silver breastplate for the more basic bronze; she said it was a stupid mistake, one by an angel so blatantly not taking his celestial duties responsibly. Gabriel had not even blinked at this. He merely raised his arms towards the Heavens and allowed a minion to try and strike him. Once the hellfire blade touched the bronze there was a loud explosion, choking smoke, then the minion was gone. Alethea was left speechless.

What a pompous fool. He merely could have spoken, instead he had to demonstrate and needlessly risk his own existence. From that one sentence I caught a quick glimpse into Alethea's soul; she cared for Gabriel and regretted that her dalliance with Miltiades and her enforced torture with Lucifer had kept her away from him. For now, though I shut that information away in a part of the mind even Alethea couldn't access. I wasn't sure Alethea knew about love, or at least the type of love like I had with Rowan, but I would talk to her about it later.

I felt a pair of golden eyes on me,

"If you have finished conversing with death, mortal, may I have a word?"

"I... I'm sorry but she can't talk right now," I was ashamed of myself for stuttering, but I *was* still trying to get used to talking to celestial bodies. If it had not been for Rowan, I would have likely had myself committed long ago. My mind still tried to tell me that none of this was real, that as soon as I came to the end of the dream I would wake up in my own bed with Rowan and I could go about my life as usual.

"And why is that?" Gabriel asked, moving slightly closer to me, perhaps in an act of intimidation.

"Because she... she's keeping her strength for the Second Coming."

"Ah," Gabriel seemed happy this was mentioned. He moved away and took a seat on the step in front of me, Raphael leaning on one of the wooden beams like the shadow he was. He at least refused to say anything to me. "I came here to speak with Alethea about that very fact. I was even willing to come into this Him-forsaken realm in search of you."

"Why?" I demanded with more strength in my voice. These were essentially supposed to be the good guys, why were they stalking someone like me? Was Alethea that essential to the winning of the War? *I do not know; I cannot imagine that I would be,* Alethea replied.

"Why? Because Lucifer has grown in power since his exile. He has converted many of the fallen and consolidated his power base. He has even embraced the mortal magics that so few of us will even consider. We need to take counter measures;

many of us are trying to convince the aspects to fight for Him once more. Several archangels have gone to love, peace, deception, all who fell, all who never gave in to Lucifer. We must fight the evil he has become."

I could hear Alethea sigh and felt like sighing myself. I couldn't understand how all of these higher beings, with all the power they possess, could not simply end this and save all Worlds from certain destruction. I felt frustrated; I however had no interest in this. All I wanted to do was find Rowan and the girls and go home. There I could forget any of this happened and go back to my boring life. Thankfully I could feel that Alethea had no interest in this either.

"No Gabriel," I was amazed I dare use such a casual tone. "All I want to do is find Rowan. Now you can either help me do it or get the hell out of my way."

"You do not speak for Alethea mortal; how dare you presume to do so?"

"Actually Gabriel, I do. Alethea has no interest in your little war..." I listened for a moment, "and she says if you don't help us get to the Court of Madness now she will 'break out of here' and beat it out of you."

I waited for the divine retribution I knew must be coming. I had spoken back to an angel and not given him the answer he wanted. He must be angry. Instead I was surprised to hear him chuckle.

"Ah Alethea, I have missed you." I felt a surge of almost happiness come from the back of my mind, but it was pulled back and all that was left was Alethea's usual cold presence and minor anger at Raphael's groan. "I will help you mortal, but I insist that I come back to speak with both yourself and Alethea as soon as your love is safe. Agreed?"

"Fine, fine, but please hurry. I fear Rowan is in so much trouble and I need to save him. Alethea can't help me, and I don't know what to do," I knew I was babbling but couldn't stop myself from doing so.

Gabriel smiled at me, only me, and I felt reassured by it. Just from that one smile I knew I was going to save Rowan and get them home safely. I knew I had to otherwise I doomed them all. Gabriel raised his right hand and with the same smile, clicked his fingers. Suddenly I was overtaken by golden flame... and the World went sparkling black once more.

***

The blackness was stripped away to reveal silver sparkling marble. I had to swivel in the air just to avoid colliding with a column. I landed on my feet, much to my shock, next to a pile of black and silver cushions and a fire pit that burned bright black, as Illaria had conjured in Rowan's rooms.

I sighed. I somehow knew I was in Illaria's temple and I could swear that I was hearing Gabriel's laugh echoing around me. Perhaps he too knew of my dislike of the woman and her interest in Rowan. Or perhaps he was just laughing at the situation Alethea found herself in, I didn't know.

Probably the latter, child. Alethea commented. *Gabriel is not Worldly enough to understand the intricate nature of jealousy, and he is male...* Alethea left that hanging in the air. I laughed despite the situation I was in. I was beginning to like these exchanges with Alethea; I was never alone now, and her dry sense of humour was a refreshing change to Vale's venom and Lyria's flightiness.

Shaking myself, I turned to what I now must do. I hoped Illaria would help me find Rowan otherwise I knew I may be lost here for a while.

"Illaria?" I called, hoping I would find the seer here. There was a rustle of black satin towards the back of the temple and I withdrew the scythe. I was pretty sure I knew how to use it and didn't want a surprise attack while I was trying to sneak in. There was another rustle and I moved cautiously towards it, the gun end of the scythe pointed towards the curtain.

"Illaria?" I asked again, this time a little quieter, wondering if this was Illaria trying to hide from me. Once I'd reached it, I used the gun end of the scythe to lift the curtain slowly and a pure silver wolf pup trotted out. I sighed and let down my guard slightly. The wolf pup put its tiny paws on my leg and yipped, almost welcoming me into the temple. I was instantly in love; he had pure black eyes that were a wonderful contrast to his soft silver fur.

"Hello beautiful one," I crooned, leaning my scythe against the wall. I knelt down beside him, "and who do you belong to? You are stunning; I can't imagine Illaria would have the nature in her to care for another." I scooped the pup up, hoping it wouldn't bite me. The pup licked my cheek, paused and then growled over my shoulder. I turned slowly, knowing something was stood behind me. Something *must* be stood behind me, I had let my guard down and that was when it usually happened.

I knew I should always trust my instincts; Illaria was stood behind me, menace in her eye and holding my scythe. The pup began growling even harder and Illaria turned a look of contempt upon it, trying to dismiss the pup into the nether realm.

"Why have you returned?" Illaria demanded. She was set in a warrior's stance, grasping the scythe with a death grip and waiting for me to make the first move. I sighed and put the pup down. I had no idea what I would do now that Illaria had the scythe, but I hoped it involved violence. I didn't like Illaria and was becoming irritated that she was in the way of my rescuing Rowan.

Click your fingers came the vague instructions. What would that do? I moved to obey anyway. I had to trust that

Alethea knew what she was doing and what I should do; and so I clicked my fingers. The sound echoed through the Hall and silver light poured through the windows. The scythe began to respond, vibrating slightly and moving even more towards me. Illaria hardly noticed; she was too focused on the pup that was trying to attack her legs. I clicked my fingers once more, instinctively knowing to do so, and the scythe was wrenched out of Illaria's hands and flew to me. I caught it with both hands and held the bladed end towards Illaria. I didn't want the seer to know all the secrets of the scythe just yet, just in case I would need them later.

"Damn you... damn you to the nether realm," Illaria screamed "Why couldn't you stay gone? Mikhail's return meant I could attain him as a lover once more. He deserves more than some snivelling mortal. Why have you returned?" She paused in her venomous rant to kick the pup in its hind quarters.

I had had enough; I was tired, cold and Rowan was still missing. Without realising I did so, I grabbed for the power within me and embraced it. This woman had no right to talk to me like this, no right to stand in the way of finding Rowan, no right in assuming she had any claim on him and definitely no right to kick the pup I had already claimed as my own. I could feel the wind pick up around me and I sent it in whirls and eddies to Illaria. It surrounded her, becoming a tornado of force and might. My eyes lit on fire with silver flame and I blew a kiss towards girl and wind; it immediately ignited into silver flame. I could hear a scream come from within.

A dry chuckle sounded in my mind. *I am enjoying this Child. It is you that called for my power, not I. It feels good, does it not?* It did but I wasn't going to admit it. I was almost appalled at what I was doing right now but I needed Illaria's help and what better way than reminding her who I (technically) was?

"Do not question me again. I am the angel of death; I am and I will always be..." I paused for effect. "Now you will help me find Rowan. Hinder me and I will see you gone!!!" Another dry chuckle sounded in my mind as another scream echoed from within the flaming eddy.

"Fine," came the reply. "I submit. I will help you with the prince. Please stop with your torture." I smiled and blew on the tornado; just as suddenly as it appeared it dissipated on the wind. Illaria was left standing, a little scorched but unharmed. She glared at me as if she hated me.

"I prefer the Lady," she mumbled as she went to get something from her rooms. I chuckled, at least now I had some help in this forsaken place, albeit unwillingly. I had a little more chance of success. Now I had to turn my mind to finding Rowan, and I would find him regardless of who tried to stop me. My sudden conviction scared me a little but I couldn't lose focus now, not when I was so close.

Illaria returned moments later, still sulking, and carrying something silver and shimmering. The part of me that loved silver was drawn to the garment but I remained dubious.

There was not a lot of the garment and it had on the same shimmering scales that adorned not much of the seer.

"To have you move freely through the Court we'll have to disguise you as a seer," Illaria held the scrap of a garment up to my front, "though I do not know who would believe it. I hear..." and here Illaria did falter, "... I hear that there will be an execution at the gathering this eve. They are already beginning, and the pyre is almost built. I fear that it is Prince Mikhail they want to murder. His father is mad with power and does not realise that he will need his heir." My heart thumped in my chest. Surely his own father wouldn't have him killed. I had to credit Illaria with some emotion at least, she seemed genuinely distraught at the thought. Clarity dawned on me. She was speaking with a sliver of guilt in her voice.

"It was you who told the king about Rowan wasn't it? When you ran off from the guild. Why? Why tell the mad king anything?"

"I was jealous. Mikhail had never looked at me the way he looked at you, and we were together fifteen years. A part of me thought if I told his father and got him reinstated, he would leave you for me. I didn't expect this... this..." she shuddered. "Hurry and change."

I changed quickly, uncomfortable both with the amount of skin on show and the company I now kept, and hoped I was not too late. Rowan had to be alive, I would feel it if he were dead, wouldn't I? I always felt such a close bond with him that there had to be no way I couldn't feel it. Alethea would feel our connection break and she had said nothing at all about it. I returned to Illaria with doubt on my face. They had to at least try to save Rowan even if nothing came of it.

"Hmm, you will do I suppose," Illaria said with a nonchalant air.

"What about my weapons?" I asked, uncomfortable at leaving them. They lay in the corner, beckoning me to them; I felt safe and protected when I had them on me.

"Leave them. You must present the image of a true seer and we have no need for weapons. The scythe should come to you when you most need it, the others should be summoned." I sighed as Illaria led the way from the temple. I didn't trust the seer, but she was the best chance I had to make it to Rowan in one piece. The wolf pup, that I had already decided to call Fenris, trotted at my feet keeping his wary eyes on the she-devil. She led the way to a silver sledge pulled by pure white horses. More of the seer bards were inside waiting for them. They didn't seem to care that I was there only that they got to the palace and the King in time. I somehow gleaned that they were eager to find out who would be the next Queen as was the custom. I wanted to vomit.

The trip took longer than I liked. The sled reeked of perfume; it was giving me a headache. I focused only on Rowan and what state he may be in. I had no clue.

Will you take over? I asked Alethea directly. It was

something I had rarely done before, but I didn't want Illaria to know they were in constant contact.

I cannot Child. I am still weak from escaping from Pandemonium and I need to conserve my strength for the penultimate battle. I will guide you through what you must do however, I will not leave you. You know how to reach for the power now, call on it once more. We will save your Rowan.

I was shaken. I was in a foreign World with people I did not know, and I was the only one able to rescue Rowan; I longed for him desperately, and Vale and Lyria. Where could they be? Were they with Rowan?

Eventually they came to two great pure silver doors adorning a thick silver wall. The palace itself was gorgeous; it had cherubim carved into silver columns rejoicing at the purity of life. There was a large shadow looming over the scene but the figures didn't seem to be afraid of it, instead they seemed to thrive on it. The guards on duty parted to let the sled through. The large silver doors had opened while I was studying the palace and they closed with a resounding boom after they had entered. What was I getting myself into? In the courtyard I dismounted the sled as the seers did and hoped I blended in; I didn't need people asking questions. The party strolled down several silver corridors and I once again found myself looking at a statue of myself; well it was of Alethea, but essentially it was me. I looked away so that no one saw the dramatic similarities. Eventually they came upon large oaken doors; I could make out orchestral music in the background. Illaria stopped and turned to me.

"We need a plan once inside. I do not know how we will free Mikhail, but it must be quick, and it must be powerful. Will the Lady take over for this?" she asked in an almost hopeful plea. I almost wanted to give her what she wanted but Alethea could not take over; I knew Alethea would not have her full power until she was complete again but I did not know what that meant for me, my power was the same as Alethea's, relishing in the death of the world but mine was erratic. I could not think on it until Rowan was safe again.

"No, she can't, but she will walk me through what we need to do. Do you know the transportation spell?"

"I do, but I do not see what..."

"When I nod to you, just start the spell, okay?" I interrupted. I was usually more polite than that, but they didn't have the time and I was confident that Alethea knew what she was doing. If I was honest, I had no real desire to listen to Illaria's input; time was ticking on.

"Fine," Illaria replied curtly. Evidently, she didn't like being told what to do by me but for now she would have to just put up with it. With perhaps a little more force than necessary Illaria shoved open the doors and we were treated to a sight I had never seen before. The throne room, sparkling with pure silver and black fire, was full of what could only be the upper class of this world. Finely clad people were milling, dancing, laughing and smiling. More of the bard seers were already there, dressed as Illaria and I were, serving the guests and acting as entertainment for the more bored patrons. Vale was off to one side, frozen in her animal form. Lyria was frozen mid light spell. My anger began to rise.

This almost seemed serene to me, people enjoying themselves amidst all the gaiety and bravado, but something was wrong. In the middle of the room was a great stake ready for burning someone and I already knew whom. I moved further into the room while desperately searching for the one I had longed for since this all began. The pup dashed between my feet, not drawing attention but finding Rowan like an arrow.

Eventually I found him and what I saw shocked me. It was evident that Rowan had been beaten badly; blood streaked down his arms and his broad chest. He was shirtless and only had on his tight pants. Black fire bound his arms behind his back and gagged his mouth; this seemed to hurt terribly and burn his skin. A dome of black light surrounded him so no escape could be made, or rescue attempted.

I wanted to rush straight to him but was blocked by one of the patrons. Damn, damn, damn, how would I explain this away? The figure blocking my way removed the mask from his face to reveal it was Azazel. I gasped.

"What are you doing here?"

"Fear not Fair One," he replied in the same smooth voice. "I am not here to hinder you. I was released, it is true, but I find myself intrigued by the events playing out and I think

I will merely watch for now. I am curious as to what role you will play in regard to Lady Death. Give her my regard. With that he smiled, mock bowed and replaced his mask. He then danced away with one of the seers seeming to take great pleasure from the debauchery and sin. I would have to ask Alethea who he really was but for now I had a job to do.

At that point Rowan looked up. His eyes connected straight with mine and I felt his piercing gaze straight to the very core of my being. He didn't want me to rescue him! His head shook ever so slightly; I was to run, save myself and leave Rowan to his fate. Yeah right, like I was going to do that, didn't he know me by now? I had to think of a way to get closer to him.

Suddenly, a drumbeat began from the musicians that had been hidden by the crowd. I could see the other seers moving to the middle of the room, facing each other in a circle. As the rest of the music began the seers' hips began to sway and they reached out to one another. As their fingertips touched, they raised their arms into the air and Illaria appeared between them in a black flash of power. Each seer then turned to the throne and began to dance towards the King. It was understandable; the King was a handsome man, the exact replica of Rowan but with a few silver hairs. If even one seer caught his attention then she could be the next Queen of this realm and have dominance over the rest.

I saw my opportunity to get closer to Rowan. Joining the seers, I hoped I danced in the same seductive way they did; I prayed that the disguise would not let me down either. The bards didn't wear a lot and I wasn't very secure in it; but on I danced. Gradually I had gotten close enough to make a move for Rowan without anyone knowing.

A shadow fell over me. I hoped it wasn't one of the guards, I wasn't as adept as Alethea with the scythe and didn't know how stable my power would be.

I looked up, dreading what I would see but already knowing it was something bad. Stood in my way, with his arm outstretched was the King, blocking my view of Rowan. My panic began to rise slightly. How was I to get past this powerhouse of a man? Could I even dare to try?

"Who... are you?" asked the King, as if he were trying to see something. "Have I met you before?"

You must seem to him that you are from this place, Alethea advised silently. *He cannot know who we are or where you come from. He shines with power so much more than any of the others, bar your Rowan. I would not anger him with me in this weakened state.*

"I... I am no one, Sire" I replied hesitantly, and then had an idea. "I am also more than I seem." I concentrated with more effort than I had ever put into anything. I could feel Alethea's push as well and my great ebony wings unfurled. Everyone gasped and stood in awe as my hips began to sway to the music.

"I am your salvation... and your damnation," I continued as I spread my wings to the greatest width they could go. I could see the Kings pupils become a little dilated. He seemed to be concentrating on the sway of my hips a little too intensely. I was uncomfortable with this but knew it was what Alethea wanted. I nodded to Illaria.

Good Child, keep him occupied, keep his focus on you or all is lost. I inwardly groaned but put more of a swing into my hips. I could feel a mild stirring within myself, almost like warm fingers caressing a frozen cheek, and silver mist began to gather around them. The King groaned and took a deep breath, smelling something I could not. Others in the room began to sway towards me, intoxicated by the mist and by me as well.

Now, raise your arm, behind our wing, and point it at Rowan as well as your friends. See the image in your head of their binds weakening. Remember, magic is merely willpower; will them free and it will be so.

Pushing my doubts aside, I focused on doing just that. Trying to bring the power forward was hard whilst I was trying to keep the Kings attention on me, but I realised I no longer had to try. The King seemed enthralled, and despite my doubts I took advantage of the fact.

I raised my hand; hoping, wishing, praying they were free; and watched in amazement as silver light poured forth to encompass the black magic holding them. I could see the dark prisons begin to dissipate but gasped when the King began to turn, feeling his magic break. Thinking quickly, I brushed up against the King and sighed in contentment. The King's attention was no longer lost; he turned back to me and tried to grasp my arms. I managed to sway out of his reach, all the while keeping my light on Rowan. Finally, I felt the King's magic shatter and knew I could grab Rowan and the girls. I prayed Illaria had been doing her part of the plan to escape.

"Illaria, duck," I shouted and threw up my other arm. A silver fireball shot out to hit the wall where Illaria had stood only seconds before. Luckily, she had heeded my instructions to duck and was crouched on the floor shivering. I was happy to see she was also a little singed.

The magic held in the fireball coalesced, then spread to encompass the intricate drawing Illaria had made moments before. The magic became a solid silver doorway and I took everyone's focus on that as the perfect opportunity to make our escape. I ran, grabbed Rowan, secured the girls on enchanted ropes, and asked Alethea to lend strength so I could fly us out of there. The great ebony wings beat at the air and we were airborne. I didn't have time to ensure Rowan's comfort, so I hoped I wasn't hurting him too much. I became enraged as I felt his warm blood trickle slowly down my hands; the King would pay dearly for that. I felt the girls fly and hoped they didn't shout too hard at me for the mode of transportation.

Child put aside your thought of retribution for now and grab the seeress as we fly past. The King will not hesitate to torture her for information regarding you. After what I have done to him, you will be very lucky if you never see him again.

I didn't like the dreadful sense of foreboding I got from Alethea's words. Why did I have to grab Illaria? Surely the little witch could take care of herself; and what had Alethea done to the King?

I knew Illaria wouldn't like what I was about to do and smiled at the thought of it. I would grab the little witch but only because it would royally piss her off; I would take whatever she dished out afterward. I lovingly held Rowan with one hand, ensuring I hurt him no more than I was and as I passed, I threw the enchanted rope around Illaria by the hair, propelling all five of them through the portal. I could hear Illaria cry out in pain and a little bit of me, the little bit I suspected was affected by Alethea, smiled. Fenris jumped through the portal after us and I smiled. I was fond of the wolf pup.

The scenery quickly morphed from silver marble to open, silver tinged blue skies. I knew we were still in Alethea's realm but was happy to be out of the Court. Twisting in the air I dropped Illaria, let my friends float on the enchanted rope and made sure Rowan would be cushioned by my body. Glancing above his head, I could see that the silver portal was still open. Panicking that someone would follow I threw a fireball at it and watched in satisfaction as the portal quickly closed behind them. We landed with a soft thud in the tall grass that was becoming so familiar; they had landed here the first time. How had Illaria known to transport us here? *It was not the seer but our magic that brought us here. She knew only to transport in this realm, you knew to come here far from the court.*

"Why, in the name of the Lady, did you bring me with you?" screamed Illaria, furious that she was now out of the Court, the centre of power she had run to, betraying Rowan. She stormed over to me and Rowan, intent on exacting revenge on me for it, but stopped when she saw Rowan had blacked out.

"Be quiet witch, and let him rest," I demanded, scared that Rowan looked so small and frail. My robust lover, my strength in this lifetime, needed my help and I would be damned if I let Illaria keep me from helping him. *We are damned anyway child,* Alethea commented with regret. *Let us get him to a sanctuary where he may heal. Although this one is very annoying and far from useful, the Temple of the Seers is a profound place of healing. Take him there and he will recover.*

"How do I do that?" I replied aloud, not caring that Illaria could only hear one half of the conversation.

Focus on him, on the love that you share in this life and the next, and wish him to float. Focus with all your soul. I did this, hoping it would work and that I wouldn't look like an idiot if nothing happened. Surprisingly, after feeling a slight mental nudge from Alethea, Rowan floated into the air on a wave of silver cloud. I kept my thoughts only on Rowan as I turned to Illaria.

"Take us to the temple of the Seers," I instructed. "I don't know where else to go and he has to heal." I could see

Illaria was about to balk again. She seemingly hated taking orders off me, but she looked at Rowan and obviously changed her mind. As cold and calculating as she was surely even she would not leave him in pain.

"It is this way," Illaria commented and turned in the opposite direction. I focused more on Rowan and willed him to follow Illaria. I hoped Illaria was not lying to me, but I had no other choice but to trust her. I checked to make sure the scythe had returned to my back and the sword to its sheath and walked after them, the wolf pup trotting at my feet, and I grabbed the ends of the rope floating my friends, their faces still frozen in what torture the King had inflicted on them. They would kill me if I forgot them. I let out an evil little chuckle.

10

Rowan

There was darkness all around me. I fought through it, desperate to get to Anahlia and see what his 'father' had done to her. The last thing I remembered was seeing her, dressed as the seers dressed in court, moving towards me with a look of panic on her beautiful face. I had tried to tell her to go back, to save herself from his father, but I didn't know if she had caught the message. His father's magic, tied to that of the throne, had dampened his own considerable gift so he could not break free. He was also considerably rusty at death spellcasting, having spent far too long on Earth. I found that now, when I needed it, the ability would not come to me.

Panic and fear rose like bile in my throat. Like adrenaline, the terror I felt kick-started my abilities. I threw fire, lightning, anything that would come to me, into the darkness. Where was I?

"Calm yourself Deathling," came a booming male voice. "Your woman is safe, until you do her some damage yourself. Return from the blackness and open your eyes to the light." Rowan knew it wasn't his father's voice even though it had the same authority within it. He soon found the silver light, and followed it to the waking world.

***

My eyes opened to quite a scene. There was scorched marble and rug work all over the temple. I was sure that I had not been there previously. She was crouched behind a large shield made of golden light, a burn up her left arm, and a tall golden haired angel stood by her, another with his pure silver sword to Rowan's throat; the first held the shield in front of her, his emerald wings masked her sides and he too had his sword drawn.

I panicked that she was in such a vulnerable position. I thrust my elbow into the midriff of the angel who held the sword to my throat, rolled away and used my magic to pull her through the air to me, not having a clue why the power I had woven into her ring had not worked. I pushed her behind me and drew a circle of black fire around us both. Conjuring several spears of golden flame to me, each blade unquestionably lethal, I confronted the assailants.

"What have you done to her?" I demanded. I seethed that someone dare touch his woman, let alone harm her in any way. I would take great pleasure in defeating these opponents, and removing their wings one feather at a time for all the pain they caused her. The angel that had held the shield to her gave him a withering stare.

"It is not I that harmed the mortal," he began, placing his sword back into its sheath. "While you were unconscious your magic began to spiral out of control. It flared out in fire, lightning, all of the elements, striking your love and would have done worse had I not been there to shield her."

The news sunk in. I had done this? Caused the terrible burn to her? I flinched and immediately put out the fire around us. How could I do that? She was the most important thing to me in this arduously long life. I paled visibly and turned to her immediately.

"I'm so sorry I... I would never hurt you, even think of hurting you... I..." I felt a distict, shattering pain in my heart and was stopped by her placing her fingers on my lips.

"Don't... Just don't. I saw what you went through. What they must have put you through. A little display like this is hardly shocking," she replied, all the love she felt for me evident in her words. I hugged her, really hugged her, putting all I felt into a single movement. I would never be able to express how much I did love her, and I would do anything in the worlds to ensure her happiness.

Eventually I let her go, questions overtaking the outpouring of feeling I was going through.

"How did we escape my father?" I asked, dreading the answer.

"I can answer that," Illaria declared, striding into the

temple once more. "Your little angel appeared in my rooms begging for my help to rescue you. So of course knowing you were in danger my prince I selflessly came up with a plan to distract your father and get you out of there." There was a snort of disgust from Ana, Gabriel and Raphael as there came a growl from the corner of the temple. The silver wolf pup came trotting over to Rowan and jumped into his arms. It licked his face as he nuzzled the familiar smell.

"What actually happened," she began, giving Illaria a scornful look, "is that I asked Gabriel to transport me to the court as I didn't know how to get there. Illaria was unwilling to help me as she saw your return as an opportunity to seduce you away from me so I... uh... convinced her to help. We came up with a plan to find you and it began to work but I was confronted by your father. Alethea did something, something that's worrying me, and we just managed to escape. Alethea instructed me to bring Illaria with us so that she not be tortured for information." I saw her give me a long look.

"Do you know that wolf? It followed us through the portal when we rescued you and has been with us ever since. It's essence seems somehow vaguely familiar to me and at least *it* was useful," she smirked at Illaria.

"Yes, this is the spirit guide I created just before entering the Court," I replied in a matter of fact tone. "I wasn't sure what was going to happen, and I didn't want you to turn up there and find no help. It's quite old Death magic. I took a small portion of my soul and bound it to a large part of my power. It seems to have taken the form of my favourite animal." I stroked the pup affectionately.

Realisation dawned. "No… where are Vale and Lyria? They were with me when we were captured. That sadist froze them so they could be sold to the highest bidder. I swear if he hurt them…" I felt a rage like nothing else build in me.

"Fear not mortal, Lady Death here saved them at the same time she did you. They are in another chamber in a deep sleep as a result of that freezing spell.

I watched in some amusement as it all tried to sink into her mortal brain. She was learning a lot about herself and the universes she lived in too quickly and even I could see the sensible part of her mind trying to reject what I and the angel said. I felt so guilty about everything that had happened to her in such a short time. How long had it been? A day? A week? I swore to myself that I would return her to her life as soon as I could. Then we could get married and have the normal life I knew both of us longed for.

She eventually spoke. "Well, let's call him Fenris for now. I like the name and the little pup is growing on me." She smiled as she stroked his fur. She was focusing on the mundane, I knew, but she was allowed anything that helped her focus on the here and now.

"Fenris it is," I replied and placed the pup on the floor. It didn't matter that my life was a little shorter for creating the pup; I still had many long and happy years together with her. A wing brushed my cheek and I almost baulked when I knew that Gabriel was so close but then I realised the wing was midnight deep ebony. "Love, your wings are still out," I said with quite a bit of concern, Ana liked to have them hidden most of the time. Alethea was supposed to be the one with the control over most of the power and all it came with. Why were the wings out when Ana was in control?

"I know," I replied dejectedly. "I can't seem to get rid of them. Alethea thinks it has something to do with being in this place and the ultimate battle with Lucifer, or something like that. I've kind of gotten used to them being out all the time now, I suppose." She looked at them and moved one. My heart ached for what she was going through. I had caused it, it was me that had brought this madness into her mundane, safe world. How could I possibly protect her from it?

"I'm so sorry my love," I said as I went to embrace her. "How could I have done this to you?" I placed a kiss on her soft forehead, noting that her essence, her aura, had changed dramatically since I last saw her. A single tear slid down my cheek.

"Ok, that is enough," Gabriel stated, parting them from one another. I was going to ask how the angel dare separate me from her but one look from her, a look that said *I'll tell you later*, kept me quiet. An almost uncomfortable cough came from the corner of the temple. In truth I had forgotten the angels were there, it was so good to feel her weight against me once more. I banished away the heartache of knowing my father didn't care, the torture he happily put me through and the annoyance that I had lost to my father. She brought light, warmth and love into my life and I could never repay her. I would protect her with my life, give it for her gladly and return her to the normality she's used to. I wanted to embrace her once more as I was afraid someone would come to take her away.

"Fear not mortal, you may stay apart," came the sarcastic comment from the corner. "You never brought this into her life... Alethea did..."

I couldn't believe my ears. Was Gabriel actually blaming Alethea for what was happening to her? Alethea was as much a victim here as she was.

"After all," Gabriel continued, "If Alethea had not sided with Lucifer against Him then his infatuation would not have grown and he would not now be obsessed with her. He would not have cursed her to reincarnation..." Gabriel threw a crafty look at her.

Oh by golly, the angel of death took over then, dammit.

Alethea

"How dare you place the blame of everything that has occurred upon my shoulders?" I demanded as I stalked towards

Gabriel, my fury blazing like a thousand suns. "I have suffered beyond your imagining, cursed to bring Death to the loved ones of my mortal body, and He stood by and watched. Do not say this is all upon me!" I took hold of Gabriel's shoulders and threw him towards the far wall of the temple. There was a high pitched scream as Illaria stooped to avoid impact but she was spared the indignity as Gabriel slowed just before her and righted himself with his wings.

Raphael had already withdrawn his sword and pointed it at Alethea's chest.

"Back off, Lapdog," I snarled with as much venom as I could muster. "Must you also revel in my torment?"

"I do not come to cause you discomfort, Death." Raphael stated in his cold tone, "It is merely pleasure for me that it occurs. I come to ensure he does not do something that I will make him regret." I was confused at this.

"What could you mean?" I demanded, uncaring that there were two very confused mortals in the same chamber. Raphael did not reply, he merely placed his sword back in its sheath and went back to staring. I screamed my frustration. Gabriel in turn cast a mischievous smile at me and bowed.

"Ah Lady Death, how wonderful it is to be speaking to you once more." I looked at him with rage which soon became barely contained laughter at his look, despite the run in with Raphael.

"You goaded me into taking over, you devil."

"Well," Gabriel said, and actually blushed. "I could not relay the magnitude of what is about to happen to these mortals. They would understand but not as well as you yourself would."

I sighed. He was going to talk of the Second Coming once more. I had wondered why my wings would not disappear; even now when I was in complete control they would not go. This suggested that Lucifer was even closer to fulfilling his plans then I realised. This was not a good sign.

"Alethea," Gabriel said in all seriousness, walking towards me. "He has asked me for your help in the Second Coming. He knows you have grown in power and knows that you regret what you did so very long ago. You have embraced the nature of your being and have unlimited power to draw upon. Please consider the Hallowed Halls when Lucifer makes his move. Do not let Raphael deter you."

I could have laughed out loud. He was begging for my help? He who cast me out and branded me a traitor; He who stood aside and let me suffer. What if I were truly to blame for the entire situation as well? Would I dare step foot in those Halls again? Or even fight for them?

"Gabriel, I appreciate the situation you find yourself in but I cannot take sides in this War. I will have to use all of my power just to defeat Lucifer, and the power he holds over me, when he comes for me and he *will* come for me; he always comes for me. I have to ensure the safety of this one," I pointed towards Rowan, "and figure a way for this mortal soul to survive should I take over the body once more. I just have no time to help; or the inclination if I'm going to be honest, but I did not want to seem rude." I smiled smugly at Gabriel, happy to decline his 'generous' offer.

"Is there no way I can convince you otherwise Alethea? It is not wise to decline an offer from Him," Gabriel put his hand on the hilt of his sword. This quickly enraged me as I could see the threat in Gabriel's stance.

"And it is unwise to enrage me once more archangel. You forget who I am. I am the angel of death, one of only two constants in this universe and any other. Be gone and do not bother me hence."

To accentuate my point I took the scythe from my back and pointed it towards Gabriel. Burning with the silver of my magic, it was my fury given form.

Gabriel bowed. "Very well. We will depart, Lady Death, but we will not go without a word with the mortal you inhabit." He lifted his hand and golden fire spread forth to pool on the floor. It spread towards me and before I could erect a barrier it consumed me and I fell...

****

Anahlia

I felt disoriented. I was also a bit disconcerted; the push of Alethea's soul had been forceful this time in its fury. I heard a string of expletives coming from the back of my mind and I smiled; so Alethea did have some human traits after all.

"Let me guess mortal," Gabriel began moving towards me. "Alethea is not happy I took her control away from her."

"Ah, no she isn't, she's even swearing in a language I don't recognise now." I couldn't help but smile at that.

"Make no mistake mortal, if Alethea had full control over the body again I could not do that, she is far greater in power than anyone, perhaps myself included, realises." Gabriel shook out his feathers. I still smiled.

"You wanted to say something to me?" I asked, though in truth I wished the celestial beings were far from here.

"I did. I am sorry to tell you this mortal but Alethea did something to the King of this realm that perhaps she should not have. She only wanted to save your love here, but she unleashed something even she has no control over. To convince Alethea to fight for him, Lucifer infected her with Desire, as you know, but to keep his control of her he stored the essence of the original Desire within her soul. This way his obsession could grow and in theory she would not be able to break free of him. The silver mist she unleashed on the King was pure

Desire, unbreakable and focused on the one looked upon at the time, namely yourself. It worked in rescuing this one from his father but it will have far reaching repercussions, I fear. Make no mistake on that score." I shivered at the tone in the angel's voice. I didn't want any repercussions from that; I just wanted to go home with Rowan and live out our lives together.

"Wait, there's something I realised when I woke up in Hell. Alethea took my place in a nightmare once I had blacked out and Lucifer pretty much showed her she was at fault for the first uprising. Is it true? Alethea is sulking at the moment so she doesn't know I know." Gabriel looked at me for a long second.

"It is as the seer told you. I am afraid Lucifer infected her. It sounds like he took advantage of the situation with the nightmare to instill doubt in Alethea. She knows better than to believe him, the original deceiver," Gabriel finished with frustration.

"To be fair all of her memories haven't returned to her yet. Part of her life is still a blur," I argued. I couldn't believe Alethea was being chastised, especially now of all times.

"Still..."

Gabriel cast me one last pitying glance, almost as if he could read my thoughts, and summoned his golden light. Both he and Raphael stepped through almost reluctantly, leaving the two mortals, the pup and the demi angel alone with our thoughts. What would Rowan and I do now? We were stuck in a world I at least knew nothing about, with an apparently obsessed foe coming for us, and nowhere to run. I turned to Rowan.

"Would your father really try to find me?"

"Yes," he replied simply, and far too quickly. "My father has always desired power and you exhibited that in spades. Then there's the fact that Alethea unleashed Desire on him," he visibly shuddered. "I am surprised he's not here already to be honest." I walked up to him and hugged him around the middle, seeking comfort as well as giving it. A groan sounded through one of the arches and my friends staggered in. I was so thrilled to see them moving once more that I hugged them both tight, regardless of the wounds they had. Vale gasped and pushed me from her, her astounding strength hardly there. I wanted to cry, what had my friends gone through that their power was not interwoven into their very beings as it was normally?

"Just... just leave off the hugs until I've had coffee yeah?" Where was the banter? Where was the insults? A single crystalline tear slid down my cheek as I went back to Rowan's arms.

"What can we do now?"

"I don't know..."

***

The King

The throne room was quiet. It would usually bother me that it was this quiet; I enjoyed people with their emotions and their dramas and their lives. Now however I had better things to concentrate on, I wanted no one around to distract me from the vision before me.

I used the pyre I was going to burn Mikhail on. It still grated on me that the little traitor had escaped my grasp once again; I had planned so many torments for him. First his mother dared defy me and then when I had groomed him for the throne; for the power, the responsibility and the ruthlessness that comes with it; my coward of a son ran away to the one place he had no dominion. Well, one of the places. I had no dominion in the Lifer's realm, I merely enjoyed causing them upset.

When I sensed my son had returned to this realm, I had assumed it was to usurp my power, it is what I would do. He had been gone for almost seventy-five years; surely he had grown in power in that time. I had gone straight to Illaria's guild, I remembered my son had had a minor fascination with the seer, and it was where he'd felt his sons' power return. However the treacherous little seer had interfered and his son had vanished once again.

The King toyed with the pendant that had disappeared when Mikhail had. Imagine my surprise when my son's power returned once more to court. He brazenly strolled straight into court demanding to know where 'she' was. I had thought it was some sort of ploy, and my son had returned to defeat me once and for all. I was shocked that the boy had been so easily captured. I had taken great pains to torture Mikhail for information but he had merely stared at me, his hateful gaze becoming angrier as more of his blood slicked to the floor. Perhaps my son had a strength in him I had never before realised. It almost made me want to return my son to his place of power; almost, but not quite. Mikhail must suffer for turning his back on his people and now his father had the perfect tool to perform this.

My gaze was drawn back to the fire that burned black before me. The drumbeats had started once more and I watched as the seers gathered around the beautiful enigma before me. She was stunning with midnight blue black curls cascading over ivory skin. I watched in amazement as large ebony wings unfurled from her back. Now I could see what she had done to free the little whelp from his imprisonment. Silver light poured forth from the arm concealed by a wing. It was powerful and worked through my magic easily. A chord of familiarity struck in my mind. Who *was* she?

I moaned aloud as I watched her brush up against me, much as I had at the time. I had to have her!

"Lazar."

"Yes my Lord," answered the shadow moving towards me. Shining silver sparks began from its centre and a handsome man stepped from the darkness. This was my most trusted general, decked out in the ceremonial armour of my people. If I gave Lazar an order he would execute it perfectly, even if it went against everything he believed.

"I need you to discover the whereabouts of my treacherous son and the vision he keeps with him. Discover all you know about her, who she is and what she's capable of. If possible take her from him and kill him. I have no need for my son any more." If I had given that order to anyone else I would have had a mutiny to deal with. Most of my people remembered my son, his courage and his valour. I knew Lazar would not falter however.

"It will be done, my Lord."

I did not watch as my general swiped his hand in front of him, gathering the magic from the air, to consume him in transportation. I did not also see the pitying look my general gave me. Oh how the mighty had fallen...

***

Anahlia

I found myself sat around the makeshift fire we had erected in the centre of the temple. I sat as close to Rowan as I could. I didn't trust Illaria in the slightest and knew she plotted to steal Rowan away, perhaps in retaliation for bringing her here. I felt that maybe I should have left her at the court to rot.

I heard laughter come from the back of my own mind. *You would not have done that Child*, counselled Alethea. *You have far too good a soul to condemn someone to that. Alas, it is my essence that is corrupting you and for that I beg your forgiveness.*

Don't worry. I felt the need to comfort the celestial being. *You are as much a victim in this as we are, perhaps even more so since you have had to endure this since the beginning of time.*

I thank you for your kind words Child.

I could feel guilt emanating from the area of the mind that was Alethea. I had to ignore it now however as I and the others had to figure out what was to be done next. The weight of Fenris snuggled at my other leg provided as much comfort as Rowan himself did; I hoped creating the pup didn't affect Rowan too much. I needed him above all others. I watched with a glare as Illaria walked back into the room, a platter of food in her hands. I gladly served Rowan, giving him my most sultry smile, I helped Vale and Lyria dish out, but threw the platter in front of her. I picked up what looked like chicken and glared at the seer. Yep, I definitely should have left her.

"We must leave here," Rowan began, after finishing off his meat. "My father will stop at nothing to possess you now, especially if what Gabriel says is true. If my father has been infected with the original Desire then nothing can stop him. I must get the pendant back too. It is a royal pendant so my father should have it but it is *mine*." I was shocked to hear the hatred in his voice. I'd never heard it before and hoped it would never be directed at me. I could feel anger replace the guilt in my mind. Alethea had not known Lucifer had stored the original Desire within her; corrupted her, changed her essence so she was permanently stuck with it. She had thought she was merely affected by the original Desire. I wondered how the angels had not warned her of this; yes she had fought against them but she had meticulously stayed out of their affairs since then. She felt betrayed.

"I merely want to go back to court," Illaria pouted, nibbling on a grape like a gerbil. "I can handle your father; I have always been able to. I am not some cowering mortal who runs at the first sign of trouble." She glared at me as hard as she could. I merely laughed and listened. Rowan walked over to Illaria and crouched before her.

"Look at me Illaria." When she didn't he took hold of her chin and forced her to look into his eyes. "My mother was three times the seer you are and he still managed to kill her in cold blood." He let go of her chin with a disdainful push. "Do not forget who Anahlia really is. She is Our Lady and the love of my harshly long life. Pay her more respect." He got up and stalked over to the other side of the temple. I reeled from his almost archaic dialect.

"F...forgive me my Lady," Illaria said as she watched me get up and walk over to Rowan. I ignored the seer; I would have worried about being rude with someone else but not Illaria. I wished Illaria far away.

"What's up?" I asked Rowan, placing my hand on his arm.

"This is so screwed up," he replied, still not looking at me. "When I escaped here I thought to never return. I wanted to live out my long life on Earth. When I found you everything seemed perfect; you seem to be the other half of my soul. Now I've got you mixed up in all this and I don't know how to fix it." He kicked the wall in anger.

"The way I understand it," I moved my hand from his arm to his cheek, making him look at me, "is that I got you dragged into this mess for being who I am. You had escaped this world and this life and I brought you back to it. I am so sorry my love." I hugged him close to me, uncaring that my wings might get in the way.

They all heard a voice boom out.

"I am the Metatron..."

Suddenly Alethea took over.

Alethea

I pushed the boy away from me. Metatron was coming which could only mean bad things were coming with him.

"Ana?" Rowan asked, a little hurt I had pushed him away.

"Trust me mortal," I said, looking into his eyes. "This is for your own good." I waved my hand the length of the room and watched in amusement as both the mortals and the pup froze. The part of my mind that was Anahlia was frozen also, a curious experience but one I could not look too closely into for now. Metatron was coming.

"... the voice of Our Lord, He who guides and protects us..." I was becoming impatient. Metatron always felt the need to announce himself and it bored me to tears. Why could he never just appear? In annoyance I waved my hand and Metatron appeared in a flash of silver light. He would be angry that he had been summoned but it was nothing I could not handle. In fact, the concept rather amused me.

"Why did you summon me Lady Death?" he asked in rather a petulant voice. It always grated on me that he sounded more like a spoilt brat than a celestial being.

"You were taking far too long Metatron. I know my life is unending but this mortal's is not. Why do you come here?"

"Be easy, angel of death," Metatron began, taking a seat by the frozen fire. "I am not here to convince you to fight for Him, though you know as well as I that we need your help."

"Get to the point then messenger." I took a seat by him.

"I am here to help. You have gone through far too much in your existence angel of death, and you need some time to figure out what you will do now. You know the mortals' time is running out. As you get stronger the mortals' soul will die. I know you wish to avoid this so you need some help."

"So what do you suggest?"

"Perhaps you should hide in Miltiades' realm?" I gasped.

"Have you lost your mind messenger?" I demanded. "My foolish need to get away from Lucifer affected Miltiades too much. I did not have enough control of the Desire hidden within me and now I must deal with Miltiades's obsession as well as Lucifer's."

"Think on it, Lady," Metatron replied, remaining seated. "You cannot return to Earth in the condition you are in; the Second Coming rapidly approaches and to survive it you will have to be complete and whole once more. You cannot remain here either; the King searches for you relentlessly. He is now under the thrall of your Desire. He will not stop until he has you completely, and these mortals will suffer." I knew he spoke the truth but it hurt my pride to hide in Miltiades realm, as ex-lovers went he was a bit... feminine.

"On a side note," Metatron continued, "why are the mortals frozen? It would be beneficial to all if they could hear this plan as well." I did not answer; instead I laughed to myself and unfroze the mortals. Metatron was right, it would be better if they could hear this too, but how could I explain that I was saving the mortals from Metatron's unending chatter? He took his role of messenger seriously and never *ever* stopped talking.

Rowan was the first to react. He saw the newcomer as a threat and thrust me behind him. The part of my mind that was Anahlia melted at the act. Rowan would always love her completely and I had to admit that I did feel a slight twinge of envy that I would never experience the same. Vale and Lyria took up positions on each side of him. When did they get so close? It warmed my heart. Their strength was still returning to them but I was happy to see their power came to them easily.

"Who are you?" Rowan demanded as he gathered golden fire in his hands. He intended to protect Anahlia with his life and I wanted to stop him from making such a foolish decision.

"This is Metatron," I said as I moved from behind Rowan. "He is the messenger of Him and an old friend of mine. He usually heralds a portent of doom. Now however he is here to help... I think."

"Why does he come now?" Rowan asked me directly. I was unsure if he was aware he spoke to me and not Anahlia.

"He has a plan that should help us avoid unnecessary trouble until we can devise how to save both you and Anahlia..." I began tentatively. Anahlia had already read from my mind what I planned and warned that Rowan would not like it. Anahlia knew little of the world we found ourselves in but knew Rowan had an aversion to his polar opposites.

"...We are going to hide in the realm of Life. That is Miltiades's realm. It is the only realm that for now is not an imminent threat to us all."

"Miltiades?" asked Illaria, resplendent in her ignorance.

"Miltiades is my polar opposite. He is the angel of life, he who stands for growth, change, creation... and ignorance," I sighed. "He is also my former lover."

"Nope," Rowan began. "No way, it's not going to happen. You may be in charge of the body at the moment Lady Death but you inhabit the body of my soul mate. Any of the Lifers there could take the opportunity to steal her. Miltiades may very well mistake her for you and take her anyway. She can no longer dismiss the wings, as you can't, and he could take the opportunity to strike. I could defeat any Lifer that comes for us but I have no chance at all against a horribly obsessed angel."

I waited patiently for Rowan to finish and then replied.

"Make no mistake mortal. This body is mine. It was foretold I would be reincarnated back into it. Granted, I do not want it. If I can find a way for Anahlia to retain control I will but do not think to dictate to me on my safety." I took a deep breath. "I can mask both yours and the seers' death essences. It is a simple matter to make it look like you belong in Miltiades realm. It is even easier for me to mask the shifter and the light essence. For me however it is a little more difficult. I believe that with Anahlia in control her mortal soul should mask my essence. The wings will be of little matter, we will just avoid all that dwell in that forsaken place. Please mortal, consider it. We need to decide what to do and how we all will survive the coming torment. Do not coddle each other; Lucifer advances his plans at a rapid rate now that I am awake. He will use the confusion to come for me and if we do not have a plan all will be lost."

I could see Rowan considering my words. I knew that all he wanted was to return to Earth with Anahlia and the others and live out their lives together. Part of me wished it could be so. I had no desire to ruin their lives at all. I wanted to fade away into oblivion and leave the pain and suffering behind. I could not however and as I must face my duties with courage, so must the mortals.

"Okay, my Lady," Rowan said with more resignation then I deemed necessary. "Let's hide in the Lifers realm. We'll figure out what to do and how to save us all." I was strangely grateful for his support. If Anahlia knew Rowan supported me then it would make the entire affair easier on all of them. I turned to the seer.

"If it is my Lady's wish, then we will travel to the cursed realm," Illaria replied, though I could not help but feel she was trying to conceal something. I was aware that the seer was treacherous and hated my mortal host with a passion.

Be careful of this one child, Alethea warned silently. *She thinks to manipulate us all to gain her own desires. Be mindful.*

Don't worry about me, came the confident reply. *I can handle her.* I had to smile at the confidence in Anahlia's voice. Now that she was aware of the other woman's desires, the Child felt she could handle it.

You do realise, Anahlia continued, *that it is very likely a trap we're getting ourselves into? I can't quite put my finger on it but something seems wrong. I read from your mind that although he willingly Fell too, Miltiades is still loyal to Him?* I was actually touched that Anahlia decided to use my terminology for our Lord.

He is. He feels that while he indulges in all the mortal pleasures and sins, if he stays loyal to Him then one day he should be able to return.

Hmmmm, I just don't like it, Anahlia counselled. I could feel something was wrong but I didn't know what. I could understand her sense of trepidation. I too felt something was wrong but it was our only option. They had to go somewhere they had time to think and where they would be mostly safe. I turned back to the others in the room.

"It is agreed then," I began. "We will travel to the realm of life and create a plan to combat all our situations." At least I hoped they would. "Come closer to me mortals. I or Anahlia will transport us. It will be a smooth spell and one that is completely undetectable by our enemies."

"Lady Death," Metatron began. "Do you need me to accompany you? We would have strength in numbers and I can provide some protection." I was again strangely touched by his gesture. He was one of the unfallen angels and indifferent to most affairs yet he offered to help us. I placed my hand on his shoulder.

"Thank you old friend," I began, sincerity shining in my voice. "I cannot tell you how much that means to me. I must urge you to return to Him however. I can feel Lucifer's insidious nature creeping upon us all and He will need all his able fighters at His side when the time comes."

"As you wish, angel of death," Metatron replied and with an indifferent shrug of his shoulders he disappeared in a flash of golden light. I almost laughed; no words of caution or wellbeing from him. I turned back to Rowan, a smile still on my lips.

"I am going to let Anahlia take over once more mortal. Until I am complete again these periods of control tire me." I could see Rowan start to object but held a hand up to silence him. "Fear not, I will talk Anahlia through the transportation spell once more. I would leave neither her nor you all unprotected."

I bowed my head and allowed the mortal to come forward once more. As our souls passed I gave her a mental hug. It was going to be extremely hard for all of us from now on; I hoped they all had the strength that was required.

***

Anahlia

I came to. I had been privy to everything that had happened and felt a horrible sense of foreboding. If the angel of death, the sole point of origin for all death everywhere, had resorted to hope then how would they survive it?

I turned to Rowan. I had to begin the transportation spell and get them out of there. I also hoped to steal some momentary comfort from him. I felt utterly exposed and terrified.

I took one step and had to lean on a column for support. The temple began to spin around me at a dizzying speed and just as I felt myself fall, the world went sparkling black...

***

I sighed once more. I was face to face with a startling set of hazel eyes which had warmed to melted chocolate. My heart did its usual stutter; the face I looked into was an almost perfect replica of Lucifer's and that fact had always made me uncomfortable.

"Why do you feel the desire to leave me now?" demanded a smooth voice, like silk rubbing against one's skin.

"Because Miltiades," I began, holding onto my patience with a white knuckled grip, "Lucifer is no longer a threat to me. There have been no attacks in nigh on two hundred years. Even Lucifer has a tendency to become bored should he not attain that which he desires."

"But what of our deep and endless love?" I actually felt bile rise in my throat. I had never felt any love for Miltiades and had accidentally infected him with the excess Desire Lucifer had left within me. It had proven problematic at first but then I had realised that Miltiades provided a stoic defence against Lucifer's unending attacks and attempts to get me back. We had shared bodies numerous times but I had shared very little else with him.

"Listen to me, Life Lord," I began in my most appeasing tone, "I do not know how to love anyone. I was never infected with Love as Lucifer deemed I would be too weak to help him. I cannot be what you want me to be." I was disgusted to hear

Miltiades sniff. He turned away from me to hide the tears I knew were appearing.

Miltiades's softer side had always made me a little uneasy. He was such a competent warrior with so much power of his own, yet he seemed to me a little too... feminine. We may have been made as complete polar opposites but I was still able to admire his prowess with a sword. If I were completely honest I could admire his prowess for other things too but I was unwilling to look into that too deeply.

It was strange for me to see this softer side of him; Miltiades was the exact replica of Lucifer. Same long golden hair, same golden wings, same hazel eyes and same beautifully toned body; however, Lucifer was far more masculine than Miltiades could ever be. That thought brought me up short; I did not think I could compliment Lucifer in any way. I had to get away from this place as soon as I could, that was evidence enough that my thought process was severely off.

I watched with trepidation as Miltiades turned back to me and carefully took hold of my hand.

"...Please... do not leave me..."

***

I slowly opened my eyes. It took just a moment for my

vision to focus and I could see Rowan's worried face with Vale and Lyria's hovering above mine. They must have heard the fall and rushed in. I love my friends, my brain was randomly thinking on a tangent. What was happening to me? Why was I fainting now of all times and places?

"Oh thank the Lady you're awake," Rowan sighed as he helped me up. "What happened?"

"It's strange," I replied. "It almost feels like little parts of my soul die every time Alethea takes over." I shook my head, not realising I had started to look inwards, and laughed. "How melodramatic does that sound?" I smiled at Rowan, if only to banish the look of worry on their faces.

A second pair of hands came to steady me, and I was amused to see it was Illaria with a shadow of concern on her face. I couldn't decide whether she actually cared or she was doing it to merely endear herself to Rowan further. If the latter, she would fail miserably.

I am sorry Child, came Alethea's saddened voice. *My memories can become... overwhelming for a mortal mind. You are seeing things no mortal should see; I wish I had not seen them myself. Your soul is not dying every time I take over.* I could almost feel the reluctance pouring from Alethea. What was she hiding? *As... as I take over more, our souls begin to recognise one another and work to help each other. It is a symbiosis rather than an end. We will not merge as you think of it, rather while we are both in here our souls work to help each other. I think.*

I didn't like that sound of that. I had become used to the mad conversations within my own head and had even started to view Alethea almost as a friend and protector. I didn't want anything bad to happen to any of them if it could be helped; but what could I do? I felt a horrible sense of foreboding creep upon me.

Fear not child, once Lucifer has been defeated and the world is once again righted we will see to your life and that of your love. Now... Alethea carried on in my matter of fact tone... *we need to see about saving us. As much as I hate to admit it, Metatron is right. We will be safe in Miltiades's realm until we can think of what to do, and as long as Miltiades does not discover my presence. May I have control of just your feet for the time being?*

Why just my feet?

Because I always loved to dance.

I could feel my mental smile. *Do you remember my telling you that magic, power, is just force of will? You can do anything as long as you will it. Repeat it often enough and it will happen. Dancing is so rhythmic, so seductive, it never fails to work in whatever spell you wish.* I had to smile at that myself.

Then feel free to control whatever you wish. I couldn't do much for Alethea but at least I could give her this small sense of happiness before what was to come.

I turned back to Rowan and the others.

"Alethea is about to start the transportation spell," I explained. "If I do anything odd, don't laugh at me," I said while smiling. I brushed Rowan's cheek and stood on my toes to brush my mouth softly against his. I had a worrying sense of dread creeping up on me and I couldn't help but feel that I may not live to see out the life I planned with Rowan. I clasped hands with my friends, Vale scarily quiet. What happened to her while frozen by the King? I would end him if he caused her harm.

"We cannot leave until I retrieve the pendant."

I resigned myself. "Do you have a plan to get it back?"

"Yes... but neither you nor the Lady will like it." He stated with worry tinged with that egotistical determination. I began to worry.

"What is it?"

"I need you to walk into the throne room and distract my father..."

"Nope, nuh uh, no way, not going to happen," Vale piped up, standing in front of me to protect me from whatever Rowan had planned. I couldn't believe Rowan was even suggesting it. Why did he desire to throw me to the wolves, quite literally? I still feared what effect the desire had had on Rowan's father. What if they got into worse trouble? I watched dubiously as Rowan took me by both arms.

"Ana, I know you're scared but I need to get the pendant back. My mother made me promise long ago that it wouldn't fall back into my father's hands, you see..." and here he faltered, "... if my father has that, the power of the crown, the throne and his own considerable gift then he will be unstoppable. His plans have always been to have dominance over both the realm of death and the realm of life. Given half the chance he'd go for the mortal realms as well."

"But isn't there an angel in residence in the realm of life?" I asked, remembering Alethea's exasperation at the fact that she would have to go anywhere near Miltiades.

"Oh believe me when I say at full strength with the entire power of his position my father is more than a match for any angel."

I shivered. "I guess we have to then. But I'm not thrilled with the prospect of seeing your father again. I dread the thought of him being as obsessed as Lucifer." Rowan hugged me in what could only be described as glee.

"Don't worry love, you can handle my father." He winked at me in a cocky, self assured way.

"I thought you just said that he's more than a match for any angel?"

"He is, but don't forget this very universe was created from Alethea's power. Should you have need merely tap into the essence of the realm."

Oh is that all? Alethea asked sarcastically from her secluded position. I had to smile.

"Okay, lets do this." I said.

I made sure the scythe was in situ on my back and Alethea swore that my other weapons were concealed on my body using the strongest death magic she knew. Vale was with Lyria in the far corner, both determining the strength of their power. Together the three of us were nigh on unstoppable, but I still fear what had happened to them as a result of my own apt stupidity. I turned in time to see Rowan hold up his right hand.

Concentrating acutely, he held out his index finger and I watched in amazement as a tear of black energy appeared in front of him, hovering in the air. He carefully withdrew a pure silver breastplate and donned it over the black silk shirt I hadn't even seen him find. He still wore his tight pants but I couldn't really complain at that. Rowan quickly reached in once more and withdrew a pure silver longsword, which he placed in a sheath on his back (again where had that come from?) and a pure silver dagger which he placed in his belt. He then flattened his hand to almost caress along the energy tear.

I was impressed. I knew full well that my logical mind was trying it's hardest to make sense of everything that was going on around me but I couldn't help but notice how very well Rowan fitted in this strange place. He was mouth-watering in a business suit but I thought my heart might actually stop seeing him dressed in his warrior regalia.

It won't came the dry reply to my thought. Honestly. Did Alethea have to crush all my thoughts?

I watched as Rowan searched inside the tear and found a pure silver box. Within was a gun, very similar to the guns at home but this had a chamber that *glowed*. Rowan placed it at the bottom of his back in the waistband and I remembered my question.

"Rowan, how are there guns here?"

"Oh well my grandfather went to the mortal realm on many a visit. He was a promiscuous old sod mostly occupied with the ladies but he did find a fascination with guns on one of his last visits there. He bought one back and had our engineers work on our equivalent. He always wanted to go back but didn't have chance as my father murdered him about a week later." He said the last bit with sadness and my heart constricted.

"Oh Rowan I'm sorry. You must have loved him."

"I did but he had had a long and full life so at least he was fulfilled. I just wish he hadn't met such a grisly end, especially at his age."

"Was he very old?" I asked watching Rowan become distracted by the gun once more.

"Not really old, he was only seven hundred and thirty two." I gasped, surely Rowan was joking with me. No one lived that long.

"Erm..." Rowan looked at me then and saw I looked rather confused.

"What?" he asked, also confused.

"Erm... people don't live that long."

Rowan chuckled. "They do here. Because this is the realm of death women struggle to carry children. If they do become pregnant they are restricted to bed rest for the entire nine months to ensure total peace and calm for the baby. To compensate for this Alethea made it so that unless we are killed or take our own lives we live for a very long time. It usually becomes the case that people become bored of existence and take their own lives and so we're not entirely sure how long our life spans are. I think the longest one recorded was a thousand years." I didn't know how to take this in. My damnable curiosity got the best of me and I determined to ask a question I wasn't sure I wanted to know the answer to.

"Rowan... are you really twenty eight?"

"Ah..." and here he paused. "No, I'm not. I'm really two hundred and fifty three years old. I'd actually lived in the mortal realm for seventy three years before I met you."

"I'm still me though, the man you agreed to marry." It actually felt like my brain had gone out to lunch and there was an answering machine in its place. *Leave your message after the beep...*

"If you two have quite finished can we return to the

court now?" Illaria interjected. She too had donned armour and weaponry and looked at them expectantly. I could hear laughing in my mind and was glad to see that both I and Alethea agreed that Illaria looked ridiculous. At least, however, it was something concrete to concentrate on to take my mind off the fact that Rowan was a hell of a lot older than I thought.

"Yes, let's go if we're going," I replied and quickly walked out of the temple without waiting for any of them.

Outside I dragged in a lung full of clean, fresh air. I would not hyperventilate even if my mortal mind said otherwise. I didn't know how much more of this I could take without cracking under the pressure. My safe and secure life was gone, replaced by this madness.

Calm down Child, Alethea tried to soothe. *Things will sort themselves in time. It is only apocalyptic events that deem these things necessary; and I can already feel your mind turning towards your love. Do not worry, he will be out momentarily, he is just threatening death upon the seer should she harm you.* I warmed at Alethea's words. That was just like Rowan to think of me first. I felt my love for him swell and felt the boon of a longer bout of sanity so I could further assist Rowan. Vale and Lyria came out and I could now see the shadows in both of their eyes. I didn't know what to say as guilt consumed me. I walked up and embraced them both which they returned. A single crystalline tear fell from all three of us. We did not see them coalesce and create a beautiful crystal flower.

Eventually both Rowan and Illaria appeared from the temple. Rowan had conjured four black robes with silver embroidery for them. They were gorgeous and I felt the urgent need to don mine. I'd never seen such exquisite silver lining before. I smiled as Rowan cast one around my shoulders and it landed perfectly to hide my wings. The others he cast around himself, Vale and Lyria and I was once again struck by his very masculine beauty. They clasped hands as they covered themselves with hoods and followed Illaria to the Court.

I was once again in wonder. I could really grow to love this place if I were given enough time. The majestic silver archways with their resplendent brickwork towered above them. The crystal blue of the ponds and rivers they passed was elegant in its beauty and even the greenery was a bright and vivid emerald green. This place held so much beauty it was a wonder that they who ruled it could exhibit such evil tendencies.

Gradually we came to the doors of the court once more, but I wasn't really paying attention. As we had walked I had been conversing with Alethea about the origins of the realm and I hadn't noticed that I had begun to walk with a stronger gait, or that my eyes had taken on a permanent silver sparkle, or even that my hair was more lustrous in its ebony darkness. Alethea knew though; she could see her aura taking over that of the mortal's and feared what Lucifer said to be true. Now that they were more angel than mortal Anahlia could draw on death at her own will and use it to cow all before them.

.. It was very likely she would not even be aware she was doing it as her mind was already attuned to the power. A proverbial tear fell in the part of the mind that Alethea hid in. She had no desire to see this child's end and had wanted to find a way to save her but it looked like that was becoming an impossibility. It seemed she was cursed to cause Death for all.

You will need to knock the seer unconscious, Alethea said and I caught the note of sadness in her voice. What was that in aid of? *If she enters the court with you she very well may betray you to the King. We do not want that.*

She was right and I knew this would cause some shock but to be honest I was tired of all this cloak and dagger bullshit. As they got closer to the door, I snaked my right hand out and a ball of silver flame shot out and crashed into Illaria. I watched in satisfaction as the seer flew into the wall and was knocked out.

In one fluid movement I threw the cloak off me, withdrew the scythe and shot both guards at the entryway in the knees; not a fatal blow but enough to incapacitate them. I saw that Rowan was frozen in shock.

"Wh...?"

"Alethea told me to do it as she believed that the witch would betray us," I said as I blushed. I didn't know how I had called on the power so fast but for now at least it felt as natural as breathing. I wanted to smile at the seer in her prone state. Rowan shook his head and Vale and Lyria stared. I wasn't an assertive woman naturally, my pacifism and anxiety making me so, but damn it felt good.

"I was expecting her to, you know. I can handle her." He sounded like he was pouting, and he threw off his own cloak, realising it wasn't necessary now; Vale and Lyria followed suit, again keeping unnaturally quiet. I laughed and readied the scythe as Rowan readied his sword and dagger; a quick look behind showed Lyria calling the light and Vale tapping into her animalistic side. Knowing I had everyone at my back made me certain we would survive whatever may came. With a nod to each other I blew lightly on the doors and they flew open in a silver gale. Shouting was heard and several guards tried to rush us. A wicked smile graced my plump lips.

I watched as a guard swung at me with his silver sword. I ducked and raked the blade of my scythe across his legs. As I span, I brought up my right hand to push the guard nearest Rowan away with another silver gale. I kept spinning and brought up the bottom of the scythe. I fired as I span, felling guards where they stood. One fell after another, unsure of what was happening or even how to stop it. None were critically wounded. As I fought Rowan had also made a significant dent in the infantry. Even as I span, I marvelled at his lethality and competence in such a deadly sport. Was it wrong that I seemed even more attracted to him now? Seriously, the guy was rocking some major sexiness. Lyria was in the middle of encasing someone in a cage of solid light, while Vale was chewing on another; I had to stifle my chuckle, she reminded me of any sought of young pet chewing on their favourite toy.

I came to a stop at the end of the long hall and I was amused to see there was only one lone guard left. He looked around him for support and when he found none, he decided to charge us anyway. I had to smirk. I focused on him and my eyes lit with silver flame. The walls and the floor vibrated and all of a sudden, the guard was imprisoned in silver tinged marble. I walked up to him and patted him on the head.

"Good boy, stay there." I turned to see how Rowan fared and I was a little surprised to see him finished with not a hair out of place. That was Rowan, always impeccable in his appearance. I turned to survey what they had done, and I was a little shocked to see so many bodies. I had thought I was only wounding them, but had I got carried away? A small tear ran down my cheek and intensified to see Rowan walk off without a care. Had he been this heartless before we met? Hell, had he been this ruthless during our relationship? I shuddered at the thought and followed after him, realising there was nothing I could do for them now. My heart ached. My friends followed suit and I could feel a sense of guilt consuming them. I wish we could talk over a bottle of red wine like we used to. I think that chatty night would be too emotionally unstable though.

They came to the great silver doors of the throne room and I took a moment to steady myself. My nerves were already shot and now I had to face down someone who was already obsessed with me; it made my skin crawl.

"Are you okay?" Rowan asked but the caring note that was always present in his voice was long gone. Was that what it took for him to be a stone-cold killer? I knew he would never hurt me, but did he have to distance himself so much?

"Just gathering my nerves," I replied, not entirely sure how to broach the subject.

Rowan must have seen what I was thinking. "Yes, I do need to distance myself from my emotions. It's the only way to survive in this Him-awful universe." The coldness in his voice made me shiver. I couldn't reply and I wouldn't even if I could. Taking a deep breath, Rowan signalled me, and I pushed open the great doors while he remained outside. The room was darker than it had been before. I could barely see the hardly lit throne in front of me. The king sat and stared into his palm as if he was watching the dearest thing in the world. I didn't need to guess hard to know who he watched. I adopted what I hoped was a sultry walk.

As I got closer, I addressed him in a throaty tone.

"Your Majesty." The King's head shot up as if I had screamed his title from miles away. He blinked several times before he focused on me and I could feel my stomach lurch at the lust I saw in his eyes.

"You!" he declared. "You have returned to me!!!" He got to his feet in very little time and almost ran down the steps towards me. My skin crawled at the thought of him touching me, so I danced out of his reach.

"I have. Who could deny such a virile man?"

"But what of my son?" he asked, wariness entering his vision momentarily.

"He could not satisfy my desires, so I ended him," I gave him a sultry smile and could see the effect my words had on him. He seemed to gain an uncomfortable bulge in his too tight leathers that made me want to vomit. Come on Rowan, where are you?

"He was such a pathetic child. I'm ashamed he was all that sap of a wife could give me." He began to take off his armour, "now come here so I can show you what a real man can do." I tried to smile at that, but disgust won my inner battle.

Suddenly there was a glare of bright light from the doorway and the King was hit with a crystal like substance that grew to encompass him, leaving only his neck and head bare. Rowan stormed up to them, rage in his every step.

"A real man, father?" he demanded. "A real man would not fall for such an easy trap." I could see that the King paid no attention to him but seemed consumed with breaking the crystal to get to me. Were the effects of the Desire that bad?

Rowan could see it too which only served to infuriate him more. He grabbed the pendant around his father's neck, yanked it off, placed it around his own neck and proceeded to punch his father. I could see that black fire surrounded his fists, so it was no wonder the King was immediately out. So much for

Rowan being rusty at magic; his power seemed to have grown tenfold since he had returned here. It made me worry for him all the more. Rowan sighed in disgust and clicked his fingers. I watched in amazement as the crystal grew further to engulf the Kings head. Somehow, I knew it wouldn't kill him but it would hold him for a while.

Rowan stomped his way over to me and grabbed my hand, roughly leading me out of the throne room and further out of the court. I wanted to tell him that he was hurting me but I knew it wasn't intentional. He seemed stuck in his own thoughts and to be honest I didn't have the energy to deal with that right now. We were flanked by my silent friends; protective, powerful but oh so silent.

Eventually we came back to where we had left Illaria. She was just waking up as they approached her, and she shot me some deadly looks. I merely smiled at her. I didn't really want friendship from Illaria anyway.

"What did you do that for?"

"Oh, you know," I replied. "I had no desire to be betrayed today." Disgust dripped from my voice. I heard Illaria bitterly sigh.

"Well, now you can leave can you not? You have no need of me anymore."

Take her with us.

I didn't ask why. I knew it would anger the seer and I

myself was so stressed at the moment that I loved that idea.

"Sorry. Alethea wants to start the transportation spell," I said with glee. I could tell Rowan was about to say something but suddenly I pirouetted to the right, my feet performing intricate steps around Rowan, Vale, Lyria and Illaria. I knew I had a look of wonderment on my face but couldn't help it. I was dancing but I was not in control of anything. Even my body took on a rhythmic, almost seductive movement that I couldn't help; I could see that it was having an effect on Rowan, however. He almost drank my movements in, memorising them and the intricate detail of my body.

Within my own mind I could hear Alethea chanting softly. She had told me that magic was always will alone but now she chanted a spell in a language I didn't know but could understand, asking for extra protection in the dreaded place they were going to. I could see the place now, Alethea held the picture in our mind so vividly; there was a forest, much like the one I had followed when I had been captured in the field, but this one radiated with a golden gleam, indicating it was different to the death realm.

Nausea welled up in my stomach and I knew it didn't come from me. Alethea really didn't want to go to the place she was sending us to. She and Miltiades were polar opposites in every way, and I did not want to have to subject myself to yet another man that had been infected by my Desire. Unfortunately, the situation Lucifer placed me in dictated I do so, at least until they could figure out how each of them would reach a happy conclusion when all of this was over.

I could feel the magic gathering around me as my body became a silver blur. Flames were left where my feet trod, and I raised my hands to coalesce the magic into one focal point. Just as it was almost over, I became aware of a quiet counter point to my spell. Someone was murmuring ancient words and now I was too far gone into the spell to find out whom. I prayed it would not affect us as we disappeared into a bright silver shine of light.

11

A brutal, raging silver storm tore the beautiful azure sky asunder. Shining emerald trees swayed in the forceful gale, some being torn from the Earth and flung far and wide. The crystalline lake, normally so quiet and still, was an angry oasis of death and destruction for nearby wildlife. Those who were not fleeing for their very lives cowered at the havoc that rained down all around them.

Amid the chaotic weather began a small silver shine in the evening's sky. It grew, becoming larger and larger until it was a swathe of silver fire stark against the unsettled golden tinged sky. It was high above the ground and one could mistake it as the fallen moon. The earth gave a small rumble, and out of this silver flame a woman was thrown out to the ground with a sickening thud.

I felt myself dizzied by the impact of my landing. I was so very cold but mercifully the wings had disappeared during the spell, although now I thought on it, they probably would have made for a softer landing than the one I had. Thankfully I still wore Alethea's archaic armour; it was bulky, cumbersome but it took most of the impact. I turned onto my back and looked into the storm filled sky. I shouldn't really be laying in the middle of a field with a storm going on I decided and moved to find Rowan so they could find shelter.

I got up slowly, and although I had a gash on my left cheek and several joints that ached, I was relatively unscathed from my entrance to the realm. I stretched to my full height, working out all the kinks I felt, and looked around me. There were scorch marks on the ground indicating the silver flame I had been engulfed in had come through the portal with me. I checked my body quickly; there were no burns, no blemishes and no sign to say I had even been alight. I was grateful for small mercies. I was however the only living being around. Where had Rowan gone?

And then it hit me. There was only one scorch mark, only one patch of crushed grass, only one impact. I had been the only one to come through this side of the portal. Fear began as a small distasteful seed in my stomach. What had happened? I had thought I had heard a quiet counter beat as the spell was being performed but Alethea could not place it. Illaria was not here either. Where were they? Had they been transported somewhere else? Or were they now trapped in an in-between place?

I started to hyperventilate with panic. I was in an unknown place with no one to help me and no comfort from the only people I relied on. I had to find them.

Calm do... Child... Spell went wrong... cast a counter tran... spell... too weak to take full control... gone wrong...

Alethea, I can barely hear you. I thought, beating down the panic. What if Alethea was so weak her presence was waning? I would be lost in this strange place, with no way back, and would never find Rowan. I was now bordering on terrified.

Something is blo... my power... You must calm Child... temple nearby to hide... Fear not... is abandoned...

What was I supposed to do now? I could feel tears begin to fall down my cheeks. I wiped them away with an impatient hand as their crystal-clear beauty began to merge with the oncoming rain. Wonderful, this was all I needed. What was I to do without Rowan? I took some deep and steadying breaths to try and calm myself. I would have to wait until Alethea was strong enough to port them away again. I hoped that Rowan was safe; he *had* to be safe, I would not think otherwise.

I looked to the distance and could see an eerily similar city to the one in the death realm but this one shone with a golden light. How was that possible when there was no sunlight? Situated amid them was a golden palace and I had to assume this realm's royalty dwelt within. Given the experience I had with the last bunch of royalty I decided to avoid that place like the plague. I started to walk.

I assumed the temple Alethea almost mentioned was there. What would I find? Was this similar to Rowan's city? I had been shocked by what I had seen there. Quaint houses with billowing chimney pots were squashed together surrounding the palace. Bakery smells wafted through the air combining with strong perfumes of flowers. There had been laughter and love surrounding them. I had never felt so at home, which shocked me as I'd never felt at home anywhere.

I drew closer to the city and I was disappointed to see that it wasn't similar at all. This city more resembled that of ancient Rome. It was far more decadent with small temples adorning the paved streets, scantily clad slaves milling around and their masters lounging... being fed grapes? Seriously? There were guards there too but they seemed to be wearing togas beneath their archaic armour. They too had guns, but they only seemed to be an added extra given the number of golden blades they wore. Cautiously, I approached the small marketplace. Given the armour I was wearing I thought it best to hide myself; silver was a remote colour here. I found a small stall with an assortment of things and managed to steal myself a cloak and some dried meat. I'd need my energy to search for Rowan. Donning the cloak, luckily not to a chorus of enraged shouts, I scurried away to begin my search.

I rounded a corner of a temple and was shocked to see someone I recognised; two someones actually. What was Azazel doing here? Why was he talking to the man that knew Rowan? Something didn't feel right so I hid back around the corner and watched. Without realising, I held a hand surrounded by silver light to my ear and listened intently.

"...she entered the realm alone, of this I am sure," Azazel said, obviously about me.

"Then the seer's spell worked to our advantage," the other man... Kane?... said.

"Do not include me in your childish dealings life bearer," Azazel declared, offended that he would do so. "The only reason I do this is to detain her enough for Lucifer to advance his plans. I am not even so certain I will help Lucifer in the end. I find myself intrigued by many things in these worlds and do not wish to see them end. Have you forgotten it was I that introduced man to original sin..." Azazel seemed to have drifted into his own private world.

"As you say," replied Kane, "but I would not be one to cross Lucifer. You should not either." Azazel only smirked,

"You do not know who you deal with..."

I had heard enough. If they were looking for me I would do well to go in the opposite direction. I hoped my mortal aura masked Alethea's presence. I had no clue how to defend them otherwise. I continued on among the streets until I came to a large temple, bigger than the others, made of white marble.

It was similar to the temple in the other realm and it made my heart twinge for Rowan. We had only been separated for around twenty minutes, but I couldn't cope. I needed him. Small cherubim blazed their golden radiance at me when I entered, and I could feel disgust radiate from the part of my mind that was Alethea. I had to smile at that; whatever was happening was hampering both Alethea's power and my ability to talk to her, but that didn't stop my contempt for our surroundings appearing loud and clear. I actually chuckled to myself as I walked further in.

... try and sleep... safe here... masked by your mortality... I didn't know why Alethea was bothering. She needed to regain all the strength she could; the Second Coming was approaching with far too much speed and I needed to find Rowan before anything happened to him. I saw a pile of discarded black and gold pillows in one corner and sat down on them. I was all alone and I was not handling it well.

I drew my knees up to my chest, placed my head on them and began to rock back and forth. I could feel my mind start to shut down; I was mortal, too much had happened that I couldn't cope with on my own and I didn't have Rowan to lean on. I didn't even have Alethea to guide my anymore, or the girls' sarcasm to soothe me. More tears fell as I wondered what I should do now and felt a small amount of guilt that I was not really bothered where Illaria had gone.

Just as I was about to lapse into a full-blown breakdown, a small golden ball of light began to form on the steps into the temple. It gradually grew in length until it became a shaft of pure golden light with a muscled, extremely naked man emerging from it. I wanted to scream. The form finally solidified into the one person that neither I nor Alethea wanted to see: Lucifer.

His long golden hair was resplendent, and his golden wings were visible and held to their greatest advantage. His hazel eyes twinkled with mischief and his soft, full lips quirked into an almost smug smirk. I was a little disorientated to see his golden skin, adorned with many fine muscles, shimmered in what little light there was. Had he actually oiled himself up just for this confrontation? Within the depths of my mind Alethea let out a heartfelt laugh at that thought. She thought it was a ridiculous notion but not beyond him.

My vision continued down his body and for the life of my I wished it hadn't. Lucifer was advancing on me, clearly very aroused. The terror I felt began to reach its highest peak; I was so alone, how could I escape one such as him?

...not Lucifer... Mil... M...

I knew I should be paying more attention to Alethea, I knew she was trying to warn me of something, but Lucifer was emitting a golden mist that quickly surrounded me and worked its way into my soul; suddenly Lucifer wasn't as terrifying any more. He seemed to be the ultimate picture of male beauty. I watched and noticed little things that enhanced his features; his eyes seemed to be molten chocolate, his physique was perfect, his features stunning.

"What's the matter, beautiful one?" he asked as he came closer still. His deep voice resonated through me, and answering heat formed deep inside. How could I answer one such as he? He was far too stunning to even see me. I felt myself almost pushed over the edge when one wing brushed against me; it seemed both soft yet vibrant at the same time. How was that even possible?

This man in front of me was proving both a mystery and a desire. I missed the being cloaked in the corner. Azazel shook his head in disgust, a novel concept for one such as he. He turned and disappeared into a sheen of golden light as if he never was.

At my last thought something in my mind urgently yelled out. I almost caught it, but it dissipated as he crouched in front of me.

"I have missed you my love." I could only stare in awe and wonder as he waved a golden hand in front of me and once again my World went shining black...

***

I stood with my eyes closed; trying to regain some of the calm I had lost. The cold wind gently caressed my skin, making my hair flow in the breeze. Today my armour was quite heavy, signifying the danger I was in and the weight on my heart.

I lifted my hand, my pure silver sword comforting in my grasp, and began turning it in a figure of eight around me. I expected an attack any second, knowing the anger I had caused so many beings in so short a time. Sensing danger, I thrust my hand to the right, in time to stop an attack from an archangel, our swords clashing. I opened my eyes to see my attacker and was shocked to see it was one of the archangels I had fought against in the uprising, one that had been my brother in arms beforehand. His sword was shining with His power, his halo making his golden hair seem even more vibrant, and his heavenly aura almost blinded me. I knew what I had to do but grieved doing it to one such as he; I too had once been as devoted.

"Rest well, my brother," I said as I brought up my other hand. Clasped in it was my scythe. Taking advantage of the archangel's prone state, I thrust the blade of my scythe into what I knew was his heart. I watched the recognition of what I had done register on the angel's face, and with cold passivity I watched as he crumpled to the floor.

I was stood in the ruins of a city once populated with millions of people. All around me the buildings had fallen, the ground was scorched, and the dead were strewn across the floor. Their souls reached out to me to give them the peace they so readily deserved. They formed a sea of silver in my vision and I longed to help them, it was my nature after all. I could not however; I had to ensure that life, all life, continued for mortals everywhere. This war had to be stopped in one way or another.

Again, I began to twirl my sword in a figure of eight, guarding for any unknown attacks that may come. My scythe I kept ready knowing the secrets it held would prove useful in the battle. I turned to block the attack of another archangel, my sword stopping his while the blade of my scythe buried into his chest; I used the bottom of my scythe to blow a hole in another attacking angel, loving the effect the silver bullets had on my enemy.

The battle continued like this; the blood red magic of Lucifer's demons clashing with the heavenly gold. Interspersed were the odd flashes of silver when I myself had to intervene. All seemed evenly matched; sometimes angels won, sometimes the demon. All who stood against me fell. I was bathed in their ruby red blood with a circle of their bodies around me. Yet still I fought.

Eventually Gabriel appeared in the fray, casually side stepping all who attacked and any battle he neared too close to. He had one goal in mind, and that was me. The old sense of sarcastic cynicism which had always appeared resurfaced and I found myself straining to mock him. He smiled his most self-assured smile and I found my attention drawn to his eyes. He may have been the most pompous, self-righteous former sword brother but his eyes had always belied his intentions, informing me of what he was up to.

My attention should never be lost during battle. An archangel took this distraction as a distinct advantage and plunged his pure silver sword straight into my heart.

I could feel the triumphant pride resonate through the metal as it tore through flesh and bone and found my heart live and beating. I coughed, blood dripping down my chin to the scorched ground below. I heard Gabriel's snicker; his admission of his victory over me. I fell to my knees, the blade still buried deeply within my chest.

In my rapidly blurring vision, I could see Gabriel come to his knees beside me. He caressed my cheek softly, running his hands down my ivory skin, seeming to revel in its softness. He lowered his mouth to mine and gave me the briefest kiss, while his hand reached to the back of him. He grinned at me, a grin reminiscent of Lucifer's, and pulled out... Rowan's dripping severed head... my heart, though already pierced, shattered...

***

I tore my eyes open, trying my hardest not to scream. Tears streamed down my cheek to wet the pillow below my head. It was the same dream from before, the one where I had taken sides, only this time Rowan was to die at the hands of the archangels. Was this a sign? If I were to pick sides would Rowan inevitably die anyway? I was determined not to take any part in this war at all, but would it come to nothing? Were these dreams to signify that Rowan was going to die no matter what I did? Fear took hold of me once more.

I tried to focus on anything else so that I didn't panic. I was inside now. The building resembled the one I had been in, with its white marble and golden shine but there was now plant life inside; a great oak grew through the window archway into the centre of the bedroom. I myself was laid on a great oak bed draped in golden silk. The bed hadn't been there before, I was sure of it. A warm weight pressed me into the bed and I looked down to see one muscled arm thrown over me. Joy like no other surged through my veins at the sight. Rowan was back and he was safe. I tried to turn over to him, but something held me down. Instead I just turned my head and almost screamed at what I saw. Somehow Lucifer was in the bed with me and the moments before my dream came screaming back. I had been transfixed by him, watching as he advanced on me and took over my soul. What had come over me? I had thought him the most beautiful man in the world, forgetting Rowan even existed, and I was thoroughly ashamed of myself.

Alethea's words came back to my then. They had been strained but she had been trying to tell me something.

...not Lucifer... Mil... M...

Was this the Life Lord and not the Lord of Hell? Miltiades, if this was him, was an exact replica of Lucifer even down to the mischief portrayed in those hazel eyes. How could they be two different people... beings... whatever they were?

I watched in fear as those hazel eyes slowly opened and looked deep into my own silver ones. He seemed to be trying to read my soul, or Alethea's, whichever one appeared first.

"M... Miltiades?" I asked, amazed that my voice even worked. I was at the point of overload now and was sure my poor brain couldn't handle any more of this.

"Alethea," he replied and ran his hand down my cheek. He seemed focused on the softness of my skin and I hoped to use this as a distraction.

"You know I'm not Alethea," I replied, hoping that it didn't make him happier. "I'm Anahlia. Please let me go. I don't belong here among you all, among all this. I need to get home to Rowan and get on with my life." I hoped using my mortal outlook would convince him to release me. I looked down my body to see why I couldn't move. I was still clothed, which was a blessing, but my breast plate was gone and I just wore the black square of cloth over my chest; I could see Miltiades trying to work his way down to that area. Both of my arms were secured to the headboard with sparkling golden magic, obviously life magic, as were my legs to the bottom of the bed. I could feel revulsion well up in my mind and knew it was Alethea's influence.

"I know you are but the mortal that houses Lady Death," Miltiades began, drawing my attention back to him. "You have her body however and though suppressed you house her soul also. This should be enough to rid myself of the obsession with her I have suffered with for so long. She cursed me with that damnable desire and now... and now..." Miltiades looked away from me for just a moment. I could tell he was struggling with something, some emotion which I had no desire to name, and left him to it. He gradually turned back to me.

"I am hoping that with you in control, mortal, that this unending desire will finally end and I can be free of her."

"Wait just a moment," I started, shocked beyond belief. If he meant what I thought he meant he could piss off. "I have absolutely no intention of staying here just to rid you of your demons. I have to find Rowan and save him from whatever may come. I don't want to be your sex toy."

"Rowan? Who is Rowan?" Miltiades asked with deceptive quietness.

"He's my fiancé and the only man I will EVER love," I responded honestly. I didn't know if one could lie around an angel but I wasn't one for trying it. I could physically see the rage building in him.

"How dare you have another?" he demanded. "I have yearned for you, suffered for you, and it is never enough. I have had lifetimes to endure what you left me with."

I could feel my own rage building in response. I was still afraid, any one of these beings could destroy me with a mere careless thought, but I had had enough. I was only mortal, and not a worldly mortal at that, why did I have to put up with all this? What right did they have to inflict this on me? I knew I was just the punishment for the perceived sins of another celestial being, but I was still a person, one that wanted to be considered when things like this happened. I had to escape, and quickly.

I paused for a moment. Could I move my wings, supressed by life magic as I was? I didn't really know how to do it but it had to be somewhere within me just as Alethea was. I had used the power on and off for my whole life but it was instinct, anger and I suspected more Alethea than myself. It was like trying to grasp water. I was angry to the point where part of me felt like I could call on the very fires of Hell but I was unsure and still so afraid. I focused on the wings moving, growing, bursting into flame, anything and directed all of my energy towards it. I felt a faint stirring in my mind from the place that was Alethea, but nothing happened. It seemed both of us were too weak, or too suppressed, to control the power properly. I screamed in frustration; what was the point of housing one of the greatest origins of power if I was unable to call on it myself? Why, when I thought about it, did I fail? Luckily Miltiades was still mid-jealous rant and missed my scream of frustration; from the looks of him, he would probably join in.

Eventually Miltiades calmed down and turned once again to look at me. He had the mischievous twinkle back in his eye and he simply smiled at me. Dread crept upon me like a plague and I tried my hardest to move as he approached me. I could see he had made his mind up about me and would now undertake his decision.

"Sire," a distressed voice shouted from beyond the archway. "Sire, we need you to come quickly. It is... ah..." I could tell he was loath to admit anything in front of me, a stranger and one who emitted a terrifying aura. "...it is a matter of urgency."

Miltiades sighed and I could tell he was internally debating whether to attend to the problem or not. I hoped he would; he was daunting and overloaded my senses. I needed time to think, to discover a way to escape from him, but it wasn't going to happen while he was there demanding my attention, amongst other things. Finally, his shoulder slumped.

"Do not go anywhere Lady Death," he began, turning his back on me. "I still have need of you." With that, he walked through the archway, still gloriously nude, to deal with whatever was occurring elsewhere. I wished he had donned some clothing before he left, the sight of his behind was going to haunt me for a while, but I could tell he rarely, if ever, wore any clothes. I shook myself; what was I saying? He didn't even begin to compare to Rowan. Obviously, whatever he had infected me with before he took me was still in my system.

How was I going to get out of this one now? I had no Rowan, Alethea was too quiet although my emotions were not,

Vale and Lyria were somewhere in the ether, and I didn't even have Illaria, not that I thought the witch could do much. No, it was left down to me and me alone. What could I do?

My thoughts would have continued on to a possible escape but there seemed to be the sound of a falling tree outside the chamber. It was followed by several metal objects hitting the ground, and then several more shouts. Weapons seemed to be clashing in heated battle and both I and Alethea could feel the death that now permeated this place. Something momentous was taking place right outside the archway and I had no desire to be a part of it. Could none of these beings understand my personal need to be far away from here?

I could now hear foot falls approaching me quickly. Who could this be now? Surely the Life Lord would not send others to carry out what he planned. I knew from Alethea's memories that he was a bit of a twisted individual, but he usually liked to do things himself. I didn't know which would be worse. I almost waited with bated breath knowing one was not better than the other but I thought I may be able to handle a non-celestial being should one appear.

Eventually my question was answered; several men garbed in silver and black armour, similar to my own, piled in through the archway led by Fenris and a warrior clad as they were but one that winked at me through the visor. Azazel? Surely not. I really did not like being in such a prone and vulnerable position, but for the moment could do nothing about it. Fenris leapt onto the bed and started to work on my golden bindings, determined to free me. It seemed the pup had Rowan's fighting spirit also.

"We have come to claim you in the name of our Lord," one of the fools loudly demanded, "King Lucian el Rayan. Come with us now if you wish to remain unharmed." At this Fenris swivelled around and in his rage leapt at the guard with the demands; obviously he didn't like people speaking to me that way. At the same time what I assumed was Azazel turned on the rest of the warriors and began to fight them off.

I honestly didn't know what was worse; the all-consuming rage I felt building within me, or the abject hilarity of them demanding I move when they could see I was secured by life magic. I actually began to laugh but I could feel the rage gaining precedence in my mind. How dare they? How dare any of them? I wasn't a piece of property to be claimed by any that saw fit to do so. I may only be mortal, and I may house one of only two constants in the known universes but I had my rights, I had my soul and I had had enough. My life was continually bombarded with instance after instance of things no mere mortal should have to deal with, and they all expect me to deal with it in a dignified and gracious manner. At the moment they were lucky I had not broken down into a quivering wreck of nerves and panic.

The rage that had started within me had now become an angry black mass of swirling emotion. I had never once in my entire life been this angry before and I secretly wondered if it was some part of Alethea that was fuelling it. In any case I took a hold of that emotion and focused on it. I could feel the indignant energy working into my limbs, my soul and the part of me that was Alethea. I called upon the wings again, somehow sensing that now they would respond, and with another small mental push my great ebony wings flew up with great speed, brushing the life magic from both my arms and my legs.

I rolled quickly off the bed, wary just in case Miltiades had set a second trap for me. I had no desire to be on that bed at all, especially with so much death and destruction around me. I stretched to my full height, working out the kinks in my limbs from being bound, and stretched my wings to their full span. They felt natural being there, almost good to the point of ecstasy, and that thought alone worried me. Perhaps Alethea was closer to the surface then I realised.

One of the guards gasped at my escape and at my obvious transformation of power level. I had to use it to my advantage and escape. I thought of my silver scythe; the look of it, the feel of it and the power it held; and it appeared on my back in its holster once more. I appreciated Illaria telling me of the weapon's secret and was actually mildly happy I could accredit something positive to the witch; knowing my weapons could be summoned would no doubt save me a lot in the future, if I had one.

I turned to face the guards knowing my only route of escape was through them. I took out my scythe and pointed it directly at them. Several of them paled and took a step back not knowing how to deal with this new predicament.

I was still in control, even if I had delved into Alethea's power level once more, and I knew I couldn't kill one of them if any. None of them deserved to die as they were just doing as they were ordered but how would I escape otherwise? Alethea couldn't take control as somehow, she was still suppressed. My way of life, my passivity, was threatened by my need to survive. If I harmed just one of them, I knew I would weep for months about it; I just didn't have it in me to kill anyone. I shuddered merely at the thought of it.

Suddenly, almost like a ray of golden sunshine descending on me, I had an idea. Would Alethea's status get me out of this? Or at least confuse them enough so that I could escape? It was worth a try if I didn't have to harm anyone in the process. I just hoped I could pull off haughty and commanding. I felt a mental nudge at that thought and struggled not to smile.

"Wait," I commanded in my most condescending tone. "Do you know who I am?" The soldiers looked at me with blatant disrespect, obviously considering me beneath even their contempt; I remembered Rowan telling me that women were not well treated in his world and hoped the soldier made a wrong move.

"No," another one replied. "Should I?" I myself had to smile at that. I could feel the shock and contempt radiate from the part of my mind that was Alethea and knew her ego had been damaged. That was a mistake.

I once again stretched my wings to their full wingspan

and held the scythe directly towards that soldier. I hoped I could conjure just the right words to convey who Alethea really was and then I would find my way out.

"I am the angel of death, your Lady and your creator. You owe no fealty to the King! Bow to me and I will spare you my wrath." I would not laugh spouting this archaic language, I was determined I wouldn't. It would ruin the effect and I needed to throw the warriors off balance to escape.

They had become clearly confused, unsure whether to believe me, unsure whether to even follow their orders now. I took this opportunity to call on Alethea's transportation spell. I didn't know the exact steps but Alethea herself said magic was repetition of will so theoretically any should work. I began to circle the warriors always keeping out of arms reach.

I stuck as closely as I could to the same dance steps and felt the power gathering around me, moving me forward faster and faster, igniting me as it had when Althea had been in control. Soon I was awash in silver flame.

I didn't know how to end the spell however. Did Alethea will herself gone? How would I do that? Should I focus the power on one single point? At that thought the silver flame rushed off me and centred on the wall just next to me, creating a silver doorway to who knew where. I had forgotten to picture a place in my mind and hoped that Alethea had done so for us. I stopped abruptly next to the portal, wings outstretched so none of the warriors could close it or go through it before me.

Triumphantly, I turned my back and moved to go through the portal.

"Wait," commanded an authoritative voice. I had no intention of discovering who commanded me so well but I found myself turning around anyway. Both Miltiades and the Death King had entered at the same time. Both looked at me expectantly, as if I were to fall to my knees and beg their forgiveness for daring to defy them. I laughed aloud. If they thought I was going to do that than they really did not know me at all.

I decided to continue the haughty, commanding voice and hoped they would believe that Alethea was now in control.

"Ah Miltiades," I began. "I have no intention of allowing you to use Anahlia in this way. The desire you feel, which I did not intend for you to experience, is just punishment for you thinking you could use a mortal in this way." I heard the Death King snicker, perhaps believing I had chosen him over the angel. How wrong he was.

"Death King," I could feel the rage of how he had treated Rowan coming to the surface and I welcomed only part of it; I could not let the façade fall. "Do not think this is a victory in your name. You are undeserving of one such as this mortal; this was blatantly shown by your treatment of your own blood. Forget this girl; it will lead to nothing but your downfall."

Before either of them could argue or stop me, I leapt

through the portal showing a courage that surprised even myself. I heard their cries, and I could only smile. I was more than happy to leave them to one another. I hoped Fenris had finished with his warrior and had leapt through after me. I needed to close the portal before they could follow.

Now that they were in the nether falling towards our destination how the Hell *did* I close the portal? I searched through the silver walls that were slowly enclosing me until I could see the very weave of the magic itself. Acting on impulse, or a craftily stealthy mental nudge, I managed to snag one of the silver threads in my hand. With an almighty heave, and using my wings to increase my speed, I managed to collapse the portal after me. Those that had followed me in would now be lost in the nether and the rest could not follow. I let out a relieved little chuckle.

12

The silver weave eventually gave way to reveal a solid white wall looming just ahead. I tried my best to use my wings to slow my speed but it was to no avail. With a loud thud I hit the wall and fell to the ground. All I could do was try to avoid landing on the wings as somehow, I just knew that that would hurt. I lay there for a moment waiting for the dizziness to subside, pondering how my life had become such a haphazard collection of running for my life and rushed exits from other worlds.

Gradually I felt I could get up from my prone position, the dizziness only held me a moment and I realised that I had been transported back to my own house. A joy like I had never felt overtook me. I was home! I wanted to collapse onto my bed and pretend none of this had happened. I could curl up with Rowan and do all the normal things we used to do; watch a film, get take out and argue over the last chocolate (I always won).

Of course, you are home Child, came Alethea's dry voice, somehow stronger than it had ever been. *You were alone, with no Rowan to guide you. We start our search here for him, and also your friends.*

"You're back," I said with strong relief. "I was so afraid. Rowan disappeared with Vale and Lyria, Illaria disappeared and even you were silent for the first time since you woke up."

I am sorry about that, she replied. *In my inflated sense of myself I did not think that Miltiades was as strong or as affected by the desire as he was. I still admit that time and the curse I am under has dampened some of my memories, even though most still seem overwhelming to your mortal mind.*

"It's okay," I replied. "...but what now? What happened to Rowan? How do you know he was even sent back here?"

In all honesty I do not know he was sent back here. He definitely did not come to the realm of life with us, the lucky man, but he may have also stayed in our death realm. We must search both places, but I do not know which to check first. Alethea paused as she thought of something; *It may be as well to check Hell too. Rowan may have been sent to Lucifer in Pandemonium and if that has occurred he will need rescuing now.*

"Which do we search first?" I asked with panic rising like bile in my throat. I heard Alethea sigh.

I do not know. To the mortal, both realms pose a deep threat. Rowan's father would have no qualms about killing him, this much we know already; and because you have the misfortune of being my ultimate reincarnation, and you have Rowan, Lucifer will not hesitate in killing him just to affect me more. I am deeply sorry Child.

I felt like I wanted to cry. I had to find Rowan now but had no idea where to start; it was almost like deciding which was the lesser of two evils.

It is trying to decide between two evils, only matter of personal perspective will make one seem lesser than the other. I couldn't focus on the entire thing at once. Already I could feel my mind fragmenting, my soul crying out. Instead I focused on how I would move around outside. My wings were still out and no matter what I did they would not go away again.

They will not unfortunately, Alethea supplied, in my way trying to be helpful. *It is too close to the Second Coming. Lucifer already moves into the mortal World. Look out of the window, you will see that time now slows down.* I had not realised that our delving into the other realms had taken so long.

A wisp of cold wind touched my bare arms and I shivered. Looking out into my living room I could see the window Barachiel had smashed out of so long ago and was surprised that I had forgotten that he had done so. How had no one noticed the smashed window and not come to find out if I am all right? With a pang of sadness, I realised that aside from Rowan and my two friends I had no one else, no one to come and see if I was still alive and well. Thanks to the curse I was under, I now knew why. With Alethea still inside me I was fated to bring death to everyone I loved. I hoped with all my heart and soul that it didn't apply to Rowan also, I could not, and I would not lose him.

I moved towards the window and looked out as I was instructed. Sure enough, time seemed to be slowing down at quite a considerable rate. I glanced toward the sky and saw birds slowing their wing beat, planes almost frozen and leaves in mid drop to the ground. This was the scariest thing I had ever seen. Why wasn't I slowing down also?

Because of this curse you are stuck with, as you referred to me. It is far too close to the battle for you to freeze. Whatever is going to happen will happen soon for all of us. Apparently my never-ending existence is not long enough, no, now they have to stop time every time I turn around. In spite of the situation I wanted to laugh at Alethea's comment. I hadn't been consciously aware that she knew sarcasm and it was refreshing in the light of our danger.

I was about to turn away from the scene in front of me when I caught a pale flash in the corner of my eye. What had it been? Was it another attack on us?

What? What did you see? Alethea demanded. *I am afraid I missed it.*

"Oh, it's nothing," I replied, "I just thought I saw a pale flash of light. It was very quick and then gone, it had a slight echo as if all the horses of Hell were appearing." I had to laugh at my phrasing, now I knew I was going crazy, not to mention dramatic.

Discord! Alethea shouted, almost deafening me in the process.

"Who?"

Discord. He is my mount fated to appear when it came closer to the apocalypse.

"Right," I said, still not fully comprehending what Alethea was getting at. "So...?"

I am death. The second coming is here. My mount is looking for me.

"What does that mean?" I asked, exasperated.

It means the four horsemen have been called and Lucifer has begun his battle. We have very little time left to find your love and it will be much harder contending with the warriors from both sides. Make no mistake, they will be contending for my power, hoping that it will tip the balance in their favour. I was about to protest that I was still in control for now and I was not taking sides in this nightmare, that I had to find Rowan. *Fear not child, I do not intend to take sides either. I have no desire to play to the whims of either side ever again.*

I was mollified for now, but I knew that they couldn't afford any distractions from our search. We would have to look for Discord later.

I agree. He can look after himself and we have much to do. Have you decided where to begin our search?

"I have," I replied. "We're going to begin in the death realm. I know Lucifer is the bigger threat, hell he's the ultimate evil, but I just can't forget the sight of Rowan tortured by his own father. I can't even imagine the damage it's done to his soul. We will look there quickly and then move on." I could feel Alethea's doubt that Rowan was there but I chose to ignore it. I had to be focused in the face of all this; I would find Rowan, I would save him and we would live out our lives together. I would use any means at my disposal to do this, even if it meant giving up part of my soul to use Alethea's power level. I would give control to Alethea but until Rowan was safe I didn't want to take a chance of there being any failure.

With that certainty I felt something within me shift, almost like a lock had opened within my own soul. Silver light began to fall from my hands to pool on the ground beneath me. I could feel it bubble as my power built to peak into columns of raging silver fire. It was magnificent. It was blazing. Silver fireworks began to detonate all around me and a sense of being whole again filled my shaking body. I rose into the air, the silver tides arcing towards me like a long-lost love. I reached out a hand and the universe itself bent to my will. I could see all that lived in the world, planets, galaxies, infinite space and time. All would kneel to my power, the power of death.

I began to glow softly and radiated dim silver light that seemed to originate from my heart and move outwards. It soon shone from every part of my being and a warm, fluttering sensation began in my heart. Alethea seemed to get stronger and more capable of helping me should I need it. Strangely, the archaic armour seemed to shift and take another shape too, perhaps reflecting my determination to find Rowan, not to mention my friends. The heavy breastplate shifted to become a form fitting black tube top interlaced with pure silver to make it impenetrable. The bracer on my right arm changed swiftly into a gauntlet of pure silver to encase my right hand, each finger ending in a lethal claw. My left arm differed though; my left shoulder became completely bare while the rest of my arm was encased by a form fitting sleeve of pure silver, great protection but light. I was worried at this. I was also a bit wary of the fact that my midriff was bare. What type of armour allowed my midriff to be bare? I scoffed and wondered if there was any sort of male influence in the design of this new armour.

My legs, always shapely, were adorned with pure silver leg guards engraved with shining silver wings. A flowing ebony skirt began at my hips and ended just above the floor; two slits matched the length of my legs and ended at the embroidered belt. Strangely I had never felt so feminine. How I could do so in armour was beyond me but in this I truly felt beautiful. I wished Rowan was there to see me.

The last things I felt to change were a necklace adorning my neck and a circlet placed on my head. I rushed to the small mirror I always kept in the living room. My blue-black curls cascaded freely down my shoulders. I had never seen my hair shine or have more health before. The necklace I now wore was delicate and had a small set of pure silver wings hanging from them; I swore they radiated a faint silver glow. The circlet was plain but sparkled with pure silver and Alethea's power. I felt powerful, invincible... alone.

I have to say child, came Alethea's almost smug voice. *I am impressed with the effect you have had on my armour and weaponry. Perhaps we are not so different, you and I. We both are able to use the power, to grasp the control and to know what we must do and how to properly do it. I can see now that we shall triumph in this and be suitably compensated for the anguish these males have put us through.* I knew Alethea was just trying to comfort me in the face of whatever danger may come but I was mildly flattered by the praise. Perhaps I could do this after all; I was determined to find Rowan; I could allow no other outcome from my trials.

"How have I been able to even grasp your power level?" I asked, unsure I wanted to know the answer to the question that had been plaguing me.

As I have already told you Child, Alethea replied patiently as if actually talking to a child, *magic and power are essentially will. He who has determination will be the more powerful. Once you determined you would save your Rowan you allowed my power to work fully for you. Embrace it, succumb to it and allow my aid to guide you.*

Fear began to rise within me. *What did Alethea mean? Am I to let Alethea take over? What would that do to my soul?* I shook these fears off now and decided to concentrate on the task at hand. I would not let Rowan suffer due to my weaknesses.

I am impressed Child. I had not the strength you are showing now. I ran from this emotion, fought against it and was weakened in consequence. This alone allowed Lucifer to condemn me, a foolish act on my part. I could hear the regret in Alethea's voice and wished I could help but Alethea's problems were millennia old, what could I do?

Do not worry about me Child, though I thank you for your kindness, Alethea said with true warmth in her voice. *Now... do not forget about all the weapons at your disposal. Use the cold, hard certainty of death's power but also my blades. There is a pure silver broadsword strapped to your left shoulder, a pure silver longsword at your hip and pure silver daggers in your boots.*

I was impressed by the sheer arsenal Alethea had at her disposal, but I was filled with uncertainty. The weapons had to be masked by some powerful death magic; I had no idea how to unmask them or even how to use them.

Do not fear, when the times comes you shall know how to do so, Alethea said soothingly. *In the meantime, the scythe should be enough. Use it wisely but never be afraid to do so.*

I acted upon Alethea's advice, and placed the scythe on my back. My wings moved accordingly to make room and for comfort. It scared me how right this all felt, like I was no longer the one in control over my own fate.

Do not worry about that for now, Alethea soothed. *Unfortunately, you have been drawn into things beyond your understanding. It is scary but I need you to focus. You will have to direct most of our actions for now. I will need to reserve my strength for the final battle. Alas, we cannot rely solely on the actions of His inept warriors; it may come to it that we will have to defeat Lucifer in the end. I will have to rely on your strength and your ability to put aside your fears.*

I was flattered by the praise. I was by no means a strong person but what right did I have to cower in fear when Rowan could be anywhere? After I had seen what his own father had done to him I dare not leave him long. I would get him back then they could deal together with what they had been through, and what I had discovered in turn. I wished I had some way of sensing Rowan; I had all of Alethea's power at my disposal and yet the one thing I so desperately wanted was just out of my reach.

I could feel grief overtaking me. I needed control now more than ever, I really didn't want to turn into a weeping mess right when the penultimate battle was about to begin. I felt warm fur brush the gaps of my leg plates and looked down to see Fenris trying his hardest to comfort me. He pawed at the silver wanting to be picked up; I obliged feeling relief that he had made it through the portal before I shut it and needing to be close to something of Rowan. Maybe Fenris would be able to find him where I could not.

Alethea distracted me once more: *Do you think you*

have enough grasp of my power to do this? I lifted my right hand from around Fenris and focused on everything I had been through; the mass abductions, the pain and losing Rowan; and I watched in amazement as silver flames began in my palm and danced along my wrist.

"I think I'm ready."

Good girl echoed in my mind and I knew I would have Alethea's support in whatever may happen, I just hoped I didn't falter; both Alethea and Rowan were relying on me and I hope I didn't fail.

I shook myself. Such morbid thoughts were a doorway for said failure. I would succeed in this; I would find Rowan and I wouldn't let it end in any other way. I took a deep breath and made sure I was ready to enter the battle. This had to be the scariest thing I had ever done, more so than being buried alive, though my heart still flinched at that.

Eventually I placed Fenris carefully on the floor, moved to the door of my house and caressed the door handle. I had to take another steadying breath. What would I find on the other side? Could I cope with the signs of horror and mutilation that were bound to follow? Gingerly I opened the door, expecting the worst, to find Discord waiting for me almost bored at the fact that it had taken me so long. The street itself was completely empty, a rarity in itself, but a doom filled portent of the harsh times to come.

Discord huffed in agitation and suddenly I saw an

opportunity for more power. I remembered Alethea telling my they had worked in harmony together, each lending the other strength and power. Would it work the same for me? Heaven knew I needed all the help I could get. I placed one foot on the stirrup and waited for the beast to bolt, perhaps sensing I was not his master. To my relief he did not and actually moved closer into I as if to urge me further onto the intricate saddle. The willing acceptance touched me but I put it aside for now. I had to focus on what needed to be done.

The saddle was perhaps the most beautiful saddle I had ever seen although admittedly I hadn't seen many. It was intricately woven with the most delicate pure silver, incorporating wings into the pattern. I thought I might break it until I heard Alethea's *Oh do not be silly* come from the back of my mind. Thankfully it was far more comfortable than a saddle made of silver had any right to be. There were various sheaths for any and all extra weapons Alethea may wish to carry but there were no reins; how were there no reins? *Simply put child,* came Alethea's calm voice, *Discord has no need of them when I am not with him. Why be burdened with them when he has no rider? You just need to sit and put your hands out as if there were reigns.* I felt silly but I did as I was told; surely Alethea wouldn't lie to me now, not after everything. I also didn't think the angel had that much of a sense of humour and felt a mental kick in response. I was stunned when silver reigns began to appear in rays of silver light.

Are you comfortable now, Your Royal Highness? Alethea

asked with a smug sense of sarcasm radiating from her.

Ah, I see you were also infected with bitchiness, I replied silently to her, smiling in spite of my harsh words. I actually appreciated how these exchanges took my mind off the terrifying events that were occurring. The fact that I was essentially talking to myself had seemed to escape me recently. There was only one problem left to address; where could Fenris go? I knew he was a wolf, but I couldn't expect him to run everywhere, he was only a pup. I heard a mental sigh and had to smile as a pouch big enough for Fenris appeared on the saddle. I watched as he climbed into it and remembered that Fenris was part of Rowan's soul. It was comforting to have a bit of him with me, though I would prefer the real thing.

I smiled again and shook myself from my reverie. Surely, I had the hang of this now. Holding up my right hand I willed a portal to the death realm to appear; I wished it with my entire heart and soul. I focused on all the death and destruction I had been forced to witness, the horror of seeing Rowan tortured by his own father and the sheer need I felt to return to my own life. For the longest time it seemed like nothing was happening. I almost gave up until I saw that a small silver flame had started on the back of my hand. It stayed where it began but spread to encompass the width of my hand in a ring of silver beauty. It then spread the length of my hand until it was merely a shining torch of silver flame. Before I could lose my grasp on the power, I motioned in front of me and the flame leapt to create a solid wall of silver flame. I hoped it was a portal, it looked like what Rowan had summoned but as Alethea had done it differently last time, I couldn't be sure.

Taking a deep breath, I urged Discord into a canter. It was better to take anything that might be waiting on the other side by surprise. I hoped there was nothing, I didn't feel equipped to handle anything that may come but I dared not leave it up to fate.

I urged Discord into a gallop as my fear rose. I swallowed several times as the steed leapt through the silver fire. What would I find?

All too quickly I had been engulfed in blood red tinged silver flame and pain so harsh I thought I felt my soul shatter. I screamed but no sound was forthcoming. The intense heat began to peel back my skin in bloody strips, the flames a sharp and foreboding tool of endless torture. It wouldn't stop, it would never end. I was damned. Everything seemed to cease functioning until all that was left was a lost soul within the swirling eddies of dark magic.

13

The light and pain quickly diminished, and I found myself in haunting halls of pure white marble. Discord's silver hooves echoed as he landed upon the floor, but I didn't even notice. Instead I hurriedly patted out the remainder of the silver flames on my skin. I gasped. The pain was quickly fading but the memory of it would not go. I was sure I must be some hideous monster now, burned beyond all recognition. I turned to look into the shine of one marble column and was relieved to see I was okay, at least for now.

I looked around me. This definitely wasn't any part of the death realm I'd ever seen. It was a cavernous throne room complete with a dais and two pure silver thrones. Attached to one was a manacle, burning blood red with Hellfire magic, made of the purest Hellfire forged metal. I shuddered; I was most definitely back in Lucifer's throne room in Pandemonium. Mercifully it was empty of both nightmare and minion but still I couldn't understand how I had ended up here instead of the death realm which I had been focusing on.

Did you have anything to do with this? I asked Alethea silently, unsure who was around to hear them.

Not consciously, Alethea replied. *It could be that since I find Lucifer the bigger threat, my power brought us here first. It does however explain about the burning sensation you felt during the spell. Lucifer put in place wards long ago to deter those with magic entering his throne room. You would have died had I not been with you. Traitorous bastard!!* I sighed. I already knew Rowan wasn't here. No one was here. I could feel Lucifer and his minions already in the worlds somewhere.

If we can sense him, could we sense Rowan? I asked, meagre hope coming alive in my soul.

I... cannot, she replied sadly. *I can sense Lucifer because, for my sins, I am bound to him. Rowan, I am not, and the spell Rowan put on you was shattered the first time you came here.* I sighed and tried not to let the tears consume me. I was desperate to find Rowan and had thought I would magically find him through my link with Alethea. Even Fenris was looking around confused; obviously he couldn't sense Rowan either and it upset him almost as much as it upset me.

I had no time to grieve however as quickly I heard the approaching sound of horses. I couldn't be certain, but I thought I heard the pained screams of the damned as an underlying beat to the hoof beats. I tensed. Who could be here now? Why weren't they with Lucifer? I took the scythe from its place on my back and waited, tensed. Would I be able to call on Alethea's power level again if needed? It never seemed to work when I thought about using it. I did however hope it wasn't necessary, I was so tired of conflict already.

"Stay in your pouch Fenris," I whispered. "We may have to move quicker than we'd like." I watched as Fenris wagged his tail and licked my hand in agreement.

Three riders entered the throne room. I recognised War immediately on his flaming steed; the desire coming from the part of my mind that was Alethea was almost tangible. The other two I didn't recognise. One was astride a large blue-black horse; he was pale, slim and looked like he had no strength to lift his own head let alone anything else. His black hair, slightly too long for my taste, was greasy and clumped together. I almost wretched where I sat; his eye sockets were sunken, and his thin lips grinned at me in a smile of pure menace.

The other rider was radiant in comparison. He had flowing golden hair underneath a ring of golden laurel leaves. He was adorned in white robes and sat atop a beautiful white mount. His nose was strong, his eyes piercing ice blue and his soft lips moved into a welcoming smile.

The first is Famine, came Alethea's weary voice, *the second is Conquest. These are the other three horsemen. Be wary, they will try to get us to ride again. We do not want that.*

"My Lady," War said in the smoothest voice he could manage. It rolled over me like velvet and I felt Alethea quiver. "I am so happy you have returned. The Revelation is upon us and we four are needed to ride once more."

I could hear Alethea's derisive snort at the name given to the Second Coming. It was nothing more than Lucifer's power play to inflate his already over extended ego. He would call it a revelation; he was that self-centred that he believed he was a revelation to everyone.

I shook my head; these weren't my thoughts. Why was I experiencing Alethea's thoughts? It was a curious melding of our minds which neither of them could afford right now. I shook my head again and heard War sigh.

"Ah, you are in control… for now… mortal."

"I am, and I have neither the time nor the inclination to

deal with any of you."

"You do not have that choice mortal," War said, evident that his anger was growing. "We have been called, death included, and we *must* obey. Lucifer's will is the law of us all and he rules supreme. That does not include you mortal, you are nothing but dying."

I gasped. I knew I should ignore his words; he was just trying to goad me into a mistake, but what if he wasn't? He was a powerful being after all; did he know something I didn't? At the loss of confidence, I felt the power lessen and my heart stuttered; doubt rocked me. How could I do this now? I was, after all, essentially mortal and in control for the time being. How could I contend with such powerful beings? I inevitably lost some of Alethea's silver sparkle.

Look Out!! Alethea shouted, but it was too late. I had been distracted long enough for Conquest and Famine to surround me.

Do something, I thought, panic rising as insidious as an enemy itself. I felt both of the horsemen grab one of my arms each and watched in horror as War withdrew his flaming broadsword from its sheath. I could feel the panic consuming me and looked desperately for a way out.

Relax Child, came what was, I assumed, Alethea's soothing voice. To me it was still cold and dispassionate but at least she was trying. *I will talk you through this. There is no need to panic.*

How is there no need to panic? I thought at her. *I'm pinned by two of the main signs of the apocalypse.*

War began to advance on me and two vastly different emotions rose. I was terrified; this was completely out of my league and I longed for my previous quiet life. It all seemed so quaint now, my little house, my job and my life ambitions. How could they compare? Lust rose in the part of my mind that was Alethea; primal, instinctive and powerful.

Control yourself, I thought at her. *We need to focus, and I don't really need you jumping on the very being that's trying to attack us.*

You need to focus on our wings. Use your anger at what has occurred, as you did in the life realm, and imagine them moving; focus, until the inside of your eyelids turn silver.

I did as I was instructed. I *was* angry. I had been happy in my quiet life, being in love and just living. I closed my eyes as I focused. Rowan and I were planning a full life together. I didn't want to know about these other worlds, or that I was merely a by-product of a curse. I was a person with dreams, emotions and a soul. I counted too.

Suddenly, my vision turned silver and I felt my wings move. They came up with such force that Famine and Conquest both flew into the walls of the throne room. Famine was knocked unconscious and Conquest struggled to rise. Taking advantage of the hesitation I urged Discord into a forward kick and War was hurled across the throne room.

By now Conquest was on his feet and moving. Famine too had regained consciousness and had struggled to his feet as well. I hoped they were still disorientated and pointed the bottom of the scythe at Conquest. A loud blast echoed through the stale throne room and he was hit by a pure bullet of silver magic. He was once again thrown backward and in an explosion of silver fire, he was gone. I merely focused on Famine and blew lightly between my pursed lips. A strong gust began to pick up and in a strong torrent of silver wind he disappeared as well.

Quickly I swung around to point the bladed end of the scythe at War. I took a deep breath.

"Be gone pest. I have things of my own that need to be done." He bowed deeply.

"Forgive me my Lady." As he came back up, he bought a forceful right hand, already surrounded in his own green magic, and thrust it towards me. Luckily, I was still atop of Discord who braced when the gale hit me so I was only disorientated for a moment. This however was long enough for War to mount his own steed and flee. Conquest and Famine's steeds quickly followed suit. I laughed to myself, amazed that I pulled it off successfully and with the least amount of panic.

I urged Discord into a canter. I didn't know how big Pandemonium was, but I would search all of it just to find Rowan. I started down a long marble corridor, one I hadn't seen on my last 'visit.' It was lined in marble statues which both awed me and unsettled me to my very core at the same time. Each statue portrayed what was essentially me in intimate detail, both clothed and not. Each one had shining pure silver wings so detailed I thought I could touch each individual feather; my own ebony wings tingled in response. Someone with a loving hand had obviously crafted these and I was sickened to think who it was; Lucifer's obsession obviously ran deeper then Alethea knew.

I urged Discord on further, trying to leave behind the chilling tribute to myself. I just wished the memory would leave me as easily. My stomach churned and I couldn't think of any other man looking at me that way; either me or Alethea. Fenris yipped encouragement and I gave him a sad smile. I sat in silence as Discord's silver hooves echoed around the abandoned hall. It was eerie how silent it was. I expected at least some resistance, but there was none.

They passed along similar halls, all decked in similar statues and my sense of panic grew. I was pretty sure I was lost now with no way of knowing where I had come from. I hadn't found Rowan either and I could literally feel time slowing down. Lucifer, almost on Earth, was a black spot on our consciousness. I felt the need to hurry as a tangible thing, desperate to find Rowan and save him.

I urged Discord into a gallop to take in the remainder of the bleak halls quicker. The shining marble reflected my own desperate reflection. I was tear stained, my blue-black curls and ebony wings streaming behind me.

Eventually, having traversed countless corridors with statues, I arrived back at the all too familiar throne room. I hoped Rowan wasn't in Hell and I hadn't just missed him. If he were unable to call out to me and I doomed him because of it, I would never forgive myself. *I wish you would believe me Child,* came Alethea's dry voice. *He is not here, no one is here, I knew this once we had arrived.* Obviously, Alethea didn't believe in checking just to be sure. *I do not,* I replied, *I believe in my power, as should you.*

Shaking my head, I never noticed how easy it was to conjure a portal to the Life realm, despite Alethea's protests that Rowan wouldn't be there I just couldn't bear the thought of Rowan in the hands of any that were obsessed with Alethea. His own father would rather kill him than look at him. Lucifer or Miltiades would torture him to get at me. My panic rose.

I urged Discord into a gallop. Best to take whatever awaited them on the other side by surprise. I hoped it was something I could handle; I honestly didn't know how much more I could take. *Do not worry child,* Alethea reassured, but no other words came after. Did Alethea know something I didn't?

Silver engulfed us once more and I sat patiently, waiting for the scene to unfold in front of us and what I saw made me worry, even past the emotion that emanated from Alethea. We came face to face with both Gabriel and Raphael who seemed to be arguing in the midst of the silver tinged forest.

"I cannot let you do this Gabriel," Raphael yelled, obviously upset about something.

"You have no say in this," he replied to the irate angel. Neither had seemed to notice I was there yet. I moved Discord to hide behind a large rock not too far away. I thanked all the higher powers that the horse moved silently. Holding my hand up to my ear I wished I could hear everything they said. I missed the following flare of silver light.

"Alethea was justifiably punished. Several of our brethren fell at her hands. She allowed herself to be tempted away from Him and then in turn became the Queen of Hell..." Raphael actually sighed. "I admire your faith. I once had faith in Alethea too. She was resplendent as a tool for Him; a beautiful portent of death and destruction..." he trailed off. I could see Gabriel was getting worked up and I wondered what he would do.

"If you cannot have faith in her brother then have faith in me. Have I ever failed the Lord?"

"No."

"I do not plan to fail him now. Alethea repented years ago. I feel it time that she be free of her punishment just as we have freed others. I..." Gabriel seemed to stutter. "I would like to see her smile again." Through the silence that followed I could hear the sound of a blade being withdrawn from its scabbard. I quickly checked to make sure no one was stealing mine. Once happy I looked at the scene again to see that

Raphael had his blade to Gabriel's neck. *This is bad,* Alethea commented. *It will be an even match between the two. Gabriel is the leader of the archangels; if you look closely you will see the golden feathers nestled in between his green ones. Now Raphael is indeed his subordinate but he also holds the position of adviser to Him as shown by his golden wings. It is a position that was once held by Lucifer.* I didn't know what to think. Should I let the two fight, or should I intervene? What could I actually do?

I watched as Gabriel drew his own sword. He seemed reluctant to do so. I could see the respect and love for Raphael shining in his face. What he must do must be that important.

Soon crashes of metal upon metal could be heard intermingled with war cries and shouts. I couldn't understand how two so close could be fighting with such passion and intensity. Why weren't either using their power? Both seemed reluctant to hurt each other but Raphael seemed somewhat more determined in his goal.

I gasped as stark panic flooded my mind. I felt my body move of its own volition. What was happening now? I urged Discord forward and he moved painfully slowly. Our goal seemed to be Gabriel but why? Alethea was frustratingly silent on this front.

When eventually we got to the fight, I felt myself dismount and jerkily move in front of Gabriel. He seemed as shocked as I was. I had no control over my body at this moment and was just along for the ride. I watched as I unsheathed the scythe and blocked Gabriel's next attack. My right hand came up, surrounded in silver light, and created a powerful wind. It was enough to push Raphael back, but not far enough. He came at them again and I began to panic. Gabriel must have seen this as he pushed his way in front of me. He whispered something to himself and Raphael froze in mid-air.

"That's enough now Raphael," Gabriel said with deadly lethality in his voice. "You will return and answer for your actions to Him." With that Raphael was quickly engulfed in golden flame and disappeared from sight.

Turning back to me Gabriel raised a single golden brow and I had the distinct feeling he thought I was late. I, perhaps feeling more bold due to Alethea's power, raised my right hand with only my middle finger erect and like the classy lady I was, flipped Michael the bird. *Hahahahahahaha*, came the maniacal laughter from the back of my mind. *I do not think I have ever seen such a look on Gabriel's face. That was beyond wonderful.* I was just glad I had control back, I would talk to Alethea about my out of body experience later.

"I can now hear you too Lady Death. I am here to inform you that you need to hurry in regards to the little lost prince. The Second Coming is about to begin." I didn't know how to respond. I was just amazed that he managed all that on one long, tired sigh.

"Why are you helping us?" I asked. "Where has your shadow gone?" suspicion laced thickly through my mind and I expected an attack any second.

"Despite what you know mortal, that we would do anything to win this war, and what your own dreams have shown you…" he looked straight into my eyes, "we would not sacrifice an innocent life."

"Then tell me where he is," I begged, desperation leading me to anything that may help me find him.

"Unfortunately, I cannot. I am surprised Alethea has not told you. Our considerable power is dampened in apocalyptic settings. I can no more sense him than you can."

While distracted by my thoughts I missed Gabriel moving towards me. A soft, almost loving caress touched my forehead and Gabriel stepped back with glowing golden eyes.

"What…?" I began but Gabriel merely held his finger to his lips, smiled and disappeared in a golden ray of light.

My head felt a little cloudy and I swore I heard the sound of a key turning and a door creaking open. How was that possible?

What happened? I asked Alethea silently, worried that somehow, ultimately, I had lost my tenuous control over my own soul.

Fear not child, Alethea replied. *You are as you were always meant to be. I would not see you lose yourself.*

I wasn't sure that was meant to comfort me. If I was as I was always meant to be then that doesn't mean I was supposed to be myself. After all, wasn't I just a by-product of Lucifer's curse? I felt weakened by whatever Michael did and was worried now that I would never find Rowan.

Be brave Child, Alethea reassured. I almost longed for how she used to be; the sarcastic, dry voice experiencing most human emotion for the first time. I sighed and shook my head. I already knew nothing about my life would ever be the same, why waste time over it now?

I urged Discord onwards as I could now see the Court in the distance. It twinkled in its silver radiance, almost laughing at my suffering. Wait, silver? I had been aiming to transport them to the life realm. Why was I now in the death realm? I recognised it from its silver tinged brilliance. I had a suspicion that Alethea had interfered in the power once more but there was an ominous silence from that corner of my mind. I smiled grimly; the death users could mock me, hold me, torture me all they liked but no one would stop me from finding Rowan. I felt the panic rise in spite of itself and took a deep breath to calm myself.

Suddenly, I felt a sharp pain slice through my neck. I gasped, unable to breath, unable to scream… nothing. I sought Alethea at the back of my mind, but nothing was working as it should. I felt my heart begin to crack, the pain overwhelming and consuming me. The crack grew until eventually my heart shattered and my world went sparkling black.

14

Silver mist surrounded me. I felt peaceful and almost happy once again. How had I gone from one extreme to the other so quickly? Surely, I should worry about what happened, but I felt no worry whatsoever. I felt calm.

Instead I smiled as a familiar face came towards me. My heart stuttered and I could feel pure crystalline tears slip down over my cheeks. My mother smiled softly at me and embraced me. I wasn't sure how I knew it was my mother, she had died from an overdose when I was days old after all, but the unending love I felt directed towards me told me enough. The kindness radiated off my mother in waves; the beauty, the love and the trust made up the core of my mother's soul. This is what I had missed my entire life, the comfort and love provided by a parent. I felt whole, complete, like I was finally home.

My mother placed a gentle hand under my chin and lifted my head. With infinite care she placed a soft kiss on my forehead, and I felt the twenty three years of love I had missed out on. I wanted to cry all over again. I didn't get the chance however as somehow Azazel strode towards me. He too was encompassed in silver mist, but he had a quality around him that suggested he didn't belong here. Wait, did I?

"No Lady Death, you do not," he said, almost with kindness. "You may be unaware, but you are needed in the coming battle. Do not think on your distrust of me and my motives, just go back... go back..." Azazel removed me from my mother's embrace and forcibly pushed my mother back into the silver cloud with disdain. I felt rage rise within me at such treatment when a jolt of lightning shot through my heart with definitive pain and clarity. Another jolt shot through me and I was flying backwards, away from the happiness and the serenity of that place. I watched as Azazel grew smaller and smaller until I flew through the silver mists, his figure disappearing from my sight...

***

With a soft groan I opened my eyes to find myself flat on my back in the grass. I must have fallen off Discord during the whole strange moment in the mists. Luckily my wings cushioned me from the worst of the fall.

"What happened?" I asked, rubbing my head while I sat

up. I must have caught it in the saddle in the fall, or there was a rock hidden in the grasses.

Well, Alethea seemed reluctant for once. *You... died.*

"I died?" I asked, sure the fall had knocked my senses, the other option I couldn't quite believe.

Yes, your heart stopped. I am afraid I had to pull you back to finish what we started, she sighed, *forgive me child.*

"Will I still find Rowan?" I asked, focusing on my main concern. It refused to process the other option. As long as I found Rowan that's all that mattered.

You will, Alethea replied, and I couldn't tell what emotion was in her voice. What did she know that I didn't?

"But..."

We have to move, Alethea inserted, pouring just a drop of death magic into her will, *our time grows short.*

I got up slowly, unable to resist the pull of Alethea's will. I desperately wanted to ask more. Had I really been dead? But I was unable to, pushed on by Alethea's will alone. I also couldn't shake the feeling that Alethea was hiding something from me. If Alethea could access my mind why couldn't I access Alethea's?

I almost fainted once I was astride the saddle once more. I felt weak, weaker then I had ever felt, almost like the very core of my soul was being taken from me. What would happen if I never found Rowan?

I rode onwards, again under Alethea's will. I could sense that Alethea didn't want to be responsible for the death of another innocent. I would by no means argue this time. I felt somehow that Alethea was now stronger than I was, I doubted I would have a choice in the matter.

Eventually, I came closer to the court, its silver radiance becoming the gleaming marble I was familiar with. I had thought it beautiful, even the statue of what was essentially myself, but now I realised I had been naïve. I saw it for what it was, power, prestige and egotism. It was rife with underhanded politics and seduction. I just couldn't understand how Rowan had come from here, though it explained why he left.

I passed marble corridor after marble corridor, always searching, never finding, everything becoming the same silver tinged blur. I came across a vaguely familiar corridor and had to think where I was. It wasn't on the way to the throne room; I wasn't filled with the sense of dread that I had been last time. So where was I?

Discord sauntered on a bit more and sheer black hangings began to grace the cold marble and it struck me cold and hard in the stomach. I was nearing one of Illaria's own temples, the one I had originally visited to find Rowan. I hadn't seen the little witch since the transportation spell had gone wrong. What had become of her?

I dismounted near the entrance and rushed inside. I had a sense that somehow Illaria was involved and I would make her pay. The temple itself was cold, a breeze flowing through the chamber, the large black bonfire snuffed out; there were signs she had been there recently though. Cushions were strewn around creating swirls in the dust, candlesticks overturned in haste and belongings gone. I could feel anger rising in my mind and realised it came from Alethea.

How dare she?? Alethea demanded. *How dare she counter-spell my magic, my* power *at the risk of others?* My hands came up involuntarily and silver fire poured to the floor igniting the cushions around. *I will make her* pay.

"Calm down," I soothed, holding my hand up to conjure wind to snuff the flame. "Why are you so worked up?"

Alethea never replied but I had a brief glimpse into her mind, a rarity in itself. I could see Alethea was ashamed that her power had been affected so easily and that she couldn't live with herself should another innocent die because of her.

"Come on," I enthused. "We have lots to search and very little time to do it in." I felt Alethea calm slightly, enough so they could concentrate on the task at hand, but I would not like to be Illaria when Alethea found her.

Do we check the throne room now child? Alethea asked, reluctant to go there as she knew the King had been infected.

"Hhhmmm, let's check the guild house first," I replied.

"I don't really want to see his father if I'm honest. He's far too obsessed with you. I don't know what he would do, and I still can't believe he tortured his own son."

Let us go to the guild house then, he very well may be there.

They left the court astride Discord once more. I worried that I was wasting both mine and Rowan's time but had no other option but to look. I tried not to panic at the fact that Alethea couldn't sense him and took a deep calming breath. The guild house wasn't far from the court and they would be there soon.

They came across the familiar shop-temple and it seemed deserted as if no one had been there in a long time. They could find no sign of footprints, no sign of a struggle or panic, no signs of Rowan. I hurried into the main living area and almost stumbled over the cushion pad where we had made love, unconsciously moving into Rowan's own chambers. It all seemed so long ago now. My heart constricted; I had only ever been happy when I was with Rowan. I needed him back desperately.

A flash of silver caught my eye and I looked to the far corner of the chamber. Stood there was the spirit of Rowan's guild member, Milah. She didn't speak to me as she had before but she stared at me with accusing eyes. What could this mean? What had happened to make the spirits rise against me?

Come child, Alethea inserted. *He is not here, we move*

on.

"But…" I began.

Come, Alethea inserted, using death magic, just a drop, to make me move. I sighed. I was getting tired of being forced to obey. I didn't know when I would regain my free will. I hoped it would be soon.

We made our way back to the court, dread eating away at me. I had no real desire to confront Rowan's father but knew a confrontation was coming. If he had Rowan, I would find the courage to face him and I would win. I paused by the large oaken doors almost reluctant to push them open. What would I find on the other side? What horrors awaited me? I listened closely trying to discern whether I could hear signs of an ambush. I heard none but instead heard two male voices. One was most definitely Rowan's father.

"I need to find her," declared the King. "I feel my insides burning with need, my fingers long to brush her soft skin." I heard something crash to the floor and knew he must be venting his frustration. I could barely hear the second voice; I couldn't catch the tone or tenor, all I could hear were the words.

"Focus, Lucian."

I was surprised to feel terror rising from the part of my mind that Alethea hid in. I couldn't understand, it was the angel of death I housed, the ultimate source of death and destruction.

It is built into the weave of the spell. Lucifer sought to punish me for ultimately escaping him. It was not enough that he cursed both myself and my hosts to the endless reincarnations and death it bought but it made me fear him as well. Egotistical bastard does not even begin to describe him. Luckily with you in control the terror did not affect me as much.

I was distracted from replying by the King's own reply to what could only be Lucifer.

"I... I... I cannot bear it. I did not see her often but I need her more than I have ever needed anything. I do not understand it." I felt a little queasy at the admission; I found myself pressed against the throne room door listening intently. Despite the danger, my damnable curiosity had me wanting to find out more. One day I would learn.

"I have done what was asked of me," said the second voice. "Granted it was much to our mutual benefit, but it is done. Now it is your turn. Do not fail me." I was definitely worried about the ruthless glee in his voice.

"Do not worry Hell Lord," Lucian replied, not even trying to hide his contempt. "I will hold her until the end of the Second Coming, if she will not fight for you. The shackle you have provided will show no failure."

My knees began to shake. I didn't worry about the shackle, I had thought and kept the key Gabriel had thrown to

Alethea, but I panicked at the knowledge they were talking about me. I didn't want to be trapped, I wanted to find Rowan and go back to my life. These adventures were not for me.

The voices moved towards the throne room doors and I ran, my wings streamlining so I was able to move faster. I had no desire for a confrontation with either of those men and suddenly my desire to find Rowan was paramount. When would all of this end?

I ran through corridor after corridor hoping I was headed towards the exit. It would just be my luck that I got lost now. I finally came across an elaborate archway and stumbled out of it into the golden sunshine. Relief rushed over me in waves; I was outside, but I had no time to stop and think on this. I had to escape before either of them caught me.

Discord was waiting patiently for me, almost annoyed that I hadn't mounted him already. I did so quickly, and he broke into a gallop almost immediately.

This time it was Discord that began to radiate the silver shine. It grew stronger and stronger until I was blinded by it. I hoped Discord knew where to go as I could no longer see to guide him. Just as soon as the light had begun, it was gone, and I was astounded to find they were back in my lounge. I *was* a little nonplussed that there was now a horse in my house but I was mainly relieved to be away from that court.

It is as it should be child, Alethea stated in her most matter of fact tone. *Discord and I have always been together and worked completely in unison. He is where I am. He must have been so lost while I was forced to sleep.* I found myself hugging the horse and felt mildly uncomfortable.

I shook myself and moved to search the house. Surely Rowan was here, sheltered from the apocalypse taking place. I hoped he was anyway. Five minutes later I knew what true fear was. Rowan was nowhere in the house and I didn't know what to do. They had run out of time, none left to search the realm of life so he had to be here, I would allow no other option. I hoped and I prayed, and I tried to calm the panic that now overtook my heart.

15

Ignoring my logic, allowing the panic to take over, I rushed to my front door but then froze, suddenly unsure of myself. What had Gabriel done? What was I to do now? My world now seemed more surreal, if that was at all possible, and I wondered if it had something to do with what Gabriel had done. I gingerly opened the door and it was almost like part of me was delayed. I walked down my front steps with a faint echo of myself following two seconds after. Even so, I was still consumed by the shocking sight I was treated to. The entire world was frozen, people stood midway through each task they had been performing, oblivious to the war raging around them. Demons and angels with weapons drawn were battling amongst them, uncaring of who fell. My shock quickly became furious rage. A sea of souls of those already fallen greeted my vision, a silver mist against the chaos. How could those beings be so obtuse to the grief and suffering caused? I could see that some of the demons were trying to get the upper hand by trying to attack the mortals, and to their credit some of the angels were trying to protect them. Others openly showed their disdain and allowed mortals to die, nothing would distract them from their battle.

I found that the scythe was already in my hand. I took the longsword, masked by powerful death magic, from my thigh This couldn t continue any longer. I would put an end to it if I had to, to find Rowan and put an end to the death and suffering.

I walked calmly through the carnage with purpose, allowing none to stand in my way. I raised the scythe and used silver bullets to fell two nearby demons. I left the angels alone as they had been some that had tried to save the mortals. I walked on taking deep calming breaths as I went. Next, I calmly beheaded an angel on my left with my longsword. I smiled as I heard the wet thud to the floor. I had a deep suspicion that Alethea was behind that particular attack. I had a feint echo of a memory where this angel was so full of pride, and I had the bitter taste of hatred at the back of my throat. I walked on regardless; I knew I should feel regret and sorrow at all this death but all I could think about was Rowan.

Suddenly a barrage of Demons tried to attack me.

Do not worry child, I have measures in place to deal with them. I wondered what she meant until all the demons leapt in unison. They flew with precision and purpose until they stopped half a meter around me. They began to sizzle and shriek in pain, until each and every one began to burst into silver flame. Finally, they dropped to the floor, charred husks of the powerful demons they once were.

I love that spell. Alethea chuckled, unable to contain her mirth. I had to smile at such happiness and continued on my search but had to duck quickly as a bolt of purple lightning flew past me. *Oh holy Him, I had forgotten about Barachiel,* Alethea thought with a sigh. I turned slowly to see quite the sight. Barachiel, with flaming purple wings, glared at me with his lightning sword drawn. In all honesty I had forgotten about him also, I was too consumed in the other worlds. I let out a long and tired sigh too noting that he was surrounded by quite a number of fawning angels. *Those are a number of his four hundred and ninety six thousand attending angels. Thankfully he hasn't brought all of them. As you can see, he revels in his own importance as one of the 'hallowed' seraphim princes.* I laughed at the fact that I could sense Alethea's air quotes.

What does he have against you? I asked silently.

Same as most angels. They think if they can bring either myself or Lucifer to justice then they will gain more of His favour. I plan to disappoint them. I felt sorry for Alethea; it must be hard to be hunted and persecuted over the entirety of your never-ending life. I determined that I would at least make this aspect of Alethea's life easier and started towards him.

"Barachiel, brother, why do you come now?" I adopted Alethea's way of speaking in the hopes that he would think I had full control.

"You know why Alethea," he replied, removing himself from his stomach-churning adoration. "You committed so many atrocities, killed so many of my subjects and now you are so close to being free of the just punishment you deserve that I feel my blade is necessary. You need only exist for death to continue, sleep now and no violence will be needed." I sighed once again and took hold of the scythe. Why did the angels always pick the hard way? I had no intention of losing so evidently, he had to. I watched as he turned to his subjects.

"Do not disturb this battle. Lady Death is mine and I refuse to see more of you dead." I faltered slightly at that. He truly cared for his people and didn't want to see them hurt. My resolve to save him from himself surfaced.

"Hold Barachiel," I stated with as much authority as I could muster. "I have no desire to see your people leaderless. They evidently love you and you care for them...," I paused... "...don't hate me for what I am about to do." I lifted my hand and blew on the back of it. Where my breath hit my skin, it froze with small silver icicles. In turn I spun in place and threw my hand towards him, watching as the icicles flew proud and true, growing to encase him in their silver depth. He quickly became one large ice sculpture and I had to smile. It wouldn't hold him for long but hopefully I could achieve my goals in that time. I quickly moved on.

I eventually came across the other horsemen blindly doing as their master bid. I couldn't help myself; I felt the mischief and spite rising in me.

Is there any way I could cloak myself? I don't want to be cornered by them again but I need to knock them off balance, so they don't win, I silently asked Alethea.

Of course, child, Alethea answered, still full of glee from before. *Use the anger you have been feeling, think of those fallen souls, and imagine yourself out of sight.* I did as I was instructed and focused on my rage and my wish to be invisible. Gradually a silver sparkle began at my feet and I slowly began to disappear from sight in a silver sheen. I actually chuckled to myself as it happened. Still I crouched nearer to the ground in case of detection and focused on creating a silver gale once more.

I watched with abject glee as the winds picked up and War's great flaming broadsword was snuffed out. Conquest in turn lost his crown and had to chase after it. I had to stop myself maniacally laughing out loud as Famine's toxic breath blew back on him and he choked.

Although I was enjoying the scene, especially when the angels took advantage of the distraction, I knew I had to move on. There was only one more place Rowan would seek sanctuary and that was a church. He had always been such an advocate and went every week. Now I knew it was to escape the past he had left behind.

As I moved towards the church, I took stock of the

world around me. Buildings were crumbled from various free-flowing energies. There were bodies everywhere: angels, demons and mortals alike. I felt the sorrow welling up in me and a single crystalline tear fell down my cheek. So much death and destruction and I couldn't stop to help. I moved on, willing myself to focus on the task at hand. I would help all I could afterwards. As I walked I came across Vale and Lyria chasing something on the way to the church. They were frozen and thankfully their magical essences protected them from attack. I would come back for them afterward. I blew them a kiss, watched as it formed a silver dome over them both, and carried on my way.

Eventually the church loomed above me. It was an old church with a sprinkling of decay, but I could see what Rowan saw in it. Thinking of Rowan drew my eyes to the doorway and the familiar figure reaching towards it.

Relief rushed through me in waves. Though the world was still frozen in the second coming, I had finally found Rowan. He was stood with his back towards me holding his arms out for protection. This worried me so I took flight, my large ebony wings propelling me towards Rowan with great speed.

As I got closer towards him, I saw something that both shattered my heart and would haunt me for the rest of my apparently never ending life. Although the two were still together, someone had neatly severed Rowan's head from his body. I knew now why I had 'died' in the field; the pain had been excruciating and only part of what Rowan had felt. I had felt him die and it had shattered my heart in return.

"*No,*" I cried; I was too late to help him, to hold him, to love him, to say goodbye.

Wait child, Alethea said. *Get your scythe quickly. The wound, though mortal, has been seared shut. Only a blade of the purest Hellfire could do this.*

I jumped to my feet, although I could not remember dropping to my knees, and grabbed the scythe from my back. As I did this the familiar blood red light appeared, coalesced into a blood red doorway and Lucifer casually strolled out. Minion after minion followed him, and I had better time to study them. They were Lucifer's 'Elite Guard', the remnants of the fallen angels that had fought Him with Alethea and Lucifer. They were not faring well. Their golden brilliance was gone, replaced by horns and devilish grins. Their wings were in tatters, bone poking through at almost every angle, their lustrous green feathers dulled and dead. Their skin was thickened and marked, marring what was once celestial beauty; their golden hair matted with filth.

I felt pity for them. They seemed to have forgotten the once wondrous beings they were and served Lucifer happily, even eagerly. Before the Fall they would have found Lucifer beneath them, they were too celestial to bow to his whims.

I calmly watched them as they surrounded me and all I felt was numb. Rowan was gone, what other reason did I have to go on? I hoped Lucifer had enough power to kill me; I did not want to live without Rowan. Crystalline tears streamed down my cheeks. How could I go on?

No! Alethea cried and I could hear real panic in her voice, *no, you must go on. We must go on. If we ceased to be then the world would know suffering the likes of which you cannot imagine. Rowan's soul is not forever lost! You will find him again! Accept me, and together we will restore order to this world.*

I was tired; tired, sad and angry. I couldn't understand the reasons behind Rowan's death. No one stood to gain from it. Why was he the one to suffer? I just wanted to let go, to accept Alethea and hope that I was snuffed out of existence altogether. So I decided.

"You lose..." I said to Lucifer between heart wrenching sobs. I opened my mind and my heart to the dark being that had quickly become my friend and protector and felt both warm loving arms embrace me and the cold, hard certainty of Death consume me. I felt them merge as if my broken soul was becoming whole and I knew I was not becoming less, but more. I welcomed my fate, my destiny, with open arms and knew it would carry me away...

***

Alethea

I raised my head. I could see Anahlia's silver soul leaving my body and I did not want that, not until I could place it where it belonged, with Rowan. I quickly reached for the pendant around Rowan's neck. I captured just a small sliver of Anahlia's soul and placed it in my mind just as I myself had been trapped. I needed her influence to help me correct Lucifer's error but to be honest I needed it to lend a mortal aspect to all now I would do.

The rest of Anahlia's soul I placed within the crystal adorning the pendant. I would not lose it this way and she would be held in something directly linked to her love; perhaps this would help. This mortal could not suffer any more due to me and I would right so many things.

I looked deep into the pure hazel of Lucifer's eyes. He flinched at my look of pure hatred, my eyes burning with the silver flame of my power and anger. He was obviously distraught at the fact the terror of the spell had vanished almost with Anahlia's soul. A small part of me rejoiced at being whole again but I concentrated on Anahlia's pain, that was still palpable after what I had done, and my millennia-old contempt.

"Oh Lucifer," the combination Anahlia's voice and mine produced a sensual, velvet purr. I could see it was having a blatant effect on Lucifer which was strange given the circumstances they were in. "I have been looking forward to this for a very long time. You indeed lose," I finished echoing Anahlia's words.

I kept hold of the scythe with my right hand but from its cloaked sheath on my thigh I took my pure silver sword with my left. With how angry I was, both weapons burned with silver flame. It felt good to wield them again, it felt familiar and right. I saw Lucifer take the smallest step backward. He seemed shocked that the terror he had woven into that damned reincarnation curse so long ago was no longer there. Now I felt only anger and I revelled in the fact that I knew Lucifer knew this also.

Glancing to the right I looked at the minion closest to me. He had once been Cadmus, the angel of vengeance. I had never liked him; he was always claiming that he should have 'my destiny'. His pride in himself came from him in waves, so much so I was almost sickened by it. Even if I could abandon my lot in life, it would not be to him, even now.

I smiled a slow, menacing smile and lifted the bottom of my scythe. I could see that in his over inflated opinion of himself my smile had no effect on him. I knew I was going to enjoy this very much. Thinking aggressive, almost malicious thoughts a loud explosion sounded and a bullet of pure silver flame shot forth. Cadmus looked at the now gaping hole in his chest with some surprise and fell unmoving to the floor. I had to smile; I loved the influence Anahlia's modern soul had had on the scythe; these bullets were coming in very handy.

Still smiling I looked at Lucifer and shrugged. I knew the battle would start now and I relished it.

"Attack!" Lucifer yelled while opting to remain where he was. I actually chuckled to myself as I brought up the scythe to block a minion's attack. I heard Hellfire metal clang against my own pure silver as I sensed another attack from behind. I swept the scythe down in an arc and buried the blade deep in what was the minion's heart. Quickly I turned, sweeping my sword behind me, and beheaded the first minion in one flowing movement. This reminded me of Rowan and I felt a sharp pain in my heart, though I had to push it aside for now. If I faltered even slightly, Lucifer would win again.

The battle continued unabated. I moved smoothly, felling minions with weapons alone. I dare not call any magic; I needed to save all reserves for the final battle. My power was unlimited, death in nature was unlimited and unending, but I dare not take any chances; I knew Lucifer was trying to wear me down. I was grateful Fenris was there battling also; I did not know if he would stay with me now that both Rowan and Anahlia were lost but I hoped he would. He seemed bigger now that Rowan had passed.

I journeyed further, only part of my mind considering the scene I now found myself in. The ground was stained in rivers of blood, some black and some ruby red. Bodies were strewn where they fell and seemed to be equal casualties for both sides. There was rubble of buildings almost acting like morbid headstones for those that fell. This is what I was created for but I could not help the tear that slipped from my moistened eye. Such a tragic loss of souls and for what? A maniac's power play for something he should never have.

Eventually all were felled and only I and Lucifer remained. We stared each other down and I knew both were trying to think of the quickest way to defeat the other. Soon He would intervene, heralded by Metatron, and I would not be robbed of my vengeance. I had to make Lucifer angry and reckless so he would make a mistake, and suddenly I knew the most satisfying way to accomplish it.

I sauntered closer to Lucifer, hoping that the seductive nature of my posture would be enough to throw him off guard. Sure enough, his sword lowered slightly as he watched me, transfixed. I moved even closer, close enough so that a whisper could be heard. Lucifer seemed not to care that most of his guard was dead, instead he focused on the softness of my lips and licked his own. I used just a tiny bit of my death magic, enough to emphasize the death in my words.

"I do not love you Lucifer; I did not, could not and never will. Oh..." and here I paused for purposeful dramatic effect, "and War was a far greater lover than you could ever be."

I saw it took just a moment for my words to sink in, and then the rage that overtook him was almost astonishing. I had to bring my scythe quickly in front of me to block his enraged lunge. We fought for what seemed like an eternity, Lucifer surprisingly skilled in his rage, both evenly matched. I had to do something to offset him, and quickly.

So, I simply... blew him a kiss. The part of my mind that stored Anahlia was howling with laughter, I had just used the kiss of death, but it was enough. An almost pitiable hope kindled once more in Lucifer's eyes. That was the entire pause I needed. I spun in place, so fast I was only a silver blur, and the momentum allowed the blade of my scythe to penetrate his armour and bury deep into his chest. Lucifer looked down to see his black blood pouring out of his body.

"You... you did it!" he stuttered. "You actually did it."

"And it was a long time coming," I ground through gritted teeth. The pain of his acidic blood splashing onto my hands was nothing in the face of the relief I could now feel.

"I..." he gasped as it was harder for him to breathe. "...I still win... you know..." He coughed and black blood streamed from his mouth.

"What..." I whispered and wrenched my blade from his chest. Lucifer fell as if in slow motion, his wings crumbling to nothing, golden heaps of feathers on the floor. A pool of black blood slowly surrounded him, coating him in his own evil. I had to turn away; I knew the scene would stay with me forever anyway. What had he meant? How could he win now that he was blessedly, finally gone?

I moved toward Rowan, determined to give him a warrior's send off, when I was sure I could hear a whispered keening come from an unknown place. I turned in a circle, unsure of where it came from even as it grew in pitch and cadence. I moved towards Lucifer grudgingly, sure he had planned something and sure enough the keening grew even louder; it was now more resembling the screech of a damned soul. Just as I had crouched near the evil bastard's head his eyes flew open and blood red light poured forth. I tried to move away but I was caught in the pool of evil that surrounded the corpse. My head pounded with unadulterated rage. It was not Lucifer that I had killed, it was this puppet who was rigged with some unknown magic for when he inevitably failed. I threw back my head and screamed in frustration. Once again, I found myself at the mercy of Lucifer's machinations without a damn thing I could do about it. I tried to call my power to me but the strands slipped through my fingers like sand as the intense light grew in power, finally exploding and taking everything with it. The only sound, an impassioned scream...

Anahlia

... The explosion had been amazingly hot, loud and painful. I hit the floor with pain confusion. I had died again, and Alethea had put me in Rowan's crystal for safe keeping. That was the last thing I remembered. Now I found myself back in Alethea's armour, wings on display, Fenris nipping at me in concern and my two best friends streaming towards me.

"Gods Anahlia," Vale shouted as she got to me. "We thought you were dead. We could almost see death fighting, wearing your skin, then the world exploded and here we are, as if nothing had happened. Are..." she stuttered, which she never did. "... are you okay?"

"I don't know." I replied honestly. "I feel different, Alethea is gone, but I feel her power has merged with mine and I am something new, something changed." Clarity dawned on me. "Where's Rowan?" I demanded, remembering the mortal wound that had ended both him and myself.

They both remained quiet and pointed at the church. On the steps lay a body, the head some feet away, and the echo of golden wings taunting me. I sped over to him. I could feel rage, pure unadulterated fury boiling inside of me. This was enough. I would find his soul. I don't care how, I don't care when. I will find him and he will be whole once more.

Uncaring of my two best friends, my rage and grief exploded, propelling me into the night sky on ebony wings, all the while crying tears of blood.

Epilogue

Rowan

A calm, soft wind blew gathering fragments of rubble, dust and human DNA. The city lay in ruins. People lay where they had been struck down, unaware of the war that had raged around them. It was such a waste. Blood and scars littered the ground portraying the carnage that had been.

Towards the centre was a large blackened crater where once evil lay dead and death had ruled. Blood red explosions sounded, and all was gone. All except him. He drifted over to the crater to survey the scene. He knew he should be panicked. He knew he was done but something kept him there, some small part knowing he actually wasn't done. There had been a woman... and a vengeful man... beings with wings... and black magic?

He floated here and there, his silver tinged vision encompassed in sadness. Where? Where? Soon he came upon the sorriest sight, a body decapitated as he reached for safety. He should weep but what would be the point? He watched as time resumed and the head fell from the body. Just as recognition began to dawn a shadowed figure shot from the ground. It was quickly followed by another and another. They reeked of evil. They were heavily armed and had one sole focus, and was that shadowed wings he saw? Did they want him? Just as he reached for that bit of him that knew the certainty of death, ready to defend, the figures seized him by the arms, the legs, all they could reach and dragged him into the earth with them. The darkness was truly black, the heat truly intense and the never-ending sense of loss inescapable. He was greeted by others of the damned and knew for sure that he was inescapably lost. He let the malicious dark carry him away.

END

ABOUT THE AUTHOR

Andrea lives in Lancaster in the UK with her husband and two kids. Andrea has always had a passion for writing but decided to self-publish her work after successfully recovering from breast cancer. Aside from her writing, Andrea loves to take walks with her family, listen to any sort of music (from classical to rock but no techno) and loves to care for her friends and family. Making others smile makes her happy. Her current mood is super excited for the jack russell puppy they are about to adopt.

Printed in Great Britain
by Amazon

50053361R00177